Advance Praise

"Nancy Burke's witty, warm stories go to the heart of relationships and family life with honesty and compassion. The sisters in the wonderful opening set of linked stories return in later pieces, and it is a pleasure to watch them grow and also remain recognizably the same as they were as girls. Other stories deal with contemporary dilemmas and problems between adults in surprising ways. *Death Cleaning and Other Units of Measure* shows another aspect of Burke's range as an author who speaks to the concerns of our times with great wisdom."

> —Alice Elliott Dark, author of *Fellowship Point, Think of England, In The Gloaming, Naked to the Waist*

"Nancy Burke's stories enable you to really understand the people you thought you already knew all about. Her writing delves into situations like sibling rivalry, parent and child conflicts and marital disputes, and uncovers veins of unique viewpoints. Whether she's exploring a day at the Jersey shore, love hate relations among sisters, or the deep personal bond between a man and his GPS, Burke will keep you interested, amused, touched and wondering why you never thought of things that way before."

> —Jean Ende, Short Story Author

"Nancy Burke's *Death Cleaning and Other Units of Measure* is a wide-ranging, moving work which focuses with great sensitivity on the intersection between the inner lives of ordinary people and their daily experiences. Told from multiple points of view—young, old, men and women—it deftly captures the long-held secrets, misunderstandings, and bonds, however fraught, that make up any relationship. In Burke's world, no matter the distance between people, whether a generational or a religious divide, or a tenuous bond between neighbors, one never doubts their connection. Her wise insights about mothers and daughters, siblings, and romantic partnerships give these memorable characters weight. Stylistically, the collection encompasses linked stories, stand-alone ones, and a piece entirely in dialogue. For readers looking to dive into a rich exploration of the seasons of women's and men's lives, this is a book to treasure."

— Roselee Blooston, author of the novel, *Trial by Family*, an IPBA Gold Medal Winner, *A Chocolate Jar & Other Stories*, the memoir *Dying in Dubai*, a Foreword INDIES Book of the Year, and *Almost: My Life in the Theater*

"Nancy Burke's stories open the treacherous ground of marriage and family relations with fearless intimacy. Her clear, everyday language and realistic dialogue take us deep into the dark recesses of envy, revenge, sibling rage, guilt, and missed connections. The personal touches on the universal when we suffer the heartbreak of infertility or the ambivalent results of failed suicide along with Burke's seemingly ordinary characters, who have much to show us about our own foibles and ingrained resentments. Units of Measure is a collection for our times, our history, our pain."

— Marina Antropow Cramer, author of the novels *Roads*, *Anna Eva Mimi Adam*, and *Marfa's River*

Death Cleaning
and Other Units
of Measure

Death Cleaning and Other Units of Measure

Short Stories

Nancy Burke

Apprentice
House Press
Loyola University Maryland

First Edition

Hardcover ISBN: 978-1-62720-504-7
Paperback ISBN: 978-1-62720-505-4
Ebook ISBN: 978-1-62720-506-1

Design by Abby Benner
Editorial Development by Evi Rizas

Published by Apprentice House Press

Loyola University Maryland
4501 N. Charles Street, Baltimore, MD 21210
410.617.5265
www.ApprenticeHouse.com
info@ApprenticeHouse.com

Also by Nancy Burke

Only the Women are Burning
If I Could Paint the Moon Black
From the Abuelas' Window

This one is for my mother, Marie Burke. I write because she didn't.

Contents

Author's Note

Somewhere in my writing of these stories, the theme "units of measure" grabbed my attention and wouldn't let go. It whispered to me that everybody measures against their own 'units', whether we acknowledge them or not, weighing in on who we want to be, what choices we make, how we navigate difficulty, how we extend kindness, how we develop hostility, who we befriend or dismiss, who gets invited, who doesn't, and whether we feel like we measure up. Instilled in us by our upbringing and influenced toward change continually, sometimes we cling to the familiar measures, and some familiar measures evolve with our accumulation of life experiences. Have I overstated an obvious truth? My own daughter said, "Mom, that's a part of just about everything." Perhaps, she is right!

I wrote these stories over many years long before my own 'units' took off their masks to reveal themselves. During the COVID 19 lockdown, I observed, in the tight communities to which we were restricted, that the assumption that our units of measure are common to all, particularly among family members and partners, is often false.

"I thought that you'd want what I want, sorry my dear." – a line in *Send in the Clowns* by Stephen Sondheim says it perfectly. The units of measure in these stories are not inches, yards, miles or light years. They are far more ephemeral, numerous and difficult to define.

The Favorite

Grace came along just past our first wedding anniversary in early June 1954. She rode into life on a thunderstorm; one of those late afternoon rumbles that stir the nerves and bring torrents. Yes, they doped me up for the delivery, but through my haze I heard the skies break to herald her arrival. I held her as soon as the doctors let me, my first little girl, my first creation, wet and wrinkled, not very pretty with her head all misshapen from the birth canal, but mine. I believed, as I gazed at her little scrunched-up face, that my life was beginning too. Everything I had done before felt frivolous. Motherhood, I knew at that moment, was my calling.

We were co-conspirators, she and I, a partnership, an uneven one, and she was soon the senior partner. She ruled, as all newborns do who are fed on demand, cradled on demand, held on demand. No infant protested a wet diaper as angrily as she did. I succumbed to my new little tyrant, and humbly did her bidding. For one year. One year and nineteen days. Then, our little cocoon of love, our perfect Madonna and child bliss, was disturbed. Girl number two, Ellen, the dark-haired interloper, usurped Grace's throne and demanded love too.

Ellen's cry was high and piercing like a cat howling in an alley. I could not let her cry herself to sleep, not in her bassinet, not in the baby carriage I parked close to Grace in the high chair at breakfast, not after her bath when she was cold and her lower lip trembled. I didn't care what the Dr. Spock book said about babies learning to self-sooth, particularly because if I let her cry for just a minute too long, Grace woke up too and joined in.

Roy worked a second job, bartending at a little watering hole in West Orange and some nights, at home alone, pacing the hallway with Ellen in my arms and Grace asleep, I came to believe he worked that job so he would not be home for this, for the midnight feedings, the diaper changes, the quotidian demands that come with children. I would have gladly traded the extra income for a second pair of hands in the middle of the night.

When Roy was home, he held Ellen in his arms and crooned Sinatra songs in his silky baritone. He soothed her. And I slept.

Grace attached herself to me when that happened, those fleeting moments when Ellen was not in my arms. She stole precious moments, bewilderment, or something else, in her eye as she leaned her head against my heart and reclaimed me for as long as she could. I held onto her to restore our little bond from her first year. I prayed it was enough. It never felt like it was though. Holding an infant in one arm and a toddler in the other and trying to turn the pages of a picture book is a feat for an octopus. Add the pacifier that kept falling out of each of their mouths and forget it.

It was fun only when Roy was home or Mom came for the day with Dad after he retired. But Roy's firm started offering overtime hours to the union workers and he took advantage of that so we could save some money. He was never home. When he was, he was sleeping.

Grace was two when I missed my period and knew a third was on the way. Roy took a Saturday job on top of his overtime and bartending and we moved into my parent's house so we could save for a down payment on a house. Mary Lou was born that year and I praise God I had my mother's help. She took Mary Lou up as though she were her own. She was a calm baby. After Ellen's cries and needs she was a little angel, all blond curls. Mom loved her. We all loved her.

Grace was three when I noticed her eye after a bout of croup. A weak muscle, the doctor said. She'll need surgery when she's six, not until she's six. Meanwhile, he gave me a set of cards with a dark black line down the middle. Strengthen her eye with these, he said, holding one up and drawing it slowly in toward her face. See how long she can see just one line. Do it for a few minutes every day.

It became a game we played after dinner. I sat on the floor in the living room. Grace and Ellen sat facing me. Mother sat in her rocker and fed Mary Lou her last bottle before bedtime and watched. Dad sat with his long legs crossed at the knee, and read a book half tuned-in, half absorbed in his story. I held the card in front of Grace and slowly moved it toward her face. "Keep your eyes on the line," I said. "Raise your hand when the line looks like two lines." Grace's hand was up when the card was a foot away. Her eye never got any stronger, not after weeks of practice. Ellen, on the other hand, could bring it all the way to within an inch of her nose before she saw double. She was almost too young for this, but somehow she understood, probably from watching Grace. She was always watching Grace, following her from room to room, wanting whatever toy Grace held in her hand.

After a few evenings of our game, Grace pushed Ellen away. "My game," she said. Ellen was barely two. Her head hit the ground. How she howled! I lifted Grace into my lap. Dad dropped his book and picked up Ellen. He walked with her up and down the hallway, front door to dining room, and back, soothing her, whispering softly in her ear. When she calmed, he sat again with her on his lap.

I talked to Grace. "You must not push," I said. "That's bad. Ellen is your sister. Look, tell her you're sorry." Grace stared blankly, her weak eye turned inward, her other eye on Ellen, her finger in her mouth. She would not say it.

The eye specialist suggested we patch Grace's good eye for an hour a day so she would use the weak one. That, he said, would strengthen it. If she saw me coming at her with the gray rectangular patch, in late morning, while she played in the living room with her toys, she ran from me. The little devil. She was so cute, trying to hide behind the sofa. How she giggled when I grabbed her little ankles and pulled her out. She didn't like the patch, but the hug that came next soothed her. She found a picture book and brought it to me, there on the floor, plopped down on my lap and opened it. "Mommy read," she said. Her eye wandered wildly. I didn't know if she could see the pictures or not, so close, but I read, pointing to the words on the page, not really believing she could follow my finger or see anything but blurred lines. Ellen, of course, wanted to listen. Grace got Ellen howling again with another shove as she approached. I settled her next to me, on the floor, cross-legged, her head peering around. At least she could see without upsetting Grace, and we all read a story together.

Living with my parents was not all cozy support and convenience. Yes, my parents were saints when it came to helping me with the girls. God knows how we managed, after a year and a half with Mother and Dad, with Roy working so much, to get pregnant again. But I did. Then, I lost it after two months. When the blood and the cramping started, I was afraid. It was a very bad time for me. I imagined bleeding to death and leaving Roy with three little girls. That was how low my state of mind was, thinking the absolute worst thought imaginable. Imagining my little Grace without me. She'd already lost such a big part of me when she had to share me at such a young age. Imagine losing me altogether? Mother thought my tears were of remorse at the loss. But, mingled with that sense of sadness, I was so relieved. Not only because I realized that I wasn't going to die and leave her alone, but that there was not going to be another baby. I was barely holding on with three. The idea of a fourth was terrifying.

We hadn't bought a house yet. Mother's house had no more room. To this day I believe God answered my secret prayers. Once I recovered from the miscarriage, I went on the Pill. In Mother's very

Catholic house I had to be sure to hide them where she'd never see them. I kept them under my mattress, in deep toward the center, so even if she came up and changed the sheets on the bed she would not find them. I didn't tell Roy either.

Dad took over with Ellen when Roy was gone, which was every day, except Sunday. He looked after her. Grace went through a wicked stage and Dad protected Ellen from her. Good Lord was Grace awful. She hid toys. She hit Ellen with a doll; thank God it was a soft one. She shrieked when Ellen came near anything she was doing. Dad took to calling Grace "Little Hitler" because she was so demanding. They say at three and a half toddlers get very aware of their world, of their domain, of their separateness from the mother. Grace must have felt that. She probably felt her old feeling of being invaded, the one she experienced at Ellen's birth. It must have left her feeling threatened to have Ellen pestering her all day every day. Thank God for Dad. He kept Ellen at bay; distracted her from her fascination with everything her older sister did, and that let Grace have the freedom she needed to explore her world.

In August of 1958 Roy and I moved into our first house, a tall colonial with a shady front porch and a neighborhood full of families with kids. Roy still had to work two jobs though. I was alone so much with the three girls. Mother and Dad came over most afternoons to give me a hand.

The phone rang one lunchtime while Grace sat in a booster and Ellen sat strapped into the high chair. Lunch was cut up cheese squares, sliced grapes, and lunchmeat and Zwieback crackers. Mary Lou hadn't woken up from her nap. I ran to answer the phone. I had to stretch the phone cord out very long to reach a pen and piece of paper in the dining room to write down a recipe from Barbara, my old high school friend. Roy and I had a party planned and Barbara had a great recipe for baked beans. I was gone just a minute or two. I hung up and turned to check on the girls and saw Ellen turning blue. Grace stood next to Ellen's high chair stuffing little cubes of Velveeta cheese into

Ellen's mouth. Ellen's cheeks were puffed up like a stuffed toad and Grace continued, calmly and methodically, to shove piece after piece of cheese in, with an expression of utter concentration furrowing her little brow.

"No," I cried. "Grace, no!"

She looked up at me and smiled. She dropped the last little cube back onto the tray of the high chair and brushed her hands together. Ellen was choking. The buckle on the safety strap that held her took forever to open. I worked as fast as I could. I lifted her, shoved my finger in her mouth to scrape what I could out as fast as I could and turn her upside down. I held her by her shins; I gave her a good clap on the back. A wad of yellow-orange mingled with drizzling saliva landed on the floor at my feet. I heard her intake of air. Then came that cry, that cat-like piercing wail of indignation, fear and need. Next, she vomited all over my shoes and the floor. The splatter clung to my bare shins and dripped toward my sandaled feet. I turned her around and pulled her close. Still she wailed. She clung to me; her bib pressed against my ribs, her head turned sideways, her ear against my breast. I calmed her, crooned to her, spoke in a soft whisper, there, there, it's okay, it's over. Grace was just trying to feed you. She was imitating me. You're okay now. It's over. There. Here, drink some milk. She quieted, drank and continued to cling.

These things always happen when you are alone. These emergencies. You learn how to do what is necessary, you tell the story later, you process the whole thing in your mind on the replay. And that's what I did an hour or so later, after I put both girls down in their cribs for afternoon naps, just before Mother and Dad pulled up in Dad's old green Chevy. I made coffee and lit a cigarette. Mary Lou sat in her infant chair and Mother fed her strained peas and peaches with the baby spoon. Dad went out to the porch to read. I told Mom everything.

"Thank God the wad fell out. She might have died. She was so blue." I told Mother how I'd never use that safety strap with the buckle again. I told her I would never leave them alone again, not for an instant. I told her everything except what Grace said with her beseeching look, as though she expected praise, as though she'd done a good thing. She lifted her arms to me as she said it. What still haunts me, to this day, is that I didn't lift Grace up. I didn't take her in my lap. I refused to offer her comfort. Her sorrow, the tears that rose in her eyes when I refused to give her a hug…and, that image of her little crossed eye, and her sad little mouth…I will never forget how she looked so pathetic, so confused, so abandoned. I told Mother Grace was trying to help me; she was imitating me, feeding her little sister to be a little helper, like she feeds her dolls when I give Mary Lou a bottle. I told Mother, "She was only trying to be me."

The Fissure

Mary Lou didn't cry when she split her knee open on gravel. Yes, it hurt like hell, but nobody would catch her crying like a baby. Her bike was fast, her legs strong. A boy wouldn't cry, so she wouldn't. She'd be tough, rugged, no tears, and no sissy stuff.

She slipped when she skidded to a stop after racing Ellen home from the park. Blood ran thick down her shin and seeped into her ankle sock, the cotton fiber spreading the bright stain across the ribs of stitching. Bits of blue stone stuck to her skin and stung. Her knee was split open. She looked for her bone. How cool that would be, to see a white smooth bone of her skeleton, like the fake one hanging near the blackboard at school. Just a glimpse. All she saw was blood, separated flesh and liquid oozing around tiny crumbles of gravel. The fear, as she was falling, during those few seconds before impact, was worse than the gashed knee. Now, she was past that. The front wheel of her bike was twisted perpendicular to the ground, and the horizontal back wheel continued to spin. This wasn't her driveway. She was three houses from home, at Mr. Wissing's driveway, the usual turn-around point. She'd cut the turn too fast and her tire had mired in the deep gravel.

Ellen, her sister, older by a year and a half, the loser of this race, arrived. From her spot on the ground, Mary Lou watched Ellen see the blood running down her leg. Ellen pulled up and jumped off her bike, a boy's black Schwinn; Dad had bought it for ten dollars from Lenny, the newspaper delivery boy, who'd outgrown it. The sting-ray handlebars looked good, but it wasn't fast, not like Mary Lou's old blue fenderless Murray with the chipped paint.

Ellen said, "Better go inside."

Mary Lou did just that. She stood, rubbed her hands together, and felt the tiny holes and the gritty dirt inside her skin. She ran, determined not to limp, across the sidewalk and up the path to their front door.

Mary Lou sat atop the clothes dryer in the kitchen. She felt heat rise under the backs of her thighs and heard the hum thump, hum thump of the laundry drying. That rhythmic music played in the kitchen all day long, while Mom cooked or ironed or sat with a cup of coffee and a book. Mary Lou's bloody sock lay in the sink under a stream of cold water that ran clear, then pink.

Mom dabbed at Mary Lou's knee, picking with a tweezers at the gravel in the fissure. "Sit there and hold this, she said. "Press it down. The bleeding isn't stopping." She glanced at Ellen, who had just arrived. "Racing again?"

"I won again," Mary Lou lifted her chin toward Ellen triumphantly, suggesting the injury was worth it. She was still the victor.

Ellen didn't bother defending her loss. She and Mary Lou played games all the time. Ellen had her turns at victory. This just wasn't one of them. Her nonchalance irritated Mary Lou. She wished her sister would care more that Mary Lou was tougher, faster and braver.

"Can we go back?" Ellen asked. "To the park after lunch?"

The sisters were building a path across the brook with rocks. It was part of a game. They pretended someone evil was chasing them and the brook was their only path of escape. They imagined they'd cross, move just one large rock to destroy the path behind them, thwart their pursuers. Ellen's idea. Mary Lou went along, though she'd rather skip rocks across the water than build a path.

Mom threw away a bloody gauze pad and tore the packing off another. "Not if it's still bleeding," she said. "Maybe some quiet time after lunch." She smiled at Mary Lou, who scowled.

"We can play checkers," Ellen suggested. It was one of her fields of victory. Mary Lou couldn't beat her at checkers. Couldn't beat her at Chinese checkers either, or Bobby Hull hockey. But Ellen never turned down a bike race, so Mary Lou wouldn't be able to turn down a game of checkers.

Olive Street was narrow and crooked. It bent three times in between Prospect Street and Myrtle Street. Mr. Wissing's house, where Mary Lou had fallen, was two past theirs, on the first bend. The houses were tall, vertical colonials that stood in rigid rows on narrow lots, fifteen feet or so apart. Driveways were rare. Each house had a front porch five steps from ground level, railings that ran around the edge, white spindles supporting the railings. White pillars held up the roofs. In those houses, it seemed, children were bred like rabbits in hollows. The Taylors had three: Grace was the eldest, then Ellen, just thirteen months younger, then Mary Lou. The three girls shared a single bedroom. A set of bunk beds and a single twin against opposing walls left room for little else. Their tall narrow house had only three bedrooms, and Mom used the small one for a sewing room. Next door, the Firsts had three filthy boys whose buzz cuts the girls mocked each summer. "Baldy," the sisters cried out the windows across the alley; the bedrooms of the two houses were separated only by those few sunless feet.

Jimmy First snapped his plastic shade and it whirled up toward the ceiling. "I can see you in your underwear," he said in retaliation.

"You wish," Mary Lou yelled defiantly. Mom arrived then and lowered the plastic shades, suggesting that civilized people did not shout across alleys at each other.

Two huge maples shaded the Taylor's front porch. Gnarled roots heaved the sidewalk and made for bumps to hit with bicycle tires, bouncing riders into the air. Mary Lou worked on hitting the highest point of heaved concrete to fly high. Her split knee today was not her first injury of the summer.

After lunch, Mom gave Mary Lou and Ellen each twenty cents and they walked to Mrs. Ryan's candy store. Hire's root beer, the bottles bigger than a bottle of Coca-Cola, was their shared favorite.

Mary Lou sat on the top step of the front porch, a checkerboard between herself and her sister. Ellen had gone swimming in their backyard pool, a four foot deep bowl of turquoise cool, once they got back from their walk. Mary Lou stayed out, her knee still oozing blood. Ellen was still dressed in her bathing suit, under a Charlie Brown sweatshirt. A silk-screened version of the cartoon character walked dejectedly across the front, a baseball bat over his shoulder. The quote on the back said, "How can you lose when you're so sincere?" Older sister Grace had an orange one illustrated with a dancing Snoopy. Her's read: "I've got to start acting more sensible…tomorrow." Mary Lou wore Grace's old navy blue one and insisted she was happy with it. She liked that it was not fussy.

Mary Lou stretched her leg out and down. She was in shorts and a striped tee shirt, and wore green flip-flops. Three Band-Aids hid the cut on her knee. A shadow of the earlier blood was visible on her shin and the knee was starting to feel stiff. Mom had given her an ice pack and she applied it every few minutes. Ellen was beating her in a game of Kings. Mary Lou had three men left to Ellen's five and two were trapped in corners. If she moved them, she lost. Defeat was inevitable.

"I think I want to quit," Mary Lou said. She lifted her bottle of Hines root beer to her lips and took a tiny sip.

"You can't quit now," Ellen said. "It's not fair to quit before the end."

"You're gonna win," Mary Lou said. "You already won and you know it."

"But it's only fair to finish," Ellen said. She eyed Mary Lou's bottle, then glanced at her own. Hers was still almost full. Mary Lou's was three quarters empty. That was a contest too. Who could make their root beer last the longest? Ellen's victory was certain there, as well. Mary Lou told herself she didn't care. She was thirsty. Better to drink it now, while it was still cool, even if it meant Ellen won again.

"Let's read," Mary Lou said. She took her pieces off the board and stacked them in the box. Ellen folded the board.

Mary Lou pressed the ice pack to her shin just below the Band-Aid. If only she'd taken that turn a bit slower. They'd be at the park now. She and Ellen had discovered the overpass at the far end. The bridge was made of metal mesh and ran under the parkway overpass. It crossed the brook where the banks were steep, where concrete supported the walls. The water flowed downhill there and rushed over rocks, lending the familiar trickling brook a new and unexpected energy. Mary Lou wanted to go back and read the graffiti on the concrete, the swear words, the hearts with names. She wanted to ride under the bridge while traffic rushed by overhead. She wanted to shout and listen to her voice echo off the metal and concrete, but she was stuck here. She squeezed cold water from the towel where it had absorbed the ice melt, and let it fall on her leg.

Jimmy First pedaled by on his bike. He was Ellen's age. The sisters called him 'Magilla Gorilla' because his buzz-cut hairline curved toward a point in his forehead. He had flaps for ears, and his chin was somehow shorter than chins on most humans. He seemed more chimpanzee than gorilla, still, they knew the reference to the TV cartoon tortured him.

They were of the same mind about Jimmy. He had tried to steal their kitten last year. They found it on his porch, under a screened box their mother used for sifting pebbles out of the soil in her garden. They found it after hearing mewing for hours, imagining it was trapped under one of the porches. They called its name, searching, fearful it was hurt and dying somewhere right under their noses. Dad blew his stack, called Jimmy a little thief, and suggested to his father that the boy needed stronger guidance. Mr. First had cursed at their father who took back the kitten and the screened box Jimmy had stolen from their yard. "Stay away from him," he told his daughters.

Jimmy passed by on his bike, circling from up the street to the edge of the driveway where Mary Lou had fallen earlier; he passed his own house, took some air at the bump near the maple and stopped on their sidewalk, in front of their house. He held his bicycle between his legs and stood flat-footed, watching them pack up the game.

"Who won?" he asked.

"I did," Ellen answered. She didn't look up. Mary Lou watched him even though she didn't like looking at him. He looked back with eyes too bright, too eager, annoying, begging for something the girls didn't have to give.

"Not that you should care. Maybe you should mind your own business." Mary Lou pulled one leg up under her and left the injured one dangling down the steps toward the street.

Jimmy said, "What happened to your knee?"

"She fell," Ellen said. She stood up. Her wet bathing suit had left a watery shadow on the lower half of her sweatshirt. Mary Lou saw Jimmy's gaze linger on her sister's legs. Ellen yanked at her shirt, pulling it down to cover more. Mary Lou saw the muscle in her sister's thigh twitch. She wished Jimmy's eyes would stop. It was worse when Ellen moved. His eyes followed her when she bent to lift the game, to lift her root beer bottle. They stayed on her when she straightened, her wet hair falling over her eyes. Mary Lou threw an ice cube toward him.

Jimmy laughed. "The tomboy," he said. "My mother always says Mary Lou is the tomboy in your family." He glanced at Mary Lou. "That's why you're always covered with bruises." He looked back at Ellen. "You're the girl," he said. His eyes traveled up and down her exposed legs. "You even look more like a girl."

Mary Lou watched Ellen's widened eyes. Ellen's skin flushed and she yanked again at the stretchy band of her sweatshirt, pulling it down to cover her crotch, her behind. Mary Lou waited for Ellen to say something. Surely she'd call him a name, something to mock him. Ellen just turned her back, opened the door and went inside. The screen flapped shut behind her, once, twice, three slaps against the frame, before it fell silent.

Mary Lou turned to watch Jimmy. She couldn't believe it. Ellen had said nothing. No fight, no ridicule, no retaliation. Mary Lou stared into his eyes. He was amused. He liked that he'd made Ellen squirm, that she'd run into the house to get away from him. Mary Lou thumbed her nose at him. His smile vanished.

Mary Lou wished she were a boy. She found that phrase, 'you're the girl' repulsive; she wanted to punch Jimmy. She wanted to be strong enough to knock that look in his eye back inside his skull. To her, his words were the worst insult a boy could give a girl. She turned to follow Ellen inside, and kicked her root beer bottle over in her haste. Its sticky syrup spilled across the porch and dripped down to the top step, making a line, just like the shadow of the bloodstain on her shin. She had to go back to retrieve the bottle. Her knee throbbed when she bent it and leaned over. Jimmy didn't look at her legs. He looked at the door where Ellen had disappeared, as though considering.

In a manner she didn't understand, Mary Lou felt irritated, and a wave of humiliation moved through her. She didn't want his eyes on her, but a sense of defeat, of another victory for Ellen nagged her for the rest of the day. She tried to read "The Secret of the Old Clock", a Nancy Drew mystery, and imagined herself as George, the friend, the tomboy sidekick of the teenaged heroine.

Over dinner that night, while Ellen drank the last of her root beer, in a glass, with ice, Mary Lou announced to her family that she wanted them to call her Lou. "Lou, not Mary Lou," she said, glancing at Ellen. "It's a nickname. If I'm the tomboy, it makes sense that my nickname should be Lou."

Homesickness, 1973

At nineteen, between her sophomore and junior years at the state university, her last summer's earnings plowed into a cool 1969 Firebird, Grace had gas and cash and, most importantly, an invitation from Charles to Prince Edward Island for a week.

"I can go and not have sex," she insisted. Mom flushed purple at the word and looked away.

"I won't do it, Mom," she said again, emphasis on the word *it*. Grace couldn't imagine letting Charles see her naked or put his hands on her small breasts beneath her padded bra. Her appendix scar kept her from allowing him to explore lower than where her bikini would end if she wore one, which she didn't because of her slightly rotund tummy, odd because the rest of her was thin. She wouldn't even take her glasses off in front of him, knowing her eye would roll, unless he closed his eyes to kiss her. She didn't share this with Mom, who would be appalled at the idea that she even considered letting him touch her. Instead she retrieved the family bible from its display under Mom's crucifix in her bedroom, put her hand on it and swore. That did it. Mom caved right there at the dinner table. Lou was a different story.

She rolled her eyes and made kissing noises. Ellen was silent as always. That was the way Grace liked it. Ellen keeping her opinions to herself. But Lou's mocking hurt. It hid what Grace knew to be more than mocking, her little sister Lou was jealous.

Mom finished her dinner quickly, then insisted on saying the prayer after meals, a tradition from her Catholic upbringing which she was passing on to her daughters along with her expectation that they all remain virgins until marriage. Mom left the table and retired to the parlor to read. Grace cleared the table, Ellen washed what wouldn't fit in the dishwasher, Lou stacked plates and glasses and silverware in the new KitchenAid.

"I can't believe Mom is letting you go," Ellen said.

"Why?" Grace pulled plastic wrap from its long narrow box and ripped it against the jagged metal edge.

"You've never been away from home." Ellen squirted detergent into a pot.

"So?"

"So you're going to get homesick," Ellen said.

"I'm nineteen! Please! I won't get homesick. I'm sick of being at home."

Lou dropped a handful of forks into the dishwasher with a loud jingle. "That's it, Grace. You are now a member of the Ellen sorority of boy crazy, make-up obsessed, tongue in the mouth French kissing club."

Ellen dropped her sponge. "What are you talking about?"

"Ellen, we know what you think about all the time." Grace said.

"What? What do I think about all the time?"

"S-E-X." Lou snorted with mocking laughter. "Come on. You're always on the phone with Sandy about boys."

"That's not true. Just because you're a tomboy doesn't mean I'm boy crazy."

Grace wanted to defend Lou against Ellen, but Ellen was right. Lou at sixteen still behaved like she did at age ten when she insisted they call her Lou because it fit her better than Mary Lou. Lou's distrust of Charles was fear and embarrassment, partially due to Dad, who, when he was around, which wasn't often, still sang the "Grace and Jimmy sitting in a tree, k-i-s-s-i-n-g" song if Jimmy First next door so much as said hello to one of them. There was a collective sense of humiliation in that, and combined with Mom's pressure, it imprisoned the three sisters while they watched classmates and friends engage with confidence with members of the opposite sex. Grace might just cross over that invisible moat and escape the castle their family had built, but it meant abandoning Lou, her best friend, her partner in crime, her cellmate.

"Lou," Grace said. "I'm just going because it's where the books were written. The Green Gables books."

"I wish I could go too," Ellen said. "I loved those books."

"Fat chance," Grace said. "Get your own boyfriend." She knew how to hurt Ellen. Ellen had a crush on Armand, a boy from high school who commuted to the same college she and Grace did. Ellen had never mustered the courage to speak to Armand, much less go out with him or any other boy. At eighteen, Ellen was far worse off than she was.

"Then you really are going to keep your promise to Mom?" Lou asked.

"Yes," Grace said.

Charles was the boy behind Grace in pre-Calc. He confessed one late March afternoon, when she descended into the commuter parking lot alone, the western sky streaking purple and pink behind her, that he cheated off her on the final. Then, to assuage her anger at that dishonest deed, he asked if he could use her as a model for his photography project. "You've got great color," he said. "Your hair especially." He said the right thing. Charles always said the right thing to Grace. He never asked about her glasses, he didn't notice she walked with her, toes pointed outward. He confessed he fell in love with her because her long hair whispered against his hand; it reached his desk, right behind hers, while he tried to take notes in class.

Grace lived at home and attended the state commuter college ten miles away. Ellen had, to her dismay, been accepted at the same college and, because Ellen did not yet own her own car, Grace had to drive Ellen to campus each day. That particular day when Charles and she began to date, Grace was feeling free. Free from Mom's oppressive reminders of the temptations of sex, drinking and drugs she might encounter at school. Free from the assumptions Ellen made that since they went to the same school they were responsible for each other. This vacation would free her further, she hoped.

Charles had not read L.M. Montgomery's books but Grace and Ellen had read every one of the Green Gable stories. The PEI idea came to him, he said, at Easter when he came to the house to meet her family. The books lined the shelf in the upstairs hallway. He'd spent a few summers there as a boy.

Now, Charles' bag was tucked behind the driver's seat of the Firebird on the floor next to Grace's bag, which was stuffed with books. "In case I need help remembering," Grace said. "I want to feel like I'm in the story." She imagined herself as the nineteen-year-old heroine, Anne Shirley, and Charles as Gilbert, the boy Anne married, her first and only love.

"I've got to pull over." He swerved to the shoulder somewhere along 95 and ducked behind a bush, did his business and returned.

"Girls can't do that," she said, watching his hands grip the steering wheel. "Pee outside."

"When it comes to that, we do have an advantage."

Ellen, Grace thought, glancing sideways at Charles as he drove, would probably try to date a boy named Charles too the way she did everything Grace did, right after Grace. Or worse, try to date *her* Charles. Ellen had a friend who had already done *it*, according to the diary she and Lou had stolen and read way back in tenth grade. But Ellen was not here. Grace let the window down; her hair flapped like a flag around her head. I am finally away and on my own, she thought.

I will stop thinking about home, I will, despite what Ellen said about how I'd be homesick.

Later, Charles read aloud from one of Grace's books while she drove, and by the time they hit Maine he called her "Carrots" like the boy in the book called the girl, even though Grace's hair was not red, it was golden brown with artificial blond streaks, and she was calling him Gilbert, the boy Anne of Green Gables married. Grace imagined Charles lifting her over the threshold of a house like the one in the story, carrying her into a new romantic world of married bliss. Then they'd do *it*. That was her secret fantasy not even Lou knew.

The sun set off a spectacle of glitter on the bay. Charles hung his arm around her; he pointed out seals and their wake in the water, a loon diving for fish. Behind them in New Brunswick, the ferry's distance made a dot out of a black bear rambling along a strip of forest, a mere shadow of movement. Dark descended just as they pulled to the dock on the ferry and their first night was a chaste one, her promise still intact and her conversation with Mother via the public phone in the parking lot of their motel an honest one.

PEI, Charles insisted she call it that, shone in the morning brightness and sparkled all day, just as LM Montgomery described. Charles said, "It's the northern light. It slants. The shadows are long so the contrasts are amazing." He stopped roadside on their way to the Green Gable House to take pictures while she ached for her first glimpse of the famous house. She was becoming Anne Shirley, driving down a golden road, not in a Firebird, but in an open horse drawn wagon. The year was 1910, not 1973. Charles pulled into the gravel parking lot, and on a small rise the House of the Green Gables welcomed them. Tears welled in Grace's eyes and she felt Charles' arm go round her shoulder and his face reach to land a kiss on her cheek, "Welcome Carrots!" he said, laughing at her.

"I want to live here," Grace said. "Not here." She laughed, her chin pointing toward the historically preserved site. "On this island."

Charles took her picture in the attic bedroom where Anne had slept. They walked along the path in the Haunted Woods. He taught her to use his light meter and adjust the aperture setting for dark shadow. They visited Lovers Lane, kissed under green draping foliage, and found a spot for a picnic.

Grace soaked in the ghost-like presence of beloved characters and longed to pick a bouquet of primroses from the bushes along the fence. Charles ate three sandwiches. "Can we swim?" he asked, lying back as the sun-baked air grew hotter. Grace read a brochure.

"First I need to get souvenirs."

"For who?" Charles said, "We've got a week. Let's buy stuff later." He rolled onto his side, elbow supporting his head and placed his hand so lightly on her thigh. "Let's swim, then maybe find something else to do."

Grace didn't want to kiss him in public. But, she decided, remembering her promise, it was safer here than in private. So they rolled around on the grass until someone coughed loudly nearby. And old couple, the woman wearing men's black socks and a pair of heavy brown sandals, shuffled past along the path.

"I have to bring something home for Lou," Grace said, sitting up. "I promised."

Charles lay back and stretched his arms over his head. He squinted as the sun glittered through the dappled shadows of an elm.

"Yes, I guess I should bring something home for my brother." His eyes followed a raptor high over the wood. "Just for Lou? Not for Ellen?"

Grace watched the raptor too. She lay on her back next to him and shaded her eyes. It circled, slowly, wings wide on an updraft.

"I don't think she'd care."

"Did Lou read the books?"

"No. Ellen did though. She tries everything I try."

"Yeah," Charles said. "I thought so. She's more like you than Lou." He sat up. "Lou acts like she wishes she were a boy." The sound of a can hissing open made Grace turn toward him. She watched his neck muscles ripple as he drank. She wanted to run her finger along his Adam's apple. Smooth skin, a crease just barely visible, stubble only on his chin.

"So why do you think she wouldn't care if you brought something for Lou and not her? Not that I want to spend more time in shops."

The question annoyed Grace. "I'm away from home. Let's not talk about my sisters."

"You brought it up."

"Yes, but just because I have to stop at a store at some point."

"Okay," He said. "I'll drop it. I'd rather go swimming."

"We'll go to the beach right off the national park," Grace said, showing him the island map. "I want to call home though. I'd rather check in now than wait for later." At his puzzled look, she added, "I made a couple of promises to get permission to come on this trip."

"Oh?" Charles gathered up the beach towel under them. He stuck up one finger, "Call home daily?" He waited. "What else?"

Grace flushed. "I can't tell you the rest."

"Oh, come on," Charles said. "How many?"

Grace gathered empty soda cans and plastic wrap from the deli sandwiches they'd picked up in Cavendish. "Only one." She flushed. "Sorry, you can't know."

His face serious, Charles dropped the towel. "Grace, how will they know?"

"I'm not a good liar, Charles," Grace said, turning swiftly up the path toward the garden and the parking lot. "I'm not."

"Is your mother the type to ask?" he asked, following. His voice was hushed but she sensed his, his, what was it, fear, astonishment, accusation?

"Yes…no…I don't know…She expects me to be a virgin until I get married." Grace wouldn't look at him. If she did, she knew he'd win. He could do that. Once, at home, in his dad's Buick, he'd just touched her with his fingers, inside her panties, against her skin. She'd sucked in her breath and gasped against his mouth she'd been exploring with her tongue. That look when she stopped him. "Why?" he had said. "Let me."

Now she hurried to the car. He expected it. Now she knew why he'd wanted to come away. For that. Not for the light and the sea and to show her the place where Montgomery had written her stories. Just for that. She fired the engine while he dropped the towel and his camera bag in the back seat. How to explain it wasn't just her promise to her mother. Lou would mock her. Lou would never forgive her. It would be as though she had joined forces with Ellen, the boy crazy. Ellen, who worshipped Jackson Browne, who collected pictures of bride dresses for the eventual day she'd get married. Grace wondered if Charles just wanted sex so he could brag that he'd done it. She wanted to do it after she knew he wouldn't walk away in the disappointment she was sure he'd feel afterwards. He'd find out how unbeautiful she was. What was love? What were the signs? She glanced sideways at Charles who watched the road and the sunlight. He had only said it once and not lately. She drove the short road to the red sand beach. She remembered her mother's words. No one will ever love you like your mother loves you. Unless, she mused, unless your sister does. She wondered what Lou was up to at home.

Grace sighed and Charles glanced at her. "What?"

"We're so far from home but why do I feel like they're all still here with me?"

"Who?"

"My family."

"Got to let go, girl. Got to be free. Live your own life." He rested his hand on her knee.

The line rang just once and Mother picked up. Grace wondered if it would turn up in her voice if she and Charles did it, if virginity gone could be detected that way. Immediately, Mother said, "We're keeping busy while you're gone. Hold on."

Charles was inside a shack shedding layers of clothes and underwear and she was supposed to be looking out for beach patrol people because the sign said no changing in the rest rooms.

"Hi." Grace heard Lou's subdued voice through the wire.

"How's things?" Grace asked.

"Boring," Lou said. "Ellen is sewing. Mom is reading. Dad's out of town on a trip."

"It's beautiful here," Grace said, feeling that perhaps she should temper her enthusiasm. Lou missed her. She could read it in the deadpan grunt after she told her, "We saw the house and the haunted woods…"

"Ellen and I are taking lifeguard lessons at the Y," Lou broke in. "We're riding our bikes over."

"What about her job?" Lou and Grace on bikes? Like before? Like they used to do as kids?

Lou said, "She's back at the waitress thing, it's only for early morning."

"I'll bring you back a present," Grace said. "Charles and I are at the beach."

"That's nice," Lou said. "Wait."

Grace heard a prolonged silence; felt the world of home spinning without her. Lou was a traitor.

"How is the island?" A cloud passed overhead and Grace felt cool suddenly. The glitter off the bay dulled. A crow, not a gull, cawed. Ellen's voice and her question grated on a nerve.

"It's nice," Grace said, her voice slow, vibrating at a low frequency. But it didn't feel nice. It only felt far away. She felt far away.

"Is Charles behaving?"

"What?"

"Mom said to ask that," Ellen said. Her laugh came out shrilly and made Grace nervous. She imagined Ellen writing about Grace and Charles in her diary. She answered with a simple, emotionless 'yes'.

"We're swimming," she said. Here was Charles, emerging, in a tee shirt and swim shorts.

"I heard the beaches there are red. There's rust in the sandstone.

Say hi to Charles for me," Ellen said. When Grace didn't respond Ellen kept talking. "Did you go to Green Gables?"

"We went this morning," Grace said.

"Did you say hello to Anne Shirley?" Ellen asked. Grace knew she expected a laugh. She didn't give her one.

"She's dead, Ellen."

"Well, she was never alive…unless you think of LM Montgomery as her, then she was, right?"

"Yes," Grace said. "I'll call again tomorrow. Bye." She pressed the receiver onto its hook.

"Your turn," she said. Charles fished for Canadian coins and lifted the phone while she headed to the women's room to change. Inside, spider webs with trapped flies filled filthy corners. Still more hovered over open holes into a tank from which a vague stench rose. She wished she were a boy and could stand to pee rather than sit where flies definitely must have landed earlier. Charles' voice came through the thin boards of the shack and she heard laughter as he said his brother's name and a swear word. Then he must have whispered because the caw of the crow was all she heard. Life was easier when there were two brothers, not three sisters, she thought, surprised as that realization came to her. Charles said she and Ellen were similar. No, he was wrong. She sat after placing strips of toilet tissue where her skin would contact the seat. Lou said Ellen was sewing. Grace's mind saw Mom and Ellen together, making, what did Lou say? She didn't. She just said sewing. Grace didn't do that kind of thing. The thing she shared with Mom was reading. Maybe I shouldn't have come. Maybe I'll get home and Ellen will be in my place, not just with Lou, but with Mom too.

There was no surf. The water lapped gently and formed eddies. They walked gingerly over the rough terrain strewn with smooth oval red pebbles, and lowered into shallow frigid water. Then they lay on the red sand and let the gentle water lap at their feet. Grace watched out for the huge horseshoe crabs that occasionally crept at them sideways.

"Ellen said the sand is red because it's full of rust," Grace said.

"That true?"

"Yup," Charles said. "Why didn't I know she was your sister? I never saw you two together until Easter. She was in a class with me once."

"She's a geology major. She takes different kinds of classes."

"You ever drive in together?"

"Only when absolutely necessary." Grace said. "Mom let's her use the family car. At least until she buys her own, like I did."

"Why don't you ever talk about her?"

"I am, right now."

"Yes, but you talk about Lou a lot."

"Lou is like me."

"No, Ellen's more like you."

"How?"

"Well, she looks more like you. And she read the Green Gables books."

"So did a million other people." Grace conjured Ellen in her mind. Tall, brown hair, blue eyes, thin, as small breasted as Grace, braces off, straight teeth, she walked with her feet straight and she didn't wear glasses. "Still talking about home. Let's take a walk."

Charles said, "I'm sorry."

"What for?" Grace asked, her eyes widening. She bent over and chose a flat stone for skimming.

"I don't want you to be in a bad mood," Charles said.

"I'm not," Grace said.

"Well, after that phone call your mood changed."

"No," Grace said.

"Yes," Charles said.

"No," Grace said.

"Oh, yes," Charles said. "You two don't get along, do you?"

"We get along fine," Grace said. "I just talked to her."

"Oh, what did she say?" Charles expertly skimmed a red stone. She counted five skips off the water and dropped hers with a plop at her feet.

"Not much. She said Mom said to tell you to behave. And, Lou and Ellen are getting lifeguard training." Grace stared back while Charles studied her face closely.

"So?"

"And I'm here," she said.

"Lucky you." He grinned and reached to pull her in to him.

"But, little does she know, Lou will dump her when I get home."

Charles let her go. "What?"

"We hate her." Grace found an oyster shell. "But Lou is hanging out with her while I'm away. By the time I get home, they'll be…"

"What?" Charles' eyes were large. "You hate her?"

"Well, not really hate. We're just at odds, I guess."

Charles' gaze stayed on her but she wouldn't meet it. "God, I fight with my brother but I'd never say I hate him…I mean sometimes he gets on my nerves."

Grace stopped and sat on a flat red rock. She dug her toes into the wet sand and flipped muddy piles toward the surf.

"Ellen is difficult. My mother always said that. She didn't get her period until last year."

"So?" Charles clearly was not getting this. "That's no reason to hate her."

"Now, every time she gets her period, she goes on these crying jags." Grace said. She watched Charles' face. A soulful look formed while he continued his intent scrutiny of her eyes.

"So maybe she knows you hate her."

"No, Charles. Don't you dare say that. You don't know her." Grace saw his tinge of interest, too much interest in this, in Ellen. She could lose him if this kept going. She saw him, next summer, taking her sister on this same trip. Ellen loved those books too. She'd fall in love with this place, just like Grace had. She'd want the same thing.

"Ellen acts like she's really nice. She tries to be pretty. She tries to get my mother to praise her all the time. My mother does, when she makes things, like, she sews and she writes in a diary, and she, oh, I don't know."

"Has she ever done anything really mean?"

Grace said. "She lies to hide it."

"Hide what?"

Charles sat with his back to the sun and let the surf lap at his crossed legs. He tossed pebbles and looked off across the water.

"Don't you fight with your brother? Come on. Tell me you two are bosom buddies forever." He didn't get the L.M. Montgomery reference. Anne Shirley had a bosom buddy named Diana.

"I never think about it, but I've only got one brother. I wonder if we'd be well, like rivals. Is that what you are?" Charles was in earnest.

"If you had a sister like her, you would pretend she wasn't there."

"But what has she done?"

Grace lost patience. "Can we talk about something else?"

"I guess so. But, I'm just… I don't get it." He brushed sand from his palms. "What does your mother say?"

"She doesn't say anything."

"Does she know?"

Grace studied him. "I don't know. It doesn't matter."

"Does she have any friends?"

Grace laughed. "If you can call them friends."

"Grace," Charles said.

"What?"

"Do you love me?" His skin reddened. He stared past her at the red sand cliff. He looked full into her eyes.

"Do you love me?" she asked.

"I do," he said. "I wanted to come away with you. Get you away from Hillston. See you without all the things at home, you know? See you for who you are, away from everything at school, in Hillston. Away from Lou."

"Well, we're here," she said. "This is me."

"And I just found out that you hate your own sister…but you can't tell me why."

"Can we leave?" Grace looked around toward where they'd climbed over the dunes.

"No," Charles said.

"Then, I'll leave and you can walk back to the motel." Grace got halfway to a stand but he leaned over to nudge her back down. Grace felt her eyeglasses fall onto the sand. She bent down to collect them. He beat her to it and held them up. "Oops, sorry. They're dirty. Here, let me…" He breathed on the lenses and polished them. Grace felt his eyes on her face. She kept her head down, staring at her lap.

"Charles!" Grace said. "Please just give me my glasses."

"First look at me," he said.

"No," Grace whispered. She kept her gaze on her lap and held out her hand.

"Not until you tell me why you hate her."

"I can't believe this." Grace's eyes filled with tears. "Charles. Here we are. At Prince Edward Island. We can't be farther from home. But you're bringing up all this stuff about home."

"When I met your family, on Easter, you and she talked about the books. It was my first day with your family. I was admiring that…how you all seemed so much like a story in a book…you know…like Little Women." He frowned. "Yeah, I know that book has four, but one dies. And no, I didn't read it. I watched it on TV when I was sick once. But, now I see that it's not really all roses and nice stuff."

Grace sighed. "I thought this was an escape. I thought you just said you wanted to see me away from all the familiar stuff. And you can't stop talking about home."

"Well, you said you hate her!" Charles lowered his voice to a whisper. "I can't marry a girl who hates her sister and can't tell me why. Why? What happened? Something has to happen to create hate."

"Marry?" Grace wiped her nose with the back of her hand. She hid her face in her hands.

Charles continued in a whisper. "I know we're too young. I get it. But, Grace, we're good together. I think this is what I want. You, I mean. But now I'm kind of stuck in my tracks. I don't want…I don't know… it's just I want to know what I'm getting into if I ask you."

"This is who I am, Charles," Grace said, her head still lowered. Her eyes closed. "I'm not someone else to you just because I have a sister I can't get along with."

"But why?" There was desperation in his voice.

She stayed silent. She looked past him to the sky where a flock of geese was rising toward the pink cloud of the sinking sun. The last bite of her earlier lunch rose in her throat and she swallowed hard to keep it down. It was so beautiful here but the enchantment was ebbing like the tide.

"She's doing it. She's not even here and she's doing it. She's ruining my vacation. Just like she ruins everything."

"How does she ruin everything?" Charles had a beseeching look. Underneath it, she saw that poor sad abandoned little boy look he revealed whenever she broke from his embrace. So he loved her. Mingled with the pleasure of that was this need of his to know. If she answered, it might spoil the love. She wanted to look at him, but she didn't dare. He'd see her eye. It would wander. It would repulse him.

Grace could not answer his question. Not to his satisfaction. Words would not form on her lips. One image lodged in her conscious mind and would not relent, his look of horror if he saw her eye and along with it the thought that because of Ellen, Charles would not love her. Because of Ellen, Charles would want to go home. He would break up with her, if she did not answer his question. How could she make him understand? How, more importantly, could she keep him? What, she asked herself, had Ellen done? Why do I hate her? She remembered the morning Ellen broke her Holy Water font. Could this explain why Ellen deserved her hatred? Her mind still saw Ellen lift her hand, bring it down on the font, let it fall to the floor, watch it break, then, when her mother asked, she had said, "I didn't see it," with wide open eyes.

Grace wanted to tell him. She wanted Charles to be there with her in the top bunk bed watching Ellen walk toward the doorframe and lift her hand to dash the precious gift to the floor. They were twelve and eleven when that happened. This is the kind of thing Ellen does, she wanted to say.

She turned to Charles and hoped her eye did not roll in, that maybe he was sitting just far enough away from her. She met his stare. A weak smile crossed her eyes despite her sense of hopelessness. She knew how this would sound if it came out. She'd look like a fool. It was always this way. Always small things, one after the other. Charles would mock her. You hate your sister over an accident? Yes, she would long to say. But, to keep him, she'd have to admit it was too small to sweat and that she should forgive and forget. A streak of unreasonableness, that's what he would perceive in her, just enough for her to lose him. She could not explain. It would have been like trying to tell him why she felt such relief when she wrote graffiti all over Ellen's diary and saw it later torn to shreds in the trash and knew Ellen did not tell Mom.

This, she wanted to scream at Charles, was not a big deal. Mother knew that even though they seemed the same on the surface, Ellen was different from she and Lou. But only Lou knew what Ellen was left out of and why she was different.

Then, it came to her. Grace knew what to tell Charles, to keep him. To keep the idea in his head of her, that he loved her.

"If you hand me my glasses, I'll tell you."

"Promise?" Charles said.

Grace nodded. He handed her the glasses. She slid them on. She knelt on the sand and leaned toward him, her elbows on his knees, her face close to his. She said, "Ellen is different from me and Lou. Ellen likes girls."

Charles sat back. His mouth opened. It closed. He breathed in. He sighed. "Oh," is all he said. "But you could accept that, couldn't you? Unless, did she try to like, you know…"

Grace dropped her small smile. She frowned. "Yes."

"To Lou too?"

Grace waited for understanding to fill his eyes, loosen his furrowed brow, slacken his mouth.

"Now can we leave?" Grace let her hand rest on his leg, near his knee, and slowly, deliberately, with her eyes softening into his, slid it up as high as she could to his inner thigh. "And go to back to the motel?"

"I'm sorry," Charles said. "I made you tell me a secret."

"That's okay," Grace said. "Now you can tell me one. Now we can share everything. But, we've got to promise to never share them with anyone else. Okay?"

Charles touched her. His hands slid up under her arms and he pulled her close. "Yes, of course."

His mouth came down on hers. At his final word she moved his hands from her sides to her shoulders. While he pulled down the straps of her bathing suit she took in a sharp, short breath of victory. After this, she told herself. After tonight, we'll go home and I can tell Lou this too. Lou must know this too. She must know this lie and promise to keep it a secret.

The Last Day

Helen followed Mama from the road through the cold, iron gate and tripped on the curb where cobblestone ended and grassy lawn interrupted slabs of stone in rows. She tucked her hands up inside her cuffs, her coat's sleeves now one long black arc swooping from shoulder to shoulder. It was here, above the cradle of that arc, that she felt her own heart pumping black in her veins, its heat pulsing to the ends of her fingers. She felt it, viscous, slow, trapped in there like she was trapped here, its insidious weight scraping along the coarsely textured insides of her arteries. Florence had had red blood and Helen had seen Jack's blue through the pale skin on his forearms under his sleeves. Her blood too, had once been red. She'd seen it ooze through her knee once after a fall, but that was long before she'd ever come here.

She lingered near a stone and traced its letters with her fingers. Smooth as glass. Her hand, hot within, felt cool relief. If Mama didn't notice, she would just wait here. But Mama stopped at a small rise. With the bright sky behind her, she was a pale statue, like the sandstone angel just to the west, except for the lack of wings. Mama gestured with an impatient hand and became flesh and blood again, dark clothing wrapping her from head to foot, a fluttering kerchief tied tightly over her hair. Helen ran. Helen let her mother pull her into a cold hard embrace through layers of spun wool, a dry kiss to her hair through her tight hat, then a tug toward the tiny half sized slab where their family name, SAND, flickered while the sun flirted with an overhead branch.

Mama turned her back to the blue sky and tossing wind. Helen let Mama position her by her side although she would have preferred the sun on her face. Her eyes rested on the etched name, Florence. Helen calculated her dead sister's age. Born 1904. Died 1908. Helen knew Mama thought she prayed when she stood there next to her. Like the black in her veins, the arithmetic was Helen's secret. Florence would be eight this year. I was seven when she died. I am eleven.

Mama fell across the frozen earth and buried her face in dry yellow grass; her arms embraced the little granite slab. Helen looked toward the gate and the road and saw with relief there was nobody nearby. Helen heard "Flo, my little girl, my flower, my angel..."

Helen's heart pumped her inky blood harder. She knelt down and felt a rock under her knee, then shifted until a tuft of dead grass cushioned her bony joint. She stroked her mother's back. "Mama," Helen whispered. "Let's go home." Florence. Florence always in Mama's mind. Helen tried with all she did, all she said, her little gifts of flowers after she returned from school, her obedient attention to her chores, her studies; she kept her clothes spotless, ate without prompting, all her dinner, all of it a plea to her mother to turn her eyes to Helen and smile. After every failure the inky black darkened further in her veins and made it hard to muster joy of any kind, any remembrance of Florence except Mama's sorrow. And, if Helen laughed, Mama's frown quickly shut her down and returned her to obedient grief. Gladness was something that required forgiveness now.

Did Mama's veins flow with black also? They must, mustn't they, to make those dark circles under her eyes? Helen was not allowed to ask such questions at home, but at school, from the sisters, she took in every lesson, eager to find answers her mother's silence denied her.

"Death is punishment for sin," Sister Wilhelmina taught Helen's sixth grade class. Sister Wilhelmina said, "Ask God for forgiveness every day of your life or God will take you too." At her sister's grave, Helen prayed fervently for forgiveness.

Mama wiped her nose with her gloved hand and lifted herself to a kneeling position. She made a sign of the cross. She held her hands in prayer. She glanced at Helen and waited until she took a similar pose next to her.

"We pray for the soul of Florence," Mama recited. Helen didn't dare shift even though her knees had found the rock again. She spoke her mother's prayer, but in her heart, she prayed against Sister's warning.

"Florence was too young to sin," Mama said once, her only answer when Helen repeated Sister's lesson. "Florence is in heaven with Jesus and the angels and God the Father, not hell, because Florence did not deserve punishment."

Helen mumbled Mama's prayers after her, the words digging further and further down, spinning with contradictions. She prayed that she would not sin. She prayed she wouldn't die. She prayed she would be good so she, like Florence, would not deserve to die. Yet, Florence had died. Helen added a silent one that Mama would not punish her. She glanced over and flinched at the memory of the day of her punishment, and prayed that God would keep her good, would forgive her for whatever she had done to deserve the pain she had borne at Mama's hand.

Helen had walked through her front door, a dry dusty day, that first September after the funeral, home from second grade, calling "Mama, I'm home." She had dropped her bag on the floor and entered the kitchen, Mama's usual place. The back door was open, a few leaves, brown and dead, had blown in unnoticed and lay there inside the screen door. Helen bent to pick them up and drop them outside. She descended eight steps to the grassy yard. The peach tree was empty, but the pear tree was ripening with green fruit. Helen picked one then saw Mama crawling towards her through the box hedge at the rear of the yard.

Mama brushed dirt off her skirt and dropped a bucket of water on the ground in front of her. Helen saw the wild white kitten, one of three Jack had found and saved from a deliberate drowning by the old grocer up the street. A fine trickle of blood had dried on its lips. It lay near the base of the barren peach tree, dead. In Mama's hand, she saw its brother, a tabby, hanging by the skin on the back of its neck where its mother might have grasped it with her teeth. Helen saw its grey fur as it went down into the bucket. Mama held it there, pressing down, a grimace on her face. Helen screamed, "Mama, no!" She fell as she ran the length of the yard, got up and stumbled to her mother who pressed her away with an outstretched arm and did not look at her at all.

Helen begged, "Mama, no, please!"

When Mama's hand came up, the kitten was limp, its mouth open, its eyes half shut, unseeing.

Mama's eyes were liquid, black liquid. Helen drew back. "Mama, leave the other," she begged.

"One more." Mama practically shrieked.

Helen grabbed at her arm. "Stop! No! Not mine! That one is mine!"

Mama paid no attention. Helen prayed her brother, Jack, would come home early, that someone would come.

"Little rats, they are!" Mama said. "How long were they here? Did you let her near them? Look," she pointed with her chin at the white one, "its throat, it died like Florence died. We can't have them here."

"Keep one," Helen begged. "Keep the black one. I beg you. He's mine."

Mama ignored her. Helen fell on the ground across her mother's feet. "Please!" she begged. "Leave one for me."

Mama grabbed the black kitten by its scruff. Helen, on her knees, tried to tear it from her hand. Mama lifted it high and away, and then plunged it into the water. Helen stopped breathing. She tried to knock over the bucket. It sloshed over Mama's feet. Still Mama prevailed. Helen buried her face in the grass, closed her eyes, and prayed. She could hear claws scratching at the metal bucket, then, she heard nothing. She looked up. In horror, Helen saw Mama lift the dead soggy kitten and throw it on the ground with the others. That was the moment Helen's blood turned black. Mama tossed the water onto the grass and crawled through the box hedge and fence, dragging the bucket behind her.

Florence died this way? Did Mama say that? Helen tried to speak, to ask Mama what that meant. Mama cut her off. "No questions. Don't touch them," she said. "Go up to your room."

Helen fled. Her tears unchecked, her sobs gave her hiccups and she tried to hold her breath to cure them, and slowly, her horror gave away to fear. She lay on her bed, waiting for Mama to come through the door. Helen knew only that she had woken on a summer morning to find Mama sponging Florence down with cool water. Later that day, Dr. Van Essel had taken Florence to Saint Joseph's hospital. Mama had left Helen with Mrs. Degnan whose daughter Mildred was Helen's age. Mama in the carriage with Florence. Helen lay on her bed, her hiccups calmed, and tried to picture Florence with gray mucous on her pink lips, or with her eyes rolled back, staring blankly. Helen trembled at the idea of her sister lying in a dead heap on the ground like the kittens. Florence had not died this way.

Finally, Mama appeared. "Helen," she said. "You will have to be quarantined. No school for a week." Mama quickly closed the door and left her.

Helen looked in the mirror; she saw deep circles under her eyes. She noted the black half moons there along the insides of her eye sockets. Yesterday they had been slightly blue, like the veins in Jack's wrists. My blood is the stain of sin. Sister Wilhelmina said sin brought a stain on your soul. Our blood is our soul and mine is black, she thought. What sins have I done? She would ask Jack. Jack was sixteen and her brother. Surely Jack could explain things to her. Especially now that Mama had found the kittens. Why though, had she killed them? Sick? The kittens were sick? Sick like Florence? She lay down on her bed, watched the shadows fall on her bedroom walls and willed the afternoon to pass. She would not dare look out the window at her precious kitten, dead. The white one had been for Florence, the tabby Jack had named Mo, and the tuxedo, well Helen had called it Millie, after her friend Mildred. Gone, dead like her sister, except not in heaven. Jack had saved them but now they were dead.

Jack's heavy steps on the front porch and his singsong greeting to Mama reached her; she sat up. She waited. Surely he'd come up to take off the clothes he wore to Mr. Wannamaker's jewelry store where he had apprenticed these last two years. He usually changed so he could shovel coal for the furnace, chop wood for the stove or sweep the walk to help Mama. She opened the door just a crack and caught him passing. She swung the door wide and he brought up short before her.

"The kittens are dead, Jack," she said. "Mama told me I was quarantined again. Why Jack? Why did she kill our kittens?" Helen couldn't help the tears that rolled down her cheeks. She wiped at them, expecting them too to smear her hands with black. To her surprise her tears were just clear water, and salty when she put the tip of one wet finger to her tongue.

Jack pulled at his tie and unsnapped his collar. She prayed he would be the old Jack. The one who played pirate games and taught her to read and brought her books from the library, back when he still went to school. These days she was uncertain of everything. Jack had taken to imitating Papa, important now that he earned money and put it on the table every Thursday evening, now that he was an inventor for his boss and had a patent to his name. Jack studied her wet face, her puffy eyes. He pulled his handkerchief from his pocket and held it out for her. She smiled and shook her head no. He studied it, smiled, shoved it back into his trousers and said, "Yes, I had to use it earlier, sorry."

"Am I going to die, Jack?" she whispered. "I'm quarantined again.

Mama said."

"You're not going to die," he said quickly.

"Mama said Florence died like the kittens."

"Helen," Jack said. "Diphtheria is what got Florence."

She just stood there, staring at him, trying to understand him. "What's that?"

"A sickness," he said. "Florence caught a germ and it made her sick and the doctors couldn't make her well."

"Why didn't I get it? Or you?"

"Because we're just lucky. At least this time." Jack stooped down on one knee so he was eye to eye with her. "You miss her, huh?"

Helen nodded and swallowed hard, trying to fight the urge to cry.

"Me too," he said. "And now I'm sorry I ever brought those cats home." He stood again. "Hungry? Mama says dinner in five minutes. Come on. Give me a minute. I'll give you a ride down." He stepped through the door to his room. Papa's voice echoed up the stairs as the screen door slapped shut behind him. Helen felt a flood of relief. She didn't wait for Jack to carry her on his back, but tiptoed down the stairs. Papa lifted her for a hug and a kiss on her cheek, placed her gently down while he hung up his hat and jacket.

At the table, Mama said nothing about the kittens. She said nothing at all, but silently served stew with a wide ladle and passed a basket of bread. After prayers, Papa and Jack talked about Mr. Wannamaker and the jewelry business. Papa had written the man's insurance policy and lectured Jack on the proper way to stay in the man's good graces.

Jack pulled a sample of a watchband from around his wrist and passed it to Papa, then Mama. Mama nodded silently and handed it back. "I designed this. Been working on it all week," Jack said. "We may apply for a patent on it." Helen waited until Jack passed it to her. She admired the silver shine of the metal. Jack said, "Pull on it." He reached for it. "Like this." He held it between his thumb and fore-fingers of each hand and pulled. It grew longer; as it did the width narrowed. He let go with one hand and it snapped back to its original size. "See?" he said. "It's expandable. Better than the leather straps that have to be fit to size."

"I like it," Helen said. "Can you make a bracelet like that?"

"Ah," Papa said. "Sounds like your sister has some good ideas too, Jack." Papa smiled and winked at Helen. "Smart girl we've got, hey, Lena?"

Mama nodded and ate her stew. "Helen's quarantined, Joe."

"Again?" Papa asked.

Helen's heart, which soared at Papa's praise, shuddered and sank.

"Do we need to again, Lena? She's suffered enough. She's not showing signs of sickness is she?" Papa leaned over toward Helen. "Here," he said. "Stick out your tongue." Helen obeyed. Papa pressed her tongue with his teaspoon and said, "Say ahh." She did and she heard Jack imitate her. She resisted the urge to giggle and tried to look at Mama. Papa pulled out the spoon. "Throat looks fine, Lena."

Mama stood up. "Come to the yard, Joe." She didn't wait but disappeared through the kitchen. Papa followed, a frown nestling between his eyebrows. Jack helped himself to more stew and Helen sat, stared at him, and lifted her own spoon to her mouth.

"How does Mama know about the well?" she asked him.

"She knows," Jack said. "I told her."

"I thought it was our secret." Helen chewed a tough chunk of beef. Helen saw Jack transform before her eyes. The remnants of her child playmate became Jack the adult. He sat up rigidly in his chair and lifted his glass of milk primly to his lips.

"It doesn't matter anymore," he said. "We don't need the secret dungeon anymore, Helen. We haven't played that game in years. She found the cats herself after the white one died." Helen stared at him. "Why did she kill the others?" Jack did not answer. She chewed and chewed at the stringy grisly meat. It was not getting any smaller, or softer. Rather, the more she chewed, the harder the chunk of beef became, until she knew it would be impossible to swallow it. Before she could take it out and hide it under the rim of her bowl, Mama and

Papa returned from the yard.

Papa sat. "Helen, Mama's right. You'll have to miss a week of school." The rest of the meal was eaten in silence. Helen resumed chewing, and chewing, and chewing. Finally, she attempted to swallow. The wad stuck in her throat. She gagged making a loud rude noise. The meat moved back to her mouth and she swallowed again. Once, twice, on the third try it went down. Helen gulped her milk to wash it down. Mama's eyes were on her, her face chalk white, her hand at her own throat, her eyes filled with terror.

It was the loud bark of metal hitting stone that drew Helen from her scrapbook into which she'd been pasting pictures from a magazine Mama gave her. Through the window she saw workmen trounce through her yard and past the hedge, widening the tiny opening she and Jack had always crawled through for their pirate game. Now it was wide and no one would need to bend down at all to get through. She and Jack's secret was now receiving the attention of a team of men bent on destroying it. One man, who reminded her of a bulldog with his short legs and strong round shoulders and almost no neck carried a great many pieces of flat wooden board. He tripped through the yard, back and forth, while she sat and watched. Papa stood just this side of the property line, speaking with Mr. Duffy, the man in whose yard she and Jack had found the well. The dead kittens were no longer under the tree. Where they'd gone she couldn't say and knew no one else would say if she ventured to ask. Just like Florence, she thought. Gone. She comforted herself with the idea they were up in heaven with Florence and the thought rose up that Florence was perhaps having more fun than she right now. Through the hedge she saw the bulldog-like man swing a huge hammer to the brick wall that enclosed the well. Then he kicked the brick down into the hole where she and Jack had imagined the pirates hid after stealing their imaginary gold. Her eardrums reverberated with every whack of the giant hammer and she stuck her fingers in to dull the sound. That well, she knew, was no longer used. That was the fun of it. She and Jack were sure its history was a mysterious and exciting one. Only once had it proved useful for anything other than imagining.

It was the day of the kittens. Helen remembered it clearly, a hot August day with hazy sun. Mama had instructed her to stay in the yard and watch Florence while she lay down with a headache. Helen had chanted the words to a clapping game while slapping the flat palms of her younger sister's chubby hands. The window to the kitchen was curtained and the shade pulled down. Florence grew tired of the clapping game.

The ground was littered with peaches, hard but good for pies and good for throwing against the wall of the shed that bordered the east side of the yard. She loved the wet round splat marks on the clapboard wall, the sound that echoed through the wood, the wrecked ovals, skins marred by impact, as they fell to the ground. Helen let Florence pick up the smaller pieces, to try again and again to hit the wall. They were magnets for ants. Florence tried to put pieces in her mouth. Helen said "No Florence" and took them away, remembering Mama's admonishments to keep her little sister clean. All was fine, until the gate swung open and Jack carried in a basket. "Come look," he shouted.

Helen abandoned the peaches. With a squeal, she lifted a black tuxedo kitten from the basket.

"The grocer was about to drown them," Jack said. "I couldn't let him do that. What do you think Mama will say?"

"Mama is still resting," Helen said. "We can't go inside."

Florence sat on the dirt with a peach to her lips. Helen handed the tuxedo kitten to Jack and tossed the peach into the distance, brushed at Florence's face with the back of her hand.

"Come let me wash you," she said, annoyed, pulling Florence to her feet and dragging her away.

Mama must not see this. She would tell Helen she was lazy and neglectful. An ant marched slowly across Florence's sticky cheek. Helen brushed at it a bit too hard and Florence let out a cry. A red welt formed between ear and nose.

"Shhh," Helen begged. "Come with me. I have to clean you."

Helen dragged Florence by the hand to the rear fence and crawled first through the opening, her skirt catching on a twig and tearing. Holding Florence by the hand, Helen lowered the gray bucket into the well and pulled it up. She dipped her hands and reached toward Florence's sticky face. As she made contact with her sister's pale skin with the red welt, she let the water run through her fingers, across Florence's cheeks and down her chin. Helen rubbed at the dirt and the peach juice. She flicked a wandering black ant toward the ground. Florence's clothes were a bit wet, but in the August heat, they would soon be dry. Florence said, "More." She dipped her own hands in the bucket to clean them, and then before Helen could stop her, she sucked at her fingers. Helen sighed.

Florence said, "More."

Helen said no and dumped the remaining water back down the well. She returned the bucket to its spot on the wall and lifted Florence into her arms. "We're done here," she whispered. "Want to see the kittens?"

Now, watching the men take down the well, Helen remembered how she felt at dinner last night, that Jack was changed, that she too could not be who she was before. That was the day before Florence's fever. That had been the last day. Now, she was a different girl. Florence was gone. The kittens dead. The mystery of the deep dark hole she and Jack had peered into, shouted into, voices echoing down down into darkness was gone too along with ghosts of imagined pirates, dead and long gone. I know someone who is dead now, she realized. Florence is dead. The intrigue of the dead was no longer a source of curiosity. Now, she knew it only caused tears, her own, which spilled now, and silence, Mama's silence.

The short bulldog of a man eventually stopped tramping across the yard. Papa shook Mr. Duffy's hand, and to Helen's surprise, Mr. Duffy embraced Papa while the bulldog man stood by rubbing his thick neck with a dirty hand and staring off in the distance. Papa put his hand on the man's round shoulder, paid him for his labor with a wad of bills. Helen heard Papa's voice rise and say to both. "Yes, Jack and his damned animals. They drank from that stink hole too. It's what killed the first one. Otherwise we'd never know." He turned his gaze toward the house and the window where Helen stood and caught her eye. What, Papa, she wanted to shout. What would we never know? But he quickly turned his back to her. Only Mr. Duffy, now with his hat off and placed gently against his chest, lifted his hand in a wave and smiled at her.

She went back to school for relief from Mama's silence, finding comfort in the routine of learning to add and subtract, read and write and to ask as many questions as she wanted. Sister Wilhelmina's lessons about sin swam in Helen's head along with her admonitions. God will punish you with death if you disobey his commandments. Think kind thoughts. Cruel thoughts are cruel deeds, one and the same. Stay pure and without sin, girls and boys. Helen heard her whisper to the other sister. "That poor woman," Sister said. "Pray God spares her any other grief." The other sister whispered back, "God would not punish her by taking another daughter. Would he?" Seeing Helen listening, she said, "Diphtheria punishes indiscriminately. Pray for your mother, Helen. Pray that God spares her by sparing you."

In spring, when Helen had just turned eight, she learned how to enter the little booth where the priest sat behind a screen. She knew to kneel and bless herself; what followed was between herself and God. But she stopped at the word 'sins' mute with bewilderment. She could make up some, but that would be the sin of lying. Helen said her penance feeling doubtful. She ran home and looked in the mirror. The black under her eyes, the black in her veins that made the circles, was still there, still stained. She asked, "Mama, do you know any sins I have done that I cannot remember?"

Mama said, "Helen, you are a good little girl." She kissed Helen's forehead while Helen felt the emptiness where Mama's 'no' should have been.

Sister Wilhelmina told Helen she was ready to received Christ in the Holy Bread. The sun, shining off the white of her communion dress blinded her. It made her feel clean but black still flowed in her veins, bringing her to despair. Her friend Mildred received the sacraments with her, and seemed buoyed with joy. She was beautiful in her white dress, her cheeks rosy, her smile wide, and a blue vein in her jaw prominent against her flushed skin. Helen asked Sister about how you feel when you are free from sin. Sister answered, "You are never free from sin. That is why you can go to confession as often as you need. God knows us better than we know ourselves." Helen went every Saturday still unable to name her sin.

Time passed. Helen reached the age of twelve still doing penance in earnest at every opportunity. It was only at Florence's grave that Helen heard her mother's voice. At home, Mama's silence was broken only by Jack's talk at dinner, Papa's soft goodbye as he left the house for business each morning. Helen learned to abide the silence, to honor her mother's desire for quiet. To do otherwise would be to sin, to worsen her mother's grief, to make herself more vulnerable to punishment by Mama's hand or by the hand of God. She did not want to die. Mama and Papa never mentioned Florence's name. It was hard work for Helen to recall memories from before when Florence was alive and Mama spoke of happy things and had been a comforting presence.

Helen lay in bed at night and tried to see Florence's face, to remind herself of what was fading with every passing year. She and Jack only whispered Florence's name to each other when their parents couldn't hear. She cried for Florence and for the kittens before sleep some nights and all the while she waited for death where she would join Florence. The sisters at school reported her meticulous adherence to the rules on her report cards and Sister Wilhelmina called her Helen, the Good. She would not run in the playground. She would not climb trees with Mildred. She lived in fear her blood would spill and reveal the shame of her unnamed sin.

An early morning after Good Friday Mass, after her class had attended and returned to the classroom, Helen excused herself for the ladies room. Once inside the rough wooden door of the cubicle, an ugly black puddle of wetness threatened to reveal her shame. To her great relief, it did not leak through her school uniform. After several trips back there, and an odd stare from Sister Wilhelmina, she was unprepared for the sight of red dripping below her into the toilet. She wiped and wiped, but still, it kept coming. Her back ached. She could not decide what she should do…go to Sister Wilhelmina and say she was sick and go home…pull up her clothes and go back to her desk… no, this would stain her dress if she sat down. Finally, Sister came looking for her.

Helen said through the door, "I'm sick. Something awful. I can't come back to my desk." Something was happening. Her blood was returning to its clean and natural color. Despite the pain in her back, and the embarrassment she felt whispering what was happening to her, Helen felt something she took to be a lifting, finally, of the stain in her soul. Her mind worked fast, panicked as she was, imagining this color change a signal of God's forgiveness. All her penance had finally won her a clean soul. What had she confessed yesterday in the confessional? She could not remember. Had God finally heard and forgiven her?

The nurse told Helen she was not dying. She gave Helen a medical book open to pages that explained her blood and told her to lie down on a cot and rest. Helen silently lay there, the lifting of that black in her soul, surely a sign of God's love for her, filling her with a new radiant peace she had never known before. Mama came to walk her home. Helen felt herself glowing with renewed awareness of God and a feeling she'd just learned first hand about miracles despite the ache in her abdomen and the wet sensation between her legs. She whispered of it once they arrived at home.

"Ah," Mama said, not looking at Helen, hurrying to stir whatever was cooking in the huge black pot on the stove, "The curse. You now have the curse like the rest of us."

Helen's glow flickered out. Mama chopped at an onion with a cleaver, eyes on her hands. Helen knew better than to ask her to explain. She climbed the stairs to her bedroom, lay down and curled her legs to her chest and waited for sleep to overcome the anxiety that had briefly left her but now roared back. Helen's heart beat faster; her breathing intensified and panic settled over her as she waited for the curse to hurt her further, as surely it must. She slept, waking to find the sun setting and long shadows falling across her bedspread and walls. She sat up and found her way to the kitchen where she watched Mama wash dishes and picked at the plate of meatloaf and roasted potatoes. Then, she stood up and went to the secretary with deep drawers that held all the family papers. She pulled open the lowest drawer and lifted a pile of documents. There, she found a folder with a seal of the state prominent on the cover and Florence written in faded ink across the front. Cause of death, she read, neatly printed in the blank space, diphtheria.

There, under Florence's birth certificate was a letter in Dr. Van Essel's neat hand. Diphtheria again. Helen's eyes scanned down. She tried to unfold the letter, to see the bottom half, to know how Florence might have caught it. To her surprise, the letter was torn, the bottom missing. Helen breathed deeply.

"Why did Florence die?" Helen called to Mama in the kitchen.

Through the doorway she watched Mama's hands stop. A plate slipped into the water and Helen watched her fish it out and continue with her scrubbing. Maybe it was the blood. Maybe it was because she fervently believed she'd been transformed, despite Mama's use of the word curse, but Helen was certain she had earned the right to an answer, finally. Helen felt like Jack. No longer a child, no longer a play-mate to the young. Mama answered.

"Please," Mama said. "Don't talk about your dead sister. Let the dead stay dead."

Mama's eyes never left her hands. She said, "You should rest. Go lie down."

Helen did not want to lie down. She studied her mother. Helen felt her silence now, not as a reproach, something Helen had always shrunk from in her past, but as a lock on the truth. Helen did not demur. "Mama," she said, "I miss my sister. She would be eight this year."

Mama said. "Eight…yes."

"Why didn't I catch it?"

"That I cannot answer. Just be glad you didn't," Mama said. She put down her last clean dish. She wiped her hands on a towel.

"What happened to the second half of Dr. Van's letter?" Helen asked.

"Would you like to go to the cemetery with me?" Mama asked. "Put those old documents back where you got them."

"I don't want to go to the cemetery," Helen answered. "Why is the letter torn?"

"Well, you were only just there yesterday. I'll go alone then." Mama turned and silently took her coat from the closet and her purse and hat. She left Helen standing in a slanted ray of sunlight. Helen moved to the back steps and felt a stirring of her sister's presence; saw her on her stubby four-year-old legs. The scent in the yard was earthy, musty, like wet soil. She'd remembered that day before, but now, with the burden of her fear of sin and death lifted; memory was more than a desire to see her sister's face, to hear her laughter. Helen remembered herself on that day, her obedient love for Florence and her longing for Mama's approval, for her praise. Was there more? Mama had gone inside with a headache. While she remembered, Helen left the porch and at the far end of the yard she crawled through the box hedge into the next lot. A wide plank of wood covered the ground where the round stone wall once circled the well. Helen had used the well. She'd filled that bucket, not to kill her, to clean her. Mama had never asked where she washed her and now it was gone. The well was gone.

Helen breathed deeply. She let out a sigh and felt a gush of blood leave her. How thorough Mama was. That torn letter was part of her silence. Helen knew now, that by keeping Florence clean, she had stained herself with sin and her mother with grief on that last day. Mama never said so. Mama would never say so. Helen remembered the black liquid in Mama's eyes, Mama with the bucket, killing the innocent kittens, drowning them in water from the well. She saw Papa turning his gaze from her in the window, from the unanswered plea in her eyes. Even Jack had evaded her questions. Mama would only suffer to reveal more, Papa too, their love for her greater than she, until now, could know. The stain of her sin flowed into the past, replaced with her knowledge that her penance perhaps could now be offered, and through the grace of God, accepted.

Give and Take

The sun is streaming down, the wind is moving swiftly around the trees, scattering leaves, green leaves. Branches turn over and show the leaves' white skin. The veins of traveling chlorophyll pass the sunlight to the pointed tips of their outer reaches. I stand and feel the swirling cycles of heat and cool wishing it would sweep me upward and let me soar, my own energy surging and expending itself in synch with nature. But, I am separate. I feel alien to the ones who instill life in the mix of elements that make this place.

The garden, in which I expend my energy against the chaos of nature, looks alert under my constant vigilance. The impatiens are still tiny but their leaves robust, blossoms readying themselves to burst forth from buds. The violas have expended their strength on purple petals. Hostas are bolted upward with long stalks that will hold blue blooms in just a few days. The astilbe show brown where pink reached in feathery tentacles toward the shy lilies who will close on themselves in evening, protecting their seeds from night stalkers- raccoons, rabbits and skunks.

Many things took life in this place. I think back. My choice to keep this house was borne of an ache as I beheld this garden tended so meticulously by my mother. Its beauty would be Henry's and mine to safeguard. Six years ago, Henry and I stood here, arms around each other's waists and felt the stir of God's purpose as we beheld what spring beckoned forth from the soil. It was time for those chaotic forces in our own lives to be made into something real and tangible. We would clear the tangled overgrowth of our work and the world. We would make a place for our own someone, a baby, a new joy to accept for each other.

With dirt up to my elbows and streaks of brown on my face, wiped across under my eyes with my sleeve, I realized that if I was ever to create a new little life from my own hidden sources, I would have to leave the outside world and all it's gracious taking of my gifts and horde whatever energy and creative force I could muster for the purpose of procreation. I was infertile and stressed and my doctor suggested a leave of absence from my art director position at the ad agency to relax my body into conception. And for three months, so far, in between doctors appointments, exercise and meditation classes I had expended whatever left over stress remaining in my body minding this garden, hacking at weeds, dragging bags of organic topsoil, scattering seeds of herbs and transplanting seedlings of vegetable plants, willing some control over the elements of water, sun and soil, to purge my self of utter despair knowing how alien to the forces that instill life I was.

My hands in dirt, my knees on the old rag rug, I bent over and raked back and forth destroying the weeds that threatened all this vibrant happiness. This was under my power to control.

My doorbell rang. I stripped off the yellow rubber gardening gloves. Who would ring my bell in the middle of a warm June morning? Nobody who knew I was home had any time for a visit. They were all spreading artistic pieces of themselves all over the New York advertising world for clients desperate for a larger voice on the airwaves.

I imagined a desperate teenage girl, with milk spewing forth from her milk-laden breasts, placing her precious bundle gently down on my doorstep. She was crying and turning away, rounding the corner quickly to avoid detection, her desperation a mirror of my own. Where I so wanted the warmth of that bundle to curl toward me for comfort, she was fearful, so unprepared and shaken by the very real consequence of her foolish youth.

I rounded the corner of the house and watched a UPS truck, not a desperate teenager, pull away. On the front porch was a large box. Desperate teenage girls abort their babies these days I reminded myself as I abandoned my wishful longing!

My brother had sent it, my beloved younger brother, the one with the bleached white hair that stood up on his head like cactus spines. I found a knife in the kitchen and slit the top of the box open. As I did so the telephone rang. The brother, whose animated short subject won honorable mention at the Sundance Festival two years ago. The brother whose actress wife called him from LA two weeks ago to announce she wanted a legal separation. No explanation. No tears. No emotion of any kind. Not on her part, only on his. He'd told me last Tuesday, his voice, low and deadpan. He couldn't stay in the apartment, not now, with no expectation that she'd return. He was packing his things and would I mind keeping them until he decided where he would go. "We have extra room," I'd said, "I'm spending a lot of time at home these days. You could come here and keep me company."

"I've got to think about it. Thanks."

Today his voice came through the wire reflecting chords of sorrow. I knew, the connection of shared DNA strands ringing through my heart, that he would come here. This was home. There could be no other place where comfort and familiarity could set his tilting planet back in balance. "I'll be home all day. Come on over. I'll make tea."

"It's only for a short stay."

"As long as you need."

I hung up.

The box, I discovered, was filled with his books and papers. I dragged it into the front hall and returned to my garden.

The fertility doctor had explained it all to me in the surreal language of engineering of procreation. I felt dehumanized. The human activity of two bodies joining to create new life out of love and joy and pleasure apparently had lost its function, at least between Henry and me. We had fastidiously prevented pregnancy for ten years. I think our former intent had possessed our bodies with it's own will and had taken over. Now we could not cause the joining of ovum and sperm. Not for lack of trying. We'd been tested, poked and explored, with light, sound and laser. It was all so clinical and precise. Sex had become our brick wall, our place of failure. We visited it far too often, hoping that the game of numbers would finally tilt in our favor and that statistically we'd have to get pregnant, there was no other number left to draw. We avoided contemplation of IVF. We could do it ourselves, I adamantly insisted.

I don't have a room yet. But I have a secret stash of baby things, in a closet, way back in a corner. Baby things, not sentimental ornaments of the job, but real tools of the trade of motherhood. Cloth diapers, now with Velcro instead of diaper pins. Wipes. I'd sneak into that back corner and open the plastic lid on the blue rectangular box and inhale their sweet gentle powdery smell of just bathed freshness, the essence of baby skin. A book, "What to Expect When You are Expecting." had been on the table at a garage sale along with a baby swing, high chair and changing table. I only allowed myself the book. I vowed not to read it until I really was expecting.

The first test was optimistic. I was ovulating. "But you have a tilted uterus," said Dr. Bianco. "It makes conception slightly more difficult, but only slightly. We'll check Henry next."

Henry, I knew, prayed against the role of culprit in our elusive quest. His prayer was answered. His count was normal. "Timing," Dr. Bianco said. His nurse showed me how to predict my ovulation each month. "And relax. It will happen."

We tried mornings. We tried evenings. We tried noontime on days when Henry had no business commitments. We tried location changes, the Bahamas, cruise ships, Mexico, Ireland. Henry performed remarkably well considering the pressure I'd put him under. I think his sense of humor saved him. I was losing mine. Nothing. Just a stain of old blood each month right on time like my punctual body had done each month since the age of thirteen with the accompanying pain and an increased sense of absolutely no control.

If only I could figure the exact time, of day, of night, the precise day of the month, the position. I worried that the intensity of my pleasure somehow could change the likelihood of a meeting between sperm and ovum. The positions changed as I imagined uphill vs. downhill swims, and I worried about how often was enough or too much, and if Henry's sperm count would be affected if we waited a few days in between. You only need one energetic one, plowing its way up the long tunnel to the cavern, then up one of the two tubes, a fifty percent chance that the energetic one would head toward the ovary that had not produced this month's egg. Or as Henry said, a fifty percent chance that it would pick the correct one. What wrong turns had I taken, in my long life that had caused me to miss that magical encounter that would transform me into a mother? Had I picked the wrong man? Had I waited too long? Was I too long anxious about controlling my body's productivity toward the reverse of conception? Or was it that I could not turn the direction of my prayers, or my mind to exert my will over my life.

I talked to my ovaries. I visualized ovulation. I rolled my hips up over my head and did shoulder stands on the bed after sex. Henry went to sleep, his part in this quest gratefully fulfilled. I wondered, but never asked him, because I was afraid to know if he found sex a chore now or if he found any pleasure other than relief that he'd performed once again on demand. As I lifted my hips up over my head and pointed my toes toward the headboard and tucked a pillow under my buttocks, I thought I should have asked Dr. Bianco which direction my uterus was tilted so I could know if this position was helping the little spermatozoa to swim or was I creating an upstream battle like the one salmon fight each year when they return to their spawning grounds far upriver, hurtling themselves against gravity and flowing current and against bad odds to lay their eggs or die trying.

Hope ebbed with the dropping tide of time and six years into our quest we looked at each other with a vividly shared sense of passing time, time to be parents and still be young enough, energetic enough to chase a child around the beach, the park, the backyard. Okay, we'd said. Let's at least talk to the clinic.

Shots in the arm everyday. We would pump me full of chemicals and my ovaries would become factories. Henry would give countless specimens, which they preserved, and there, in the clinic, in a petrie dish, we could accomplish the goal. Embryos, the beginnings of life. Line them all up in their tubes, like newborns through the nursery window at the local maternity ward where we'd witnessed proud fathers and mothers pointing out their new progeny to our stiffly smiling faces.

How many embryos do they implant? "We recommend that we implant up to seven. Some will fail. Some will thrive. Then we selectively abort at the end of the first trimester."

I contemplated this scenario as I planted impatiens in my front border. My pitchfork turned over fertile soil and I hacked at the clumps with the rake. I spread it evenly across the bed and added organic fertilizer. Its scent conjured up images of green pastures and herds of cows and sheep grazing along the roads we toured by bicycle in Ireland. I had held my breath as I rode past them long ago. Now I found myself doing the same although I envied the plants and the soil, uncontaminated with man's interference, no chemicals or poisons interrupting the course of nature in the recycling of life. Not so me.

The flowers took an hour to transplant. The procedure for implanting our embryos into my uterus would take many hours. I would be instructed to stay bedridden; moving as little as possible, for a few days, then the sonograms would track the health and progress of my little blossoms.

Then what? Some of the little life stems would wither and die?

Some would make it? Which ones? Early strength was certainly no sign of enduring health for the long term. I thought of Wilma Rudolph, the crippled polio victim in her youth, she won three Olympic gold medals in track and field. Then she died of brain cancer in her fifties. How do I pick? How do the doctors pick which to keep, which to abort? I pulled flowers from their place in the flat and tucked their roots down into the dark brown hummus. Packing the dirt around and flattening it, I saw that some already had blossoms, some had only buds, and some showed nothing but green leaves and were smaller than the others. I imagined myself randomly pulling up plants by their roots and discarding them. Playing God. Who lives? Who dies? Show no weakness, I warned the flowers, because if you do, you're history. I did not want to play God. I wanted God to play God and give me a baby.

Matt pulled up the driveway in his '77 Toyota Cressida. The car had 125,000 miles on it. It still purred like a kitten. It looked like hell though, rusted out bumpers, dents from careless doors in parking lots, paint gone on the front hood. Matt opened the back door and his pug, the noble Yuki, emerged from the back seat and ran at me. Matt followed her. As he approached he surveyed my work. He nodded. He wrinkled his nose.

"Why does it smell like poop?"

I laughed. "The garden is organic. Yuki can add to the pile if she's ready."

"She's housebroken. Don't worry. And I'll find a dog walker for the middle of the day when I'm at work."

"I'll walk her. I have nothing to do except relax. Hurry up and relax."

Matt looked into my eyes. "You know, they say that people who adopt get pregnant within a year of bringing the child home."

"I'll adopt Yuki then…and you, for a while. How long are you staying?"

"How about we say three weeks minimum? Is that okay? Will

Henry mind my staying?"

"Henry would probably love the distraction of a little company."

"And the dog?"

"He'll be all right about the dog. As long as she's clean and quiet."

"No problem."

We walked into the house and his face relaxed when he saw his books and papers.

"I'll bring them up to the guest room."

"First have something to drink. Tea?"

I put on a kettle even though it was June and the day was warm. He always drank tea, hot tea with two spoonsful of sugar.

I was a child of eleven when my parents brought us to this house. Matt was eight.

We moved too early in the summer from a neighborhood filled to overflowing with families of children. We waited for the school year and the prospect of meeting children our own ages, and found contentment with each other in our huge new house.

As the tea brewed I remembered my brother, his blue eyes always watching me, waiting for my bossy explanation of who he was in our games and how he was supposed to act, what he was supposed to say. He was trained at that early age, as an actor, taking direction, but he must have preferred my role, because now, at the age of thirty-three, he was the one directing the action and controlling the story. He was a freelance director. It felt right that he and I would be together again like that first summer here, long ago. At least it started out that way.

Matt drank his tea in silence. I made him a sandwich. I filled a bowl of water and placed it on the floor for the dog. I suggested he take some time off from work and hang out with me.

"I'd rather keep busy, actually," he said. "I might start driving you nuts, hanging around all day. I'm better off working."

"What have you heard from Sophie?"

"That she is sharing an apartment with Cindy, she has a personal trainer, the car that I am paying for has a new dent, she found an agent, she had new head shots taken, and she's seeing someone."

"That sucks."

"She's a whore and a bitch. She eats the liver of children for breakfast. She is swine and pond scum. She is a c-word for using me, pretending to love me, and walking out as soon as she didn't need me anymore. She's a slut too."

His brow was furrowed but the corners of his mouth were trying to resist turning upward. I detected a slow-starting glint in his eye.

"Would you take her back?"

"In a second."

"You're in big trouble brother."

"I know." He bent his head to sip his hot tea.

For the next ten days, he was gone, on the job all day and into the wee hours of the morning. He spent time with us on the rare weekends when he didn't work, eating breakfast, playing with the dog in the yard, running errands, cooking his 'unique' meals of Thai chili and jasmine rice. After his first diatribe against her and his admission that he still loved her he ignored my references to Sophie in conversation and quickly changed the subject. When, I thought, will he ever talk about this? He'd always confided in me before. What changed?

Matt brought his box of books and papers to the guest room and left them there, in the large dusty box in the middle of the room. In one of my cleaning frenzies, I came upon the box. I couldn't vacuum around it so I let the vacuum and hose drop to the floor and reached in to pull the books out. I stacked them near the wall, under the window and made a mental note to buy a shelf for the room. The notebooks were of all sizes and shapes. Each was dated. I began to sort them by date, lining them up in neat piles on the floor as I put them in order. Matt has always kept a journal. I pulled a notebook out of the pile at random and began to read.

'The Gracious Game of Give and Take.' There on the page, line after line, I began to understand my brother's silence. I felt shocked. I was horrified. I looked at the cover of the notebook to be sure this was his and nobody else's. There was his name and his familiar handwriting. But the entries... My pulse increased. My brother's majestic inconsistencies and endearingly confusing divergences from normal behavior, which I attributed to his zany creativity, showed themselves to me with the veneer of his humor and self-deprecating demeanor stripped away. His secrets lay bare. Did Sophie read these? Did she know this side of him? No wonder she left him. I would leave him too. Here he listed countless little ways he'd devised to measure Sophie's contributions to their marriage. He had a point system. A game. If she arrived home late for work, he'd deduct five points. If she called only once during the day she'd lose ten points. If she left the garbage for him to take out, late, because he always worked later than her, he'd take fifteen points. Did she agree to this point system? I read on. A dirty toilet was another ten points. Dishes in the sink, twelve points. What did she do to earn points? I read on. The location of the act determined the points earned. The bedroom was the lowest on the point scale. Two points. The living room sofa, five points. The floor, ten points. Standing, another ten. The car earned fifteen. The point scale clearly indicated the greater the risk of detection, the more points he awarded her. What happened if she ran out of points? No wonder she left him. I heard footsteps on the front porch down below; the sound came through the window. I slammed the notebook down and shoved it back in the pile. I cleaned up the rest of the notebooks and picked up the vacuum and pretended to clean.

It was Henry. He and I were supposed to have sex today, in the middle of the day. The calendar had clearly indicated that this was the fertile day. And the doctor had suggested we try early before we were tired.

"You look really ready," Henry said, expressionless.

I laughed. Then I said, "Hey, let's do it in the dining room, on the floor."

"What difference does it make? I'd rather be comfortable. Come on downstairs to the bedroom."

I thought of the point system. I laughed. "Henry, I just got a great idea…"

He looked at me as though I'd lost my mind. "A point system? For sex?"

"It will take my mind off the other purpose. It'll make it fun again."

I read his thoughts about sex on demand. To my relief he looked amused.

"I want a baby as much as you do. Why not?"

And so it began. We kept a journal. Henry kept score. I kept taking my temperature to confirm I was ovulating, measuring days on the calendar trying to isolate the precise date and time of day when we'd strike gold. Henry evaluated my housework with points for shine and clean, the garden for weedless beds and no dead heads on the stems of blossoming plants. At the end of the month he added up the score.

"You're in the negative." He frowned. I laughed.

"Well, we're not supposed to do it too often. They said that your count goes down when we do it every night. Once every three days is more than enough."

"Not for my system."

I threatened to call the fertility clinic and sign up for IVF if he didn't change his tune. He relented and doubled the number of points for each occurrence. At the end of the next month I sighed as I left the bathroom with evidence of another cycle of failure. Henry tried to cheer me up.

"You're ahead in the game though."

I didn't look amused.

Henry took me out to dinner and pried my disappointed heart with a bottle of red wine. I ate chocolate mousse for comfort.

"Maybe the forced idleness is not relaxing. Maybe it's causing you to focus too much and stress out."

"Yoga."

"What?"

"I should try yoga. It's supposed to relax and let all the yin and yang flow through your body. It releases the blocked energy."

"Your energy was not blocked this month."

"Very funny."

Matt was very much at home in our house. So at home, in fact, that his mess spread from the guest room, down two flights of stairs, to the living room and kitchen. I stumbled over his sneakers in the front hall countless times. I took to leaving them at the foot of the attic stairs. I added his laundry to ours and folded it neatly and placed it at the foot of the attic stairs for him to take up. Most of the time those items stayed exactly where I placed them. He lived from the piles. When the entire pile had been worn he carried it down to the laundry room and left it in the middle of the floor as a gift for me to give back to him later, cleaned, dried and folded. I wondered if he was keeping points on my performance as a sister. He didn't want me to get too close, he didn't want to spend any time with me, an admission I found cut my heart with hurt, he just wanted me to follow him around and wrestle his chaos back into order. I wasn't his sister; I was the innkeeper. He didn't pay rent, but I expected a little affectionate sibling bonding in response to my toil. The only bonding I did was with the dog.

His cooking was questionable. We enjoyed the chili the first time he made it. The second and third times, well, enough was enough. And if his cooking was marginal, his cleanup skills left everything to be desired. I wanted to tell him to clean up his own mess, but I was feeling for the guy, I didn't want him to think I meant clean up his life. He was still morose over losing her. That nagged at me. Of course superimpose his mood on the Gracious Give and Take Game and I could side with Sophie and blame him for his own unhappiness. He was a slob. He was lazy. He spent all his time on the job. Should I implement the point game on him? What would his response be? He'd know I read his journal. I had to keep my secret. If he felt like I was invading him, he'd leave. That might be a good thing. I didn't want him mad at me even if I was losing my lifelong enchantment with him.

My phone rang while I was carrying Matt's shoes up to the attic steps one more time. I turned and almost tripped over Yuki. She'd taken to following me everywhere as I moved through the house. They say dogs latch onto who they think is the lead dog in the pack, even if the pack is a human one. Her eyes never left me.

"Hello?"

"Margo, hi."

"Sophie?"

"Hi. Yes, it's me."

"Matt's not home."

"I though so. I was hoping to reach you while he was out."

"You did. What's up?" My antennae were on alert. What could she want with me? A girl-to-girl chat? About Matt? My guard was up. But so was my curiosity.

"I'm in New York. Could I come see Yuki?"

"When?"

"Well, now if it's convenient. I'm sorry for the short notice. I'd just like to see her. Not Matt. Not now, at least. Just the dog. Would you mind?"

Loyalty fought with my curiosity. Should I ask Matt first if it was all right with him? I should, but he was on location and, I quickly justified my decision, he should not be interrupted.

"Come on over. Where are you?"

"It'll take an hour to get there."

"Okay. See you in a bit."

Panic. But I was secretly pleased. Perhaps I'd get a look at her point of view on this separation. Matt was not talking, perhaps she would.

When she rang the doorbell Yuki barked loudly and ran in circles in the front hall. Yuki was a clean dog until Sophie showed up. At the sight of her, Yuki squatted and squirted. A large yellow puddle formed on my polished wood floor. Sophie laughed. She laughed! I ran for paper towels and felt my status as lead dog rapidly diminishing as she picked up the pug and kissed her on her little pushed-in mouth. The dog snorted and almost fainted with excitement.

She extended her cheek for me to kiss. I hoped she wouldn't kiss me after sucking face with the dog. She didn't.

We sat and drank tea. After the encounter with the dog she returned to her usual serious self. I wondered if she thought smiling would give her unwanted lines on her face. Some actresses were like that. She had flaming red hair that cascaded in wrinkled waves down her back. Her green eyes were bright. She looked dreamy. She always did, her head seemed to be engulfed in a mist of warm air, which created a distracted look that Matt must have found irresistible. I felt my own leadened heart and my abdominal cramps and knew I looked haggard next to her radiant vulnerability.

I felt like a betrayer to my beloved brother. She should not be here.

"Sophie, did you really come for the dog? Or did you want to see me?"

"I came to see Yuki. She's my dog. I took care of her. Can't you tell by the way she greeted me?"

"I thought Matt was the one who bought her."

"He bought her for me."

Hmm. An opening. A chance to score a point for Matt.

"Matt did a lot for you, didn't he?"

"Yes. Matt did. Yes."

"I don't suppose you'd have your actor's equity without him?"

I poured more tea.

"No. I wouldn't." She hesitated, and said, "I always wanted to do something for him for all the help he gave me with my career."

"Is that why you married him?"

I had an innocent look on my face that Henry would have been proud of. It didn't match the venomous taste in my mouth.

"No. We were already married."

"Is that when he invented the Gracious Give and Take game?"

That was a risk. But I had nothing to lose. She'd tell Matt, maybe. But by then I will have already told him I knew about it. I'd see him before she did.

Her eyes narrowed.

"Matt didn't invent the game. I did."

She said it like someone was trying to take something away from her.

Her words took a moment to sink in.

"How did you find out about it? Did Matt tell you? It was supposed to be our secret." Her face was beet red. She was indignant. I wondered if she had a shrink.

"You invented it? Are you out of your mind?"

"I'd come home and the house would be a disaster. The dog wasn't walked and she'd pee on the floor. Matt's mess was always all over the place. And he was never home. He was always working. He'd come and go in the middle of the night. When he got home he was always too tired for you-know-what."

I was speechless. She continued.

"I was always so in debt to him. I was always feeling like I owed him so much because of all those contacts he made for me. And he never asked me for anything so I made up my own way to pay him back."

I took a deep breath and let it out. Part of my relaxation routine.

"I realized though, I could never pay him back. I'd always be indebted to him."

"That's why you left?"

She looked like she'd just figured something out.

"I guess so."

"Matt didn't tell me about the game," I said. "I found out about it by accident. I thought, when I first learned of it that he did it to manipulate you." I looked at her. "You two have the strangest ideas. I shouldn't really be surprised, I guess…why was it in his notebook?"

At that moment Yuki took to another circle dance and ran to the door.

Matt's voice called, "Yuki, here girl."

He stood still in the doorway. His eyes ran over her, then me, then her again. Then he picked up Yuki and held her protectively against his chest.

"You're not here for the dog are you?" I read his resigned face. I saw in it that possession of the dog, with Sophie here, would soon change. He never could deny her anything.

"Matt, I…"

"You came here to TAKE her?" I whirled on Sophie. "I thought you just wanted a visit with her." I turned to Matt. "Honest, Matt, I would never have let her come if I thought that is what she would do."

"It's all right. She's right. Yuki was a gift from me to her. She's perfectly justified in taking her."

But he didn't put the dog down. He stood there stroking her short fur. The dog licked his hand.

"Sophie, I think you should leave." I took her teacup away from her and placed it in the sink. She didn't hear me. She didn't move.

"Matt, I'm sorry. I wanted to do this without seeing you. I didn't expect you'd be home early. You're never home early."

"We finished the shoot."

I wished to be invisible. I wished to disappear into the kitchen floor. I saw the whole truth in my brother's face. I saw that if Yuki remained with him, then there was a chance that Sophie would come back. That hope was coming to a rapid and joyless end right before my eyes. This time I was keeping score and Sophie was losing. But she'd walk out with her dog, and her career, and a sense of being at last in control, and leave the man without whom she'd have none of it, and feel, I saw with shocked insight, like she'd won. Only Matt felt the loss. And, I wondered if he would ever understand why. He'd done all the giving. She'd always had all the control.

I left them alone in the kitchen. There was no place on this battle-field for me. I don't know how long they stayed there. Later, when the house felt silent I ventured back to the kitchen. I saw that Yuki's bowl was gone, they were gone and so were their cars.

I went upstairs to the closet. Back in the corner, behind some shoeboxes, behind the stack of diapers and baby wipes and the pregnancy book, I pulled out my log. Six years of measuring. Six years of temperature taking before I got out of bed in the morning. Six years of charts, plotting my ovulation, my periods, estimating when to have sex, when to wait, when to pee in a cup to check the hormone levels in my blood. Six years of waiting, in vain, for my body to do the job and become pregnant. My calendars, listing every doctor's appointment, every hospital test, blood test, ultrasounds, laparoscopies to look into my tubes, my uterus, my ears if it would help. Six years of keeping statistics on the odds of my body and Henry's doing their own give and take and producing a baby. There was nothing wrong with me. Physically, I was fine. Henry was perfect. Why couldn't it work?

I took the calendars to the yard and threw them in the trash. I slammed the lid back down and returned to the house. Henry came home and found me soaking in a hot tub of bubbles. I was listening to Indian flute melodies as I soaked.

"Want to earn some points?" Henry asked me with a silly look on his face.

"No."

He stiffened at my lack of humor. He watched my face soften. My voice changed too.

I said, "Why don't you come in and join me?"

He hesitated. Then he got a little gleam in his eye. He stripped down and got in, his legs running along outside my own, his body facing me. He submerged himself up to his neck and sighed deeply.

"No more points."

"Okay."

"No more record keeping."

"Okay."

"No more sex on demand."

"How about if I demand it?" He looked funny.

"I'll take that on a case by case basis."

"Are you changing your mind about a baby?"

"No."

"Are you giving up?"

"No."

"What are you doing?"

"I'm relaxing."

"So am I." Henry sniffed at the bubbles. "I'm going to smell sweet when this is over."

We made love in the tub.

Later, Matt returned. I heard his car in the driveway and water running in the kitchen. I crept downstairs. He was boiling water for tea.

"She's gone," he said. He averted his eyes and searched for tea bags.

"I'm sorry."

"It'll fade. I'm sure."

"Might just take time." I put two mugs on the counter.

"No, I mean, she'll need me. Watch."

"After today, do you still want that?"

"I do."

"You're still in big trouble brother."

"I'm just waiting. She'll get that ache in her heart. And maybe then she'll figure out that the dog or a job can't make it go away."

It took fourteen months. Matt stayed with Henry and me until the holidays that year. We bought him a puppy for Christmas. He named it Addie. "An 'A' name," he said. "It signifies a new beginning." In spring he moved to an apartment on the West Side. I step over his sneakers in the front hall when he comes to spend the weekend. I don't pick them up and I never told him I'd read his notebook. Sophie, after a job in a TV pilot that lasted a single season, got that ache in her heart and moved back in with him. Yuki had a hard time adjusting to Addie's presence in the apartment.

I adopted a puppy and named it Zoë. When it was two months old I had to throw out all my rugs. She was housebroken by six months, but by then I'd gone to the shelter and found an eight-week-old mutt and brought him home. I named him Ozzie. Henry asked what was with the letter Z in the names I was picking. I couldn't say, I told him, except I felt like I was at the end of something.

Puppies are born in litters. Female dogs can carry eight or more babies at one time. They have enough mammary glands to feed them all. I, on the other hand, am human. I have only two breasts.

The clinic wanted to fertilize six eggs. It was hard to limit them to three and we worried when one of my embryos didn't make it. That was hard. But two are hanging in there. The babies are due in seven weeks and Henry has started to wallpaper our largest bedroom with floating puppies in hot air balloons. Zoë and Ozzie don't know what's coming. After six years of waiting, and another torturous six months of IVF effort, I decided I was now entitled to break open that pregnancy book and start reading it, once for each child. I am on the last chapter for the second time.

The garden is chaos. The sunflowers are the only things taller than the weeds. The perennials have lost their color and I never got the impatiens in the ground this year. I sit in the garden in a chair with a soft cushion, my feet bare and my toes tucked into the dark soil of an empty flowerbed. My book is opened face down on my lap. I look up toward the house. With two giant oaks filtering sunlight downward, and the air bursting in short gusts of warmth then chill, I no longer feel like I am alien to the chemical mix of elements that make up life in this place. I feel the beginnings of hope and I pray that the gracious game of give and take will keep strong the balance in all the elements of life that begin with love.

Death Cleaning

All his working life he had lunged from sleep at 5:30 a.m. to silence his alarm. It was by his own clock now, somewhere internal nudging him to open his eyes, roll to a sit and rest his feet on the carpet. Janis still slept in their bed, in the big master bedroom. He had this room across the hall, with his CPAP. He removed the mask now and took in a deep breath. Can apnea kill? Gordon was a big man, round like Hoss from the old Bonanza series and quiet.

He used the toilet, scratched his neck, grabbed a paperback mystery from the shelf and lumbered to the stairs in his pajamas and robe. On the way down, he picked up the sound of Janis's shower behind the bathroom door and felt a comforting sense of continuity, proud that he'd shared the rewards of his work with her, with their two daughters who were grown up now, the younger recently married, the elder a new mother. With the retirement party done, his thank you notes written to his staff, doing for his girls was the only thing left for him. He had earned this easier time of life through years of hard work.

Coffee cups for the Kuerig were convenient. He choose the light breakfast blend and inserted it, checked the water level, pressed the button, remembering to place his mug under the stream before it started.

It was Wednesday, the day a realtor was scheduled for a walk through. Death cleaning was his new pastime...cleaning out the house so after he died his kids didn't have to deal with all his and Janis' stuff. Janis would do most of it. He simply obeyed her requests to carry heavy things to the curb for Goodwill.

Janis had reached out to three different real estate firms and asked each to come and give an assessment of the house. He couldn't remember what time today's would show up. Janis remembered everything. Him, not so much.

The Keurig chortled and went silent. Gordon poured half-and-half and sat in his recliner in the living room, with his book and his coffee, in the silence. The mantle clock chimed. Before retirement he was showered, shaved, dressed, phone charged, car keys in hand and out the door, backing out of the driveway by now. His phone started ringing at seven thirty and he'd give out instructions to his office team via the dashboard Bluetooth, his eyes never leaving the road, his right hand free for taking gulps of 711 coffee or bites of his daily buttered roll.

His phone never rang now, unless it was Janis calling to check on him. Sitting there in his living room, near a cold fireplace, he hadn't even carried his phone from the bedroom. There was no email to check. No appointments with clients. He could sit in the quiet and read, so he did.

Janis's random phone calls had started after 9/11. That day she wasn't able to reach him for hours, the cell phone towers in lower Manhattan reporting all circuits busy because some of them were destroyed and the rest were already linking other couples, other families, some of them as they rode the buildings down into the inferno. That was the day he lost Edward, the friend whose annual charity drive he'd taken over--for multiple sclerosis--and whose boys he kept in touch with even now.

Janis recreated that morning, imagining car accidents, plane crashes, heart attacks that could take him away and leave her alone. She'd lived through his death in her mind so many times, he believed when it did come, she'd be ready since she was practiced in losing him.

Retirement was only a month old. He was sixty-six. She was sixty-three and here she was, stomping down the stairs to the hallway, turning to the kitchen first. Her body, once slim, had rounded out in the middle like an apple. She laughed and said couples start to resemble each other over time and she was finally becoming a replica of him. But, she actually looked more like her mother except for the eyeglasses she still needed for her far sightedness and to correct the weak muscle in her left eye that had wandered when she was a child. She was still pretty.

"Gordon?"

"In here." He kept the book open. It was too early for conversation, for him, but, he knew, not for her.

"I'm teaching. Holly Ciconne has a cardiologist appointment and called last night. I'll be back by one for the realtor visit."

"Hmmm," he responded.

"When are you getting dressed? Don't be like that when they come."

"I don't need you to remind me. I'll be up after I drink my coffee."

"You can go through the books," she said. "Get rid of the ones you've read."

"First I'm going to read this one. Then I can get rid of it too."

"Don't get snarky. I'm just making sure you're remembering the time. You've got," she glanced at the mantle clock, "five…"

"Hours. I can count…six which includes time for my walk."

"If you shower early you can walk out and get the paper."

"Hmmm-umf," he said.

She slipped into her coat. She set the code to disable the burglar alarm system so she could open the front door. He heard it gently close behind her then car noises signaled she'd gone.

The house was her domain, and this was as much an adjustment for her, well, maybe not quite as severe a change as for him. Thing was, it was January and he wasn't inclined to go out for an early morning walk. "You're goal driven," she must have said at least once a day since his first day home. "Relaxing isn't a goal."

"Right now it is," he had said to her last week. "I'm not planning to have a heart attack or drop dead from boredom." He had smiled, nearly laughed when he said, "Unless you're going to stress me out."

The paper was available online, but he liked a real newspaper. He hadn't told Janis, but the NY Post had home delivery and he hadn't been walking out early for it, he'd had it delivered. She hadn't caught on yet. Now he heard the thump of its delivery on the front porch and he rose to retrieve it.

Cold January seeped in around the front door. If he had been born the handy type, he would mind. He was born the other type who earned enough money to pay someone else to fix the insulation strip around the door. He had never noticed this until now. He wondered if Janis noticed. Should he look at this year's heat bill and compare it to last January to see if this was a new problem? He had time for such things now. The door vibrated as it released from its frame and swung toward him. Bright sun reflected off the snow and made him squint. He stepped out. The paper was in its plastic bag halfway down the front walk.

It was one of those falls that feels gentle as it happens, and he gave in to it rather than fight gravity. Better to be loose when you hit the ground, he remembered from his football days. But he found his arms shaking, and he was too weak to push himself to his feet. He sat on the cold brick and pulled his bathrobe close, a gesture that restored a bit of dignity. At least he hadn't exposed any unattractive body parts, and, in the January air, he needed the warmth. There was nobody out on the street. He laughed to himself as the thought flashed that this was probably one of the things Janis hadn't worried would happen, and she probably hadn't prayed against it as she had airplane crashes, heart attacks, car accidents, and other calamities. If he hadn't retired, he would not be here right now. His paper would have been waiting for him on his desk at the office. Next, he felt a start of guilt because he hadn't told Janis he had the paper delivered. She still thought he walked out to get it at the corner newsstand. Not only could he not get up, he would not have an easy time telling her how it happened that he was outdoors in his bathrobe on the front walk on a January morning. He thought about his cell phone upstairs next to his bed. There wasn't anybody he could call in this circumstance unless it was 911 and it occurred to him that there were other more important things those emergency people were needed for than him on the ground in his bathrobe. All this flashed through his mind in a matter of seconds.

There had been other untruths far more significant than this lie about walking out for the paper. They flashed now. Things he'd kept from Janis because he didn't want to worry her. Like when Edward died and his wife and boys needed him and he wrote out some very large checks. Like when Katie confided that she'd left her first job because she was groped by her boss. She had begged him to keep it from her mother. Like when the priest and he met to finalize the annulment of that foolish college-age marriage that had lasted three months, that Janis didn't know about.

Gordon measured the distance between himself and the handrail next to the two short steps that had led him to this. This was the gap between his lies and the truth. These thoughts arrived like an army silently surrounding him, staring at him with reproach. He had built his whole world on top of some very secret manipulations of the truth. Here he was on the ground and he suddenly had the feeling that these deceptions are what had pushed him. Gordon had never been to war. Vietnam was over before he was eligible for the draft. He knew guys who went. There were members of the football team who didn't come back. The guys in his year all wore black armbands while they played football; they flew the flag at half-mast at home games. The shadows on his shady lawn circled him and he felt prickly, reproachful eyes watching him, smirking, asking, 'how you going to handle this, Gordon?' His knee began to ache. Under the robe it swelled. One of his feet felt cold, the other cramped painfully. He was sitting in a puddle where the warmth from his body had begun to melt the ice under his backside.

What if he rolled? Crawled? The handrail was wobbly. Another project he was not equipped to fix. It might not support his weight if he pulled on it to get himself to a stand. There was a tree. Prickly ivy with red berries. He'd never find a good hand grasp. He sat there. Then he rolled himself to all fours, the bathrobe belt dangling, cold air breezing through the gap near his chest. He crawled to the step, then he heaved himself around to sit on the lowest one. Rock salt granules felt like knife points in his butt cheeks. He shivered in the dappled sunlight. He used his arms to hoist his bulk to the second step, then his legs were sufficiently under him so he could lean forward and bring himself to standing. The knee ached. He pressed the cramping foot down, stretching his arch to relieve it. He felt his dignity return, took a deep breath and stepped forward again, grasping the plastic wrapped newspaper in his left hand and turning toward the house, but when he pulled the storm door open the vacuum of air sucked the inner door toward the frame and it shut with a quiet thud. And locked. Gordon muttered a curse, pushed at the door and cursed again. The handle was immovable. He tried to remember if the alarm turned on automatically when the door locked or if he would have had to set it. Had Janis set it so it would lock when he went for his walk? Had she figured he would forget to activate it, or forget to lock up behind him? He was guilty of that, too.

He saw the world for a brief moment through her eyes. In her calm routine morning were assumptions he had taken a shower, dressed, and was currently wearing his sweat pants and a long sleeve sweatshirt, sneakers and his favorite baseball cap. He was wearing a light jacket (he was never cold, except for now) and he was heading down the street, walking on the cleared street to avoid the snow and ice on the sidewalks. That was the reality he'd sold her. This morning, the only worry she had about him was that he'd miss the realtor appointment if he stayed too long at the corner deli talking to Moe, the proprietor, about politics. Gordon imagined himself sitting here on the step, the realtor showing up and Gordon sending him away because he could not let him in the house. He pushed other complications out of his mind. The realtor studying him, his bathrobe and the newspaper Gordon was sure to have opened to while away the time until Janis returned with the key. The realtor using his (or her) cell phone to call 911 to summon the police to get the door open for him wasn't good either.

The sidewalk was slick, but he knew he would have to navigate the walkway, the sidewalk along the street and around the corner (their house was on a corner lot) to his driveway. He would have to go up the very steeply slanted driveway to the garage, enter the code to lift the garage door and pray the inner door to the kitchen was unlocked. His slippers were not meant for this. He was not meant for this. He considered trying the next door neighbor's front door, ringing the bell and greeting Matilda Green in his bathrobe. She lived alone. She might not remember who he was and refuse to answer the door. He could persist. She might swing the door open long enough for him to present himself and get past her early dementia to assure her he meant her no harm. She could let him use her phone. He would call his daughter. She would drive the hour necessary to save him before Janis returned or the realtor arrived.

He wanted none of this. He also didn't want to break a window and crawl through.

Around the corner he went. The driveway had a single long dry strip of pavement available and he lifted his eyes to praise God. Like a tightrope walker he put one floppy, slippered foot in front of the other. It was not easy. His body shifted from side to side and he felt like he would fall if he couldn't widen his stride. Slowly, he got to the even pavement near the keypad, flipped open the protective cover, and lifted his finger to press. And stopped. The code. What was the code? He tried his birthday, Janis's birthday, with and without the year, with and without the zeroes before the month number, his eldest daughter's, his second daughter's, the street number for their address was four numbers, but that didn't work. The sun had been shining and offering a bit of warmth on his face, but a cloud had brought the cold back and his feet and his fingers were numb. His backside where the wet circle of bathrobe touched through to his skin was cold, and he could feel it spreading up his back, tightening muscles and restricting blood flow.

Gordon's heart, despite his large girth, which he'd always carried easily, was strong, at least the doctor had said so. His only physical dysfunction was his sleep apnea. He was fully awake and breathing strong, maybe a bit faster than usual, but he was fine. It was his thoughts that were besieging him. He could not stop thinking about consequences and how this predicament was just that. He considered a long line of unconscious tasks and decisions, purchases and transactions, conversations and negotiations, his aptitudes, his intelligence and ultimately his choices that had culminated in such a stupid dilemma as this one.

Why did he even have a code on his garage? Let some fool steal his gardening tools and the lawn mower rusty from lack of use since he paid a service to take care of the grass. Why did they have an alarm system on the house? Nobody in the neighborhood had ever had a break-in. Why everything, he said out loud. I'm going to freeze to death standing in this driveway? No, he wasn't going to freeze and he knew it.

Gordon hadn't wanted the commute to the city. He had wanted to drive in his nice sedan and drink his coffee and eat his roll while he listened to the radio on his way to work. So, Edward had taken the WTC office and Gordon had taken the Morristown office. It was like they had drawn straws and Edward had drawn the short one.

He started to sing an old song, one he remembered from the days of childhood when he and his brother would sing in the car on long rides with Mom and Dad.

> Well, your toe bone connected to your foot bone
> Your foot bone connected to your heel bone
> Your heel bone connected to your ankle bone
> Your ankle bone connected to your leg bone
> Your leg bone connected to your knee bone
> Your knee bone connected to your thigh bone
> Your thigh bone connected to your hip bone
> Your hip bone connected to your back bone
> Your back bone connected to your shoulder bone
> Your shoulder bone connected to your neck bone
> Your neck bone connected to your head bone
> I hear the word of the Lord!

Gordon sang the words the way he sang them with his brother. His mother had always joined in, too. His father just drove and listened with a smile Gordon saw in the rearview mirror. This time, he finished the entire song, standing there in the cold, remembering the time before all the accumulated elements of his current life had even begun. Had he ever taught that song to his girls? He couldn't remember. He broke off these thoughts. How in the bloody hell was he going to get himself inside? His bones were cold. The wife's worry is connected to the burglar alarm, the fear of robbery is connected to the garage door opener, his money is connected to the sidewalk and driveway needing shoveling by the contractor he could afford who hadn't arrived yet. The newspaper, the need for which started this whole long morning saga, was connected to his fib, so was his current state of attire, he felt it all accumulating. He was here. Edward was gone. He understood, at that moment, why Janis prayed. It was a big thing to have gotten away with; he had been at the towers that morning, but Edward had called him to say, "Stay down there for a bit. The meeting is postponed an hour." Gordon was drinking coffee on the concourse level when the shuddering reverberated through the building. He couldn't go up.

He wanted to, but the elevators were not working, and the stairs were streaming with people coming down. So he walked uptown with the flow of fleeing people, turned and saw the end.

He hadn't wanted to learn home repair, he hadn't want to shovel his own driveway. He could hire someone to do anything he didn't want to do, or learn how to do, or trouble himself with. He hadn't wanted that job. He'd recommended Edward for it. A month before the planes hit.

He flashed back to the days in his driveway as a kid, Dad on his back under the car, with the oil pan collecting the oil from the reservoir under the hood where his Dad would call to him, okay, turn it, turn it harder, and the satisfaction when Dad would say, yes, you did it. Good boy! The accumulated accommodations to his own micro-decisions were now his foibles. No wonder Janis prayed. She was waiting for the consequences. She knew he was on borrowed time, that he had been traded for Edward and that his time was coming.

Gordon felt a strange resetting of the yardstick upon which he measured his life and his worth. He imagined, now that he was retired, that he might change some things. He might learn how to add weather stripping to the front door. He might buy a snow blower. What else could he do? The possibilities were endless. He could clean out the garage and sell the mower. He could memorize his own phone number. He could take a home repair class. He could fill his hours with all the things he owned that needed his attention. But he couldn't save Edward. He thought about his earlier sense of his days and how all he had left to do was take care of his girls, do for his daughters when they needed him for something.

There was more that he could do. He saw the trouble he would avoid by expanding his list of what he was capable of actually doing. Everything he would do from now on would be so he could avoid death, keep it at bay, keep the bones that are connected to the next bones clean and shining. As he made this observation, in the middle of this absurd consequence of such a tiny lie, he felt a bit better.

Still humming the song under his breath, Gordon bent over, grabbed the handle of the garage door where it beckoned, just above the few inches of snow that had blown against the bottom. With an intake of breath, he pulled. While he did, he bent his knees, something he had learned a long time ago from his football coach when he pushed the training sled across muddy practice fields. He hoisted. He heard the door on its metal runners, folding into itself and rising on its way up to the ceiling. The garage yawned wide and dark and welcoming. He'd done it. He was in. There was no code. That thing was broken too, like so many other parts of his world. He pushed against the kitchen door and stepped through to the warmth and light and comfort of his kitchen. Sanctuary. Then, as was his custom after retrieving the newspaper from the front steps on any day, he pulled the wrapper off, opened it on the counter, selected a flavor and made himself another cup of coffee. He didn't look up again until the doorbell rang. The realtor, he said out loud and swore at himself. But it was Janis, not the realtor.

"There are a few things around here I want to fix," he said. "I'm gonna do them myself."

"Why?" she asked. "Hire someone to do it."

"Death cleaning," he said. By the look on her face, he knew she understood.

Sales Call

Dressed in a suit, face smooth from a clean shave, looking deliberately crisp, George walked quietly toward the door in their darkened bedroom and looked back at his wife. Her mouth slightly open, a bit of shiny liquid just glistening on the corner of her sideways mouth; she slept curled around a tucked in section of quilt. She looked awful. And, he knew, she might snap at him if his kiss woke her from the sleep that eluded her in the darkness of night. It was her insomnia, but it kept him off balance too. Kept him still and silent if he came in and out of sleep himself in bed next to her. He'd rather keep the good feelings than play with fate. He gently closed the bedroom door and left. It was five am.

"Take this," Ray, three weeks on the job, a crony of the VP, had said with enthusiasm. "It came in from the trade show. Big potential. National network. Ready to spend now."

"Thanks Ray. I appreciate the lead. I'll call today." That was last week.

"Even if they're a small operation now, George, it sounds like growth potential. Like an annuity, might keep growing."

Was Ray apologizing? There was a hint of that coming from deep in his throat despite his attempt at optimism. George could always read his type. Eagerness based on his lack of qualifications to be George's boss, and secret knowledge of George's awareness of that. Here we go again. Play the game. A lead is a lead and new bosses need stroking.

"You're right Ray. What franchises do they own anyway?"

Be careful, he told himself, don't ask him any questions he can't answer.

"Consumer products, commodity type products. Lots of repeat business."

George knew Ray was withholding details. He had his hand out to take the lead. Ray ignored it.

"I'm sorry I haven't sent many of these your way, George. I'm pushing the younger guys a bit harder than I am you."

"And why is that?" asked George, his hand still outstretched.

"I expect a short sales cycle on this one."

George nodded again, still silent. What do you consider short? The question remained unsaid. Short sell cycles mean small deals.

"What are you closing this week?"

"Ten million dollar network to Tricorp. International."

Ray's eyebrows jerked toward the ceiling. He gave the slip of paper to George.

George wondered, as he turned his back on Ray, if Ray had any idea that George knew more than he about sales and about computer networking. If he did, would he find a way for George's successes to make him look good, or would he deride them and attribute them to dumb luck? Ray had no idea how long that ten million dollar deal took George to close.

This morning, as he sped along the interstate, George wondered whether his life would get better or worse after he'd broken Ray in, the third new sales director in two years. George had to act on this lead. It was Ray's acid test, he knew, of George's loyalty to another new boss, brought in from the outside; an obvious snub by management to

George's experience and ability.

He found a classic rock radio station and drove, sipping black sludge from a Styrofoam cup, the only coffee available this early. The one person he knew to be awake and alert at this hour was his father. Should he call him? He hesitated. Then, faced with a boring four-hour drive, he dialed his father's number. It rang before he remembered the last time he'd received a phone call this early. It was too late to hang up, too late to stop his father's heart racing in panic as he groped for the phone next to his bed.

The machine with his dead mother's voice came on and asked him to leave a message. He recited assurances that nothing was wrong, just a hello, and promised to call back later in the day. He hung up. Creeping into the discomfort of the already unsavory morning came the nagging worry about why the phone had gone unanswered. Where could Dad be at five am? He turned the radio up, loud, distracting, annoying. His foot floored the gas pedal. He knew it wouldn't make the time go faster, just the car. He was tempted to set the cruise control. He heard his wife's diatribe on the subject.

"George, let me read you something…The odds are that if you are using cruise control and fall asleep at the wheel from boredom or fatigue, you are more likely to kill yourself, or kill someone else. If you fall asleep with your foot on the gas pedal, chances are the pressure on the gas will lighten as you fall asleep, reducing the chance that you will hit someone or something at full speed."

His wife's anxiety about all the time he spent in the car set him on edge. He could hardly avoid getting in the car. He could only promise her he was an alert and careful driver. She found other things to worry about and countless suggestions for his safety, including jumper cables, flares, spare tires, full size ones, not the miniature donuts the manufacturers included with new cars, and a can of pepper spray attached to a key chain to protect him from imagined marauders on the highways. He supposed they reassured her.

This morning his right leg felt stiff. He wanted to flex his ankle.

But his wife's worry kept him pressing with his foot. At seven he passed a sign announcing a rest stop ten miles ahead. By then his bladder was screaming for relief. He pulled off the highway and made for the men's room. A burly truck driver in faded overalls, the only other patron of the service area let out a distinctive bad noise as he stood next to him relieving himself. The truck driver finished first, zipped up and left, passing up the sink and heading for the food concession. George washed his hands and followed him to the coffee counter, slipped some sugar packets into his pocket and made for the car. He carefully placed the coffee in his rack, tossing the empty one in the back seat. He backed up and spun the wheel to blaze back to the highway. Once merged with the sparse morning traffic his mind wandered back to his father's unanswered telephone. He pulled the sugar packet from his pocket and looked down at the coffee thinking he should've mixed it at the counter. On long drives with his wife she stirred the cream and sugar into the cup for him. He tore the packet and lifted the plastic lid from the cup. He noticed too late his swerve from the right lane to the center. The blare of a car horn jerked his attention back up. He was too late. From behind and to the left a small commercial van bore down on him. Time slowed. The unmistakable sound of crunching metal filled his head and he felt the car lurch. Like a cat landing on its feet, George's car managed to stay over its wheels. He hit the brakes wondering if he slowed down would he only stay in the way of the car behind him, inviting more impact. He couldn't see where the van had gone. He felt the wheels crunch gravel and he was on the shoulder of the road. Looseness in the steering wheel, he turned rapidly from side to side, trying to regain a sense of control. He screeched to a halt and watched as his new cup of coffee splattered the windshield and the dashboard. It hit him with scorching heat right in the eyes. He looked around for the van. It was lying on its side just off the shoulder.

The driver's side door, which faced the sky, opened upward and a small gray haired man climbed out. George made to open his door and remembered to look behind him. He was close to the traffic lane.

He lifted his feet over the center console and put them on the floor on the passenger side, hoisted the rest of his body over and shoved the passenger side door. He stepped out and heard traffic roar past him. A semi roared by; its horn honking. The driver was the guy from the men's room. He changed lanes while flashing his lights. The gray haired man approached as George turned to his car for his phone. Grasping the cell phone he swung around and he and the man were face to face.

"If you're trying to commit suicide, don't do it on a highway you son of a bitch. You'll take people with you who don't want to go."

"Suicide? Me?" George thought the man had possibly been hit in the head.

"Oh, you expected to live after that move?"

George's hand felt in his pocket for the packet of sugar. His fingers closed around it and he curled his fingers into a fist and pulled it out. He dropped it on the ground behind him. The man saw and bent to pick it up.

"What's that? Are you a druggie or something? White powder. Trying to dump it before the state police arrive? I'll just keep this if you don't mind."

"It's sugar."

"And I'm Santa Claus."

"No, really. I was drinking coffee. I just stopped at the rest stop just back a mile or so." He recalled the truck driver who knew he was there, saw him in his minds eye whizzing past in his semi.

"The trooper's will get you for careless driving." The man's voice faded.

George wondered if he was hurt. He looked closer at him. "Would you like to sit down? Do you feel all right?"

"I'm fine." George saw the man's eyes in the early dawn light. They were dilated unevenly. He took a staggering step and George grabbed his arm to keep him from falling. He jerked his arm away.

"Maybe I'd better sit down."

George opened the rear passenger side door for him. He sat with his feet on the gravel and put his hands up to his head.

"Bit of a headache."

"Don't lie down. If you get drowsy tell me."

George pressed the send button on the cell phone. In moments a dispatcher took a description of the accident and an estimated location.

"State police will be here in a few minutes."

"Tell them to send EMT's?"

"They will. Do you have any family you want me to call for you?"

"No. My wife is dead. My kids are grown. They live out of state. I'm alone. I'll call my son in Illinois when I get home."

In emergencies, George handled only the information he felt was pertinent to the occasion. From the man's words he plucked only the word no. He didn't respond to the rest. Not now. He had an appointment to keep. He was going to be late. Ray's lead. His subtle score keeping. He was losing ground. He was derailing his relationship with his new boss. The results of the appointment didn't mean much. Showing up, however, did. And now he was going to be late, very late.

"I'm going to call my wife."

George dialed home. He glanced at his watch. It was six thirty. Deirdre would be getting up now. He hoped. He heard her answer with a muffled sleepy voice. Deep. It was soft and low in the morning. "Deirdre?"

"Hi."

"It's George."

"I know."

"I had an accident. I'm okay. But my car is wrecked."

He imagined her sitting up in bed, now alert.

"Where are you?"

"Somewhere on route 78. Near Easton. About two hours from home."

"Are you hurt?"

"No. Just stuck. My steering isn't working."

"Should I come and get you?"

"Well, I have this appointment..."

"Please...you're not going to try to keep it, are you?"

"Well, Ray sent me on this one. The guy will be out of town for the next three weeks. It's the only day he can meet with me."

"George. Cancel the appointment. Come home."

George heard the plaintive voice of his wife. He resisted. He was almost half way there. It'd only be a little longer. Even if the appointment was pointless, he would get it over with and Ray would know he was a team player. A state police car pulled up on the shoulder.

"I'll call you back in a few minutes. The state police just arrived. I'm going to have to talk to them. Bye."

It was routine, except for the other driver who still seemed dazed. The EMT's took him immediately to a local hospital. George refused to get in an ambulance. He had nothing except hot coffee touch him. He told the police so. The policeman gave him a report number so he could get a copy for his insurance company. Then he handed him a ticket for careless driving. Two tow trucks arrived and took away the flipped van and George's company car. He rode in the truck's cab to a gas station. To his satisfaction he saw they rented cars. He looked at his watch, filled out a rental agreement and left his wreck on the lot to deal with later. He headed west on the highway and drove the remaining distance to the account. He was another hour down the road when he remembered he was covered with brown coffee stains. His hand reached for his cell phone and he realized he'd left it and his briefcase in his wrecked car. He swore to himself.

In the army they might give him an award for weathering the storm and still bringing in the ship. Here at Jones Franchise's, Inc., the customer, bald, sweaty and chain smoking, just looked at him funny, offered him another cup of coffee and sat him down in his office. George thought, I guess he can tell I really like coffee. He wondered if he smelled of it but now wasn't the time to take a sniff of himself.

Jones proceeded to describe plans for a network to link his

franchises nationwide. George nodded in all the right places. He asked some questions about his computers. He answered Jones's questions about high-speed data transport. He apologized that he left his brief-case in his wrecked car and asked for a blank piece of paper on which to take notes. Then he used the paper to draw a rough outline of data links across long distance. He took a Xerox of a hand drawn diagram of information flow from Jones. He let out an involuntary snort. A small smile tugged at the corners of his mouth. He handed the dia-gram back to Jones.

"Sorry, er, how many transactions a day and how often would you download files?"

"I can't tell you that. That's confidential business information."

"I can't make a networking recommendation without knowing how you will use the technology."

"You'll have to."

George sighed, looked right into the guy's eyes and told him the network to do the job he imagined, for his five 'nationwide' Jiffy Lube franchises, would cost him at least $1 million. This man knew noth-ing about networks or what they cost. George wanted to tell him that high tech toys were expensive and to get real, but he held his tongue. Ray, his sales director-in-training, he realized, had fallen for the word 'nationwide' and thought it showed 'big' potential. Jones leaned back in his swivel chair, lit another cigarette and blew smoke at the ceiling. George stopped worrying about smelling like coffee. Jones looked at him.

"I was wondering if I was wasting my time. All this technology. Supposed to enhance business efficiency. Guess I'm efficient enough, huh? Twenty minutes for an oil change."

George glanced at his watch. I'm efficient too. This appointment only took fifteen minutes. He was hungry. And his neck was starting to hurt. The brown coffee stains had dried so his shirt was no longer uncomfortable. Jones smoked silently, and because George felt a little ashamed of his scorn for the man, he said, "Would you like to have an early lunch?"

"That would be very nice. Thank-you."

"Do you mind if I use your phone? Before we go? I need to check in." He didn't share his reasons with him. He just reached across the desk and dialed. His father's line rang unanswered. Before he got his mother's recording he hung up. He dialed his sister. She was already at work. She didn't have an answering machine. Deirdre was out too.

George drove. The rental car was old and had a musty smell. He hadn't noticed when he drove it alone.

"I'm sorry we have to ride in this tank. Jim…"

"It's Jeff."

"Sorry. Would you mind wearing your seat belt?"

"I'd rather not."

George asked him to suggest a place for lunch. Jones smoked three cigarettes before they got to the main road. He gave directions and guided George into a parking lot. George didn't lock the car. What the hell, it was a rental.

In the smoking section of the Starlight Diner, they sat in a booth with a split leather seat and a few crumbs on the table. George coughed. After George politely gestured to his guest to order first Jones chose a combination lunch with soup, salad, entrée and dessert. This was going to be a long lunch. George ordered a club sandwich and a large coke and realized his head was throbbing. He blamed it on the smoke. The waitress took away the menus. He watched Jones' fingers holding the cigarette. They were yellowed around the nails. Jones' eyes were yellowed and streaked with red. George hadn't noticed back at his office.

"How long have you been in this business?"

"Few years."

"Enjoy it?"

"It makes money."

"How'd you choose Jiffy Lube franchises?"

"I went to a franchise show. Did the financials. Everybody has a car. Everybody needs to change the oil. Nobody has time. Made sense to me."

"What kind of income does it generate?" George wondered if his question was too personal. He waited for an answer. Jones drank his water.

"What got you into sales at Visnet?"

George had a long answer but gave Jones a short one.

"Good money. Technology is leading edge. Never have to worry about finding employment opportunities."

"Do you like sales?"

"Yes. I run my own show." He thought about why he was here. He thought about his father and the long ride and the accident. He thought about the gray-haired man in the ambulance. "Except when I get a new boss who doesn't know the difference between a good lead and a bad one." He regretted that the moment he said it.

"Well, fuck you. I'm sorry if I'm wasting your time." Jones stood up and walked out the door.

George froze. He looked out the window as Jones stalked across the parking lot and disappeared into a convenience store. He turned and the waitress was there, carrying three plates balanced perfectly from fingers to elbow. The other hand carried a bowl of soup. She placed the soup on the table and followed it with the other food. She smiled and said, "Enjoy."

"Ahh, Miss?"

She turned, looking annoyed.

"Yes?"

"My friend just walked out. I have to follow him. Could you bring me the check right away?"

She made a 'tsk' sound, then sighed.

It took her ten minutes to add up the check. George spent the time craning his neck toward the window to catch sight of Jones. As he signed the American Express receipt he saw a car pull up. Jones strode to the car, got in and drove away.

George got into the rental car and turned out of the parking lot and onto a local street. He found the highway. It was only 11:00 AM. He didn't want to apologize. He was no longer hungry. He wanted to go home. The day was a waste. A four-hour drive. A totaled car. A ruined suit. A hurt old man. All because Ray thought he knew more about sales than his subordinates and George pretended that was so. What a waste. If any real clients try to reach me… I really need my cell phone. And where in the hell is Dad?

He fumed silently for the first two hours of the return trip. The rental car had a radio that crackled static. George tapped his hand on the steering wheel and sang to keep himself alert. The sun was blinding when it glinted on the chrome of passing cars. His head pounded. Maybe it hadn't been the smoke. The silence was deafening. He turned the car radio back on just to fill up the emptiness. It was annoying so he shut it off. In the silence he heard his mother's voice again, the recorded voice that had startled him this morning and every time he called his dad. He thought about her loss of speech with her second stroke, how he never knew after that if she understood anything he said to her. He'd talk and talk and mourned her silence, mourned the loss of her even before the final coma and her silent exit from the world. It came to him now in the frightening quiet. It was her presence that had been the constant, always available, no appointment necessary, not squeezed into convenient time slots like the customers who had no real need of him. Endlessly cycling through the pattern. Create need, fill it, and move on.

George felt the acid churn in his stomach when he contemplated facing Ray after today. Ray could react to this either way now. George imagined all the new leads, the good ones, being handed to the rookie reps, and him being handed a walking slip. Tomorrow's ten million dollar deal was done. Ray could fire him and take the credit, and the commission check.

When he approached the mile-marker where he'd fished the sugar from his pocket, the old man in the hospital crossed his mind. He saw square blue "H" signs and followed them. It was only three miles from the highway. He found visitor parking and the main entrance. It had been six hours since the ambulance took the old man. He's probably discharged. But hell, I'm here. I'll just check. The admissions nurse finally checked the schedule.

"He was discharged two hours ago. Mild concussion."

"Did he leave a phone number or address?"

"Who are you?"

"I was in the other car. I just want to call him to see if he's okay."

"I'll give you his phone number. Not his address."

He went to the phone booth and called his wife again. He got her recorded voice. He recited a short version of his day and hung up. He imagined she'd called his cell phone a hundred times. The battery would be spent when he got back to his car. The second call was to the old man. He listened to the distant end ring six times and was about to give up when a feeble voice said, "Mike?"

"No. Mr. Sanders. It's not Mike. It's George McLaughlin. I was in the other car this morning."

"Oh, the guy who almost killed me."

"Sorry."

"What do you want? My insurance information?"

"No. The police have all that. I was just worried about you. I'm at the hospital. Do you need anything? I just…"

"Still at the hospital? You weren't hurt. Don't sue me. I've got nothing. It was your fault anyway."

"No. I just wanted to see if you're okay."

"I'm not going to sue you. If that's what you're worried about."

"No. I'm…"

" I'd like to keep the line clear. My son is supposed to call me back."

"You haven't reached him?"

"Yes. I did actually. But he was on a business call. He said he'd call me right back. But that was half an hour ago. I figured by now he'd be trying to call. I thought you were him."

George heard the disappointment in his voice.

"I'll hang up if you want me to."

"What did you say you wanted?"

"I just wanted to make sure you were all right. You were a little dizzy this morning."

"I'm fine. I found your packet of sugar in my pocket. I threw it away. You shouldn't use sugar. It's bad for you."

"It's bad for my driving record too."

"What's that?"

"Never mind."

"Well. I'm doing fine. The doctors checked me. Said don't drink anything alcoholic for a day or two. Told me not to go to sleep until after 8 tonight. Don't drive and just take it easy. So that's what I'm doing."

"Anybody looking in on you?"

"The nurse from the emergency room called a few minutes ago."

"Any neighbors?"

"My son will call me. He'll remember. I'd better free up the line in case he's trying right now."

"Okay. I'll hang up. Take it easy."

George heard a firm click in his ear. He put the receiver back on the hook.

He dialed again. His father's number. It rang three times. Then someone answered. It was his sister. Dread entered his chest and rose to his throat.

"Helen, where's Dad?"

"He's right here."

He waited a minute and his dad came on.

"Hi George."

Relief flooded him. "Where were you this morning? I called early."

"What time?"

"About 5:00."

"What'd you call so early for?"

"I was on the road. I just wanted to check in."

"I was here. Must have been in the shower."

"Don't you check your machine?"

"Oh, I guess I didn't today. Hold on."

Why is he checking now? In the background he heard his own voice playing.

"Your message is there. Sorry. I must have been in the shower. Why did you call this morning?"

"Oh, no reason. I was just driving and thinking you might be awake."

"I was. I was in the shower. I just told you that."

"I know. I guess I just wanted to say hello."

"Where did you go this morning?"

"To a sales call."

"Anything come of it?"

"Well, yes, actually." George paused. "Dad, do you ever listen to your message? The one that comes on when the machine answers the line?"

"Why?"

"It's Mom's voice."

"I know."

"How does it make you feel, hearing her voice?"

"I miss her. How do you feel when you hear her?"

"I guess it's good to hear it. It's different from looking at her picture."

"Yes, it is different. Do you want me to change it?"

"No. Leave it the way it is."

"I'll see you in a few days."

George hung up and re-dialed his home number, crossing his fingers, hoping the machine would not answer, not this time. He didn't want a recording. He needed his wife. Real contact. He closed his eyes. Waited. This time Deirdre answered.

"George, where've you been? You were going to call me back…"

"Can you come pick me up?"

"Yes." He heard her pause then speak again. "George…"

"What?"

"Were you using cruise control? When you had the accident, I mean?"

George laughed for the first time that day.

"No. I wasn't."

He heard her sigh of relief. He heard her calm. He felt her need of him and his own for her, and wondered what he'd done, what either of them had ever done, to make this need so real.

The Prayer You Answer Doesn't Have to Be This One

It was a dim day in February, 1973 when Grace walked past the Curran's tall house on her way home from the bus from her commuter college, and Susan, who was also nineteen, raised the second floor window and stuck out her head.

"Come in," Susan said.

They had been classmates up until ninth grade when they went to different high schools. Both girls were of Irish Catholic families but there the similarities ended.

Grace was surprised that after all this time Susan would invite her inside. Childhood playmates, classmates, neighbors, until, at adolescence, Susan used drugs, hung out with cigarette smoking, overly made-up screechers who swore loudly and lay on the hoods of cars in poses that suggested sex. Grace's father had said, "Stay away from that crowd". So Grace had.

Inside Susan's house, Grace held her breath against stale remnants of cigarette smoke while Susan descended the steps wearing a powder blue robe with a hem gray from dragging on the unswept floor. Susan sat on the bottom step and sized up Grace. Her Judy Carne haircut stuck out in tufts.

"I thought you were gone," Grace said.

"Uh-huh," Susan nodded. "I'm back. Short trip."

"Did you like it there?" Grace had never been anywhere.

"I went for an abortion." Susan hugged her own waist. "I could've had it at Mountainside but it was too old, the fetus, I mean. After the third month it's illegal."

They'd gone to eight years at Holy Name of Jesus. They'd had the same lessons from the same nuns. "We're not supposed to have abortions. We're Catholic," Grace said.

Susan laughed. "That you talking or the nuns? Sister Robert ran off last year with Father Fortunato, remember? Because she was pregnant."

Susan pulled a box of Marlboros from her robe and snagged one between her lips. "And, don't you know it's legal now?"

"The new law doesn't matter." Grace felt her face warm up.

"You're still a virgin. I can tell." Susan lifted her cigarette from her lower lip and studied Grace's face. "It's because of your eye. It keeps them away from you."

At mention of her eye Grace pushed her glasses higher on her nose. "It's because I want to wait," Grace said. "I certainly don't want to go through what you just did."

In Susan's hand, a BIC lighter flared and she sucked the flame toward the cigarette like a kid sips milk through a straw. "It was worth it. Every bit of it. She knows now she can't stop me." Susan blew smoke through her nose and her eyes softened. "I see that boy with the Firebird. He going to wait?"

"That's Charlie," Grace felt her voice lift and with it her chin. "We're dating."

"You like him and want to keep him, you got some re-thinking to do about all that chaste waiting."

One day in pre-calc, where he sat in the desk behind her she felt him touch her hair. She leaned back and took out the elastic that held it in a ponytail and let it fall long and golden onto his desk. He whispered, "Wow." She let him twirl tendrils while she faced forward, enjoying the attention, however brief it might be, knowing she was only beautiful from behind. But then, after he walked with her side by side to the parking lot, he asked for a date.

She loved that he ran his hand over her head, feeling her silki-ness when after their first date, for Pizza at Star Tavern in Orange, he parked near the reservation and they made out. He never asked about her glasses, not minding if she didn't take them off until her eyes were closed. After Rourke O'Day and his buddies, who tormented her into mute embarrassment about her eye since as far back as she could remember, finally, someone who didn't seem to notice it at all. She made sure he didn't. It didn't wander while her thick lenses held it in alignment with her other eye, the good one.

Grace watched Susan's face drain of color. Her lips went purple and the hand without the cigarette landed with a slap against the belt of her robe. "I've got diarrhea from the water down there. Nausea from whatever they used to make me sleep. And the blood…" Susan stood up and Grace saw it on the back of her robe. "Another gusher," Susan said and stumbled back up the stairs.

"What can I do?" Grace called after her, thinking she'd rather slap Susan than help her, blood or no blood. Every woman bled. Abortion or not. Why had Susan called to her anyway? Just so she could insult her? She was sorry she'd come in.

"Nothing," Susan whispered. She shouted toward the closed bed-room door at the top of the stairs. "Mom? I need more pads." She dis-appeared around the landing and Grace backed out, pulled the door shut and stood on the front porch.

Grace knew all about Roe vs. Wade from Mom's tirades at dinner.

She hadn't met anyone who actually had an abortion until now. Susan, Grace's mother would say, is trash. "If that girl had an intact family, she wouldn't be looking for attention, male attention of that kind. She's been trouble since that business with passing out in eighth grade."

Grace could still see Sister Robert charging across the parking lot that served as the playground, trying, in her heeled Oxfords and long blue skirts to reach Susan or one of her crowd before they fell to the ground after they did the procedure on each other. It involved standing behind a classmate, arms around her middle so tight the breath couldn't go all the way in and soon the classmate would faint to the ground. Sister Robert banished the procedure from school grounds but Susan and her gang continued to perfect it in the secluded circle of trees near the brook at Watsessing Park until they discovered pot, a safer alternative to asphyxiation. For Grace, the thought of her glasses falling off and her eye turning in was enough to keep her from joining that crowd before or after the pot.

Susan's nasty remark about her eye stung like a wasp's bite as Grace walked the few hundred feet down Olive Street to her house. It was late winter and water ran in the gutter. Tall straight Victorians with front porches and lawns that might better be described as patches of mud and weeds this time of year lined both sides, and the street meandered crookedly from East Orange to Bloomfield. Rental homes were distinguished from the owner occupied ones by the peeling paint on the window frames and spindled railings of the porches. At least there was no litter here. Lots of cars lined the two sides and if anyone drove down here, they drove slowly for there were always kids playing in the street, even in winter.

Inside, Mom was at the stove fastening the lid to the pressure cooker. Discarded scraps of carrot and onion littered a cutting board on the table. Ellen, her sister, younger by twelve months and two weeks, fiddled with the radio with one hand and dunked a teabag into a mug with the other.

"Ah, a perfect album side," said a DJ at Ellen's rock station.

Ellen said, "This is the only station that'll do this." She was obviously unaware of Mom's disapproval when Bob Dylan's voice filled the room.

Grace turned and dropped her books and purse. Ellen's guitar playing, folk music and soft rock were embarrassments to Grace even if nobody was around, but Charlie was due to pick her up at six and she prayed Ellen would not be practicing or listening to WNEW FM when he arrived.

"Pot roast for dinner," Mom said, turning the flame up under the cooker.

"Charlie and I have a date." Grace poured a cup of tea and sat across from Ellen.

"Not on a school night," Mom said.

"I've got one class tomorrow and it's at eleven. Mom, I'm nineteen." Grace looked at Ellen who caught the faint movement of her head as she shook it side to side tensing her brow.

"Mom," Ellen said. "We're both in college. This isn't like high school. Jeez Louise. A school night? I work later than her dates and you don't mind even if I've got class at eight. Lighten up, we're technically adults, remember?"

Grace braced herself against the back of her chair letting the spokes dig into her shoulder blades like penance. She kicked Ellen under the table. Mom whirled around and grabbed Ellen's arm. Then she shoved her face so close to Grace she knew she'd just eaten a carrot.

"Eighteen does not make you an adult. If it weren't for the Vietnam War and the draft you'd be minors until twenty-one. Getting the vote and getting to drink legal doesn't make you any smarter. Long as you girls live here you listen to me and play by the rules of the house. Ellen, shut off that hippie music."

Ellen turned the dial and Mom yanked the plug out of the wall. Grace hated Ellen at that moment. Hated her for her stubbornness or her stupidity or whatever made her do this, riling up Mom right before Grace escaped with Charlie for a few hours.

"Mom," Ellen backpedaled. "I only meant we're not in high school. Most girls our age are away at college. You wouldn't know what we were doing if that was the case."

"Why do you think you're still home? I heard that song. Lay lady lay."

"You've got nothing to worry about Mom. What I mean is we already know…"

"Know what?"

"Know how to stay out of trouble." Ellen turned to Grace but Grace wouldn't meet her eye. She was thinking about edging toward the door and leaving Ellen to deal with this, but Mom grabbed her arm too.

"Upstairs, both of you."

Grace went first. Ellen followed as meek as Grace wished she'd been a few minutes ago. The clock read 5:30. Charlie was coming at 6. Still time to comb her hair and change into something pretty if Ellen would stay meek and let them get through this. She had her eye on Ellen's new blouse. It was hanging on the doorknob and she might just be able to sneak it under her jacket. Served her right for launching Mom into this.

Mom took the family bible from its place on her bureau next to the statue of the Virgin with the bowed head, demure eyes and the chipped fingers on her upturned hands from the time Grace knocked it over. Grace and Ellen sat on the edge of Mom and Dad's bed.

"Bless yourself."

They did, moving their hands almost in unison from forehead to chest, shoulder to shoulder ending with clasped fingers and eyes on the face of the Virgin.

"Grace first."

Grace sighed. She raised her right hand and placed her left on the bible.

"Say the prayer."

Grace closed her eyes. In a moment of resistance she opened them again. "Susan Curran had an abortion. Mom, if that won't stop me, this won't."

"How'd you know that?" Mom lowered the good book and just for a second Grace thought she'd distracted her enough to be spared this exercise.

"I just saw her. She told me."

"Trash," Mom said. "If Mary, the Mother of God had done that, where'd we all be?"

"It's legal now," Ellen said. "Isn't it?"

"So is drinking now for you. Don't make it moral," Mom lifted the book again, held it firm and Grace recited from memory like she had every time.

"O Blessed Saint Joseph, faithful guardian and protector of virgins, to whom God entrusted Jesus and Mary, I implore you by the love which you did bear them, to preserve me from every defilement of soul and body, that I may always serve them in holiness and purity of love. Amen."

"Keep going," Mom said.

"Saint Philomena, model of virginity, pray for us."

Grace stared into her mother's eyes, letting each word penetrate and soothe the earnest concern from her expression. Right before the amen Grace's glasses slipped and she lifted her right hand off the bible to slide them back into place. That glaring ugly imperfection, it seemed no amount of prayer and no doctor's care, no surgery would ever make it go away. Grace knew Mother's prayers did nothing but soothe Mother, like her own prayers soothed her all through her childhood. Even now the echoes of taunting from the boys ambushed her in defenseless moments. She hated those boys and their words stuck inside her head that she couldn't forget. But most of all, she hated her flaw.

"Now swear," Mom urged.

"I promise before Mary, the Virgin Mother of Jesus that my virginity will be my gift to my husband after marriage. I pledge my chastity before God."

She turned to Ellen as the timer on the dinner in the kitchen blared. Ellen, Grace could see, was getting off the hook. With deliberate deadpan beneficence she said, "Nobody needs to worry about Ellen, Mom. She'll be a virgin forever."

Mom put the bible back in its place. "I'm not worried about Ellen. It's you who's got the boyfriend."

Grace grabbed Ellen's blouse from Ellen's tiny bedroom, which had once been Mom's sewing room, and ducked into the bathroom. She heard the doorbell. Ellen's blouse was pale blue, a soft gauzy fabric. She slipped it on and checked to see if the tags showed through the back. She'd sneak it back into Ellen's room later and if she left the tags on Ellen would never know. Lipstick, a bit of blush, and she shrugged her jacket on over the blouse. Her last act of preparation was to pull off her glasses and turn from side to side. Her eye slid toward her nose and stayed there. St. Joseph, you don't need to listen. If you or anyone is going to answer my prayers, it doesn't have to be that one.

Mrs. Curran was at the door in her waitress uniform, black mascara smudged under one eye, her black hair bound close to her skull by a hairnet. She smelled like her house. "Can she? I'm due at work. My shift starts. Bring back the change. Get her the big ones."

Ellen was shoving herself into her coat and taking the cash. Charlie was just coming up the steps, and through the screen Grace saw him pause in Ellen's path. Ellen was skinny, with unruly dark brown curls and her eyes were as blue as Grace's. Her flaw, Grace thought, watching Charlie speak to her, was that her nose was large for her thin face and she had almost no breasts. Her acne was bad still but, she looked from Charlie to her sister and back, his was worse. Ellen no longer wore braces on her teeth, and so now she smiled all the time, showing off her white brights. There was no artificial smile on her now. It was genuine, wide and contagious. Charlie was taking her in with a familiarity Grace's viscera objected to with a sudden contracting. Ellen was saying, "Yes, last semester. Anthropology with Flint. You sat in the back near the windows. We're sisters."

Charlie's gaze moved from Ellen to her in the doorway. "Hey, Grace, now I know why you seemed so familiar when we met. Gees, only the hair color and the glasses. Grace, take them off, really, you two could be twins."

Then Ellen said in a smooth soft voice, "Grace will never take off her glasses. I'm off to run an errand. Grace, don't forget your pledge!"

"How come I didn't know about her?" Charlie didn't exactly watch Ellen but to Grace it seemed a bit of his distracted air had to do with wanting to, and not wanting Grace to see him.

"Let's go," she said.

"Shouldn't I say hello to your folks?"

"Dad's out of town. Mom's busy with a neighbor."

Mrs. Curran came out with her car keys in hand. "This your young man, Grace?"

Grace introduced them and Mrs. Curran nodded distractedly. "Your sister'll look in on my Susan." She jingled her keys looking from Grace to Charlie, and fixated her black eyes on him. She reached into her pocket and handed him something small. "I ain't asking no questions, mind you. It's none of my business but as far as I can tell God made these for a reason."

Charlie reddened and his acne outbreak seemed to grow more pronounced, a welt on his cheek turning an ugly purple. "Let's go Grace," he said, grabbing her hand and practically dragging her to the curb where his blue Firebird idled.

"What'd she give you?"

"A pack of condoms."

"Oh."

They passed Ellen on her way to Mr. Bachman's convenience store around the corner and Charles honked. Ellen waved.

"How come I didn't know about her?"

"I don't know. I guess she's never been home when you've been here."

"She nice?"

"She's evil."

"Seems nice enough. What'd she mean about the pledge?"

"I had to take the pledge tonight because she opened her big mouth and Mom jumped all over me."

"What's the pledge?"

Grace turned toward him and watched as he paused at the stop sign. He looked to the left, then the right, then left again, so careful, so by the book, so exactly the way the adults teach you how to drive. How she wished they'd been that thorough in health class back in high school. Miss Flannery, the old maid health teacher said very little about sex. All Grace had learned was to fear the consequences, pregnancy, syphilis, and gonorrhea. The only thing Miss Flannery taught them about birth control was the percentage probability of failure for each method and the health dangers of The Pill. One afternoon, deep into a lecture that included the perils of the withdrawal method, in the class of all girls, Janet Natush raised her hand. "Miss Flannery," she asked, in a deadpan tone, "can you get pregnant from oral sex?"

Janet had been a Holy Name girl, one of Susan Curran's posse. All eyes turned from Janet to the old maid nurse who answered in an equally even tone, "There is no direct passage from the mouth to the Fallopian tubes in the human body, so no, you can't get pregnant from oral sex."

Janet nodded her head and politely said, "Thank you."

Now, after a college freshman class in human sexuality, Grace at least knew what oral sex was. How though, could she tell Charlie about the pledge? Susan's warning rang in her head.

Grace knew herself to be the oldest living virgin except maybe Miss Flannery. Even strict Sister Robert had finally succumbed to the sin everyone seemed to partake in, running off with handsome Father Fortunato, who Grace recalled had delivered the eighth grade lecture on the male and female reproductive organs. She and Ellen got the goods on the same day and at home later, they told Mom. "You don't have to teach us, they taught us at school."

"About what?"

"About sex," Ellen had used the word where Grace might have said 'the birds and the bees'.

Mom jerked her head around, sliced her pinky with the paring knife she used to dice parsley. "I expect all my daughters to be virgins on their wedding nights."

"Virgins?"

"Yes, like Mary, the mother of God."

"That's what virgin means? Someone who never had sex?"

"What did you think it meant?"

"The nuns always said it meant a young girl without sin."

"Yes, so there you go. It's only a sin before you're married."

Ellen burst out laughing. Grace stared.

"So what's the point?"

"Of?

"Of telling us now?"

"So you understand what to not do." Mom ran cold water on her finger and the stream ran red then pink into the sink. "Time for your first pledge girls. Now that your eyes have been opened."

Mom's first time was a soothing permission to remain in the safety of childhood. Now, the weight of that saintly protection hung on Grace like a disabling defect. She felt like an innocent, for whom the evidence had been fabricated and with which she had been framed and wrongly jailed.

"Grace?" Charlie's elbow broke her reverie.

In profile, he was handsome because his chin was just long enough to balance with the bones in his cheeks and brow. If only his skin would clear up.

"Hmmm?"

"She just gave me condoms."

"Her daughter just had an abortion. That's why."

"Let's use 'em."

"How?"

"How?"

"I didn't mean how." She giggled. "I meant where."

"We've got til eleven. There's a motel out on the highway. I've got enough for a room."

They were stopped at another red light near the center of town where the five and dime blinked its neon enticements. SALE it said in siren pink. BUY NOW AND SAVE!

"Because we can. Because we're ready." He turned from the window to her. "Because sex is a way to explore love and it's a way to really know each other."

"We do."

"So we know it'll be good."

"Charlie, I've never…"

"Then you'll see. The first time is the best." His skin darkened. "At least that's what I've heard."

Horns honked behind them and Charlie parked along the curb in front of Sue Dee Hosiery with its mannequins of women in thigh length stockings and little else.

"I didn't tell you what the pledge is."

"You don't want to, do you? It's what your mother does to control you. Come on, you're not in Billy Joel's song. Yeah, Catholic girls start much too late. It's already late Virginia…I mean Grace." He burst into song. "Come on Virginia I'll show you a sign, send up a signal I'll throw you a line. That stained glass curtain you're hiding behind never lets in the sun. And only the good die young."

Grace sang next. "They showed me a statue and told me to pray. They built me a temple and locked me away. But they never told me the price that I'd pay for things that I might have done. Only the good die young."

Charlie leaned in to kiss her. She felt a lifting from inside. His even white teeth peeked through an eager smile and his eyes were warm on hers. Susan was wrong. Her eye was not why she was the last oldest virgin or unworthy of love. It was all that fear. Susan's lack of it

112

gave her courage now. She didn't need St. Joseph's protection against defilement. She shuddered at the word. All she needed was what Mrs. Curran handed over with that pack of condoms. "The Lantern Motel." He put the car in gear and sped out. "They rent by the hour, I hear."

The young woman at the desk inside what looked like a tiny cabin painted white took Charlie's cash and handed him a key without making eye contact with either of them. She was more interested in her cigarette and the Cosmopolitan magazine open on the desk. Old-fashioned oil lanterns hung from poles that held up the balcony but Grace saw they were powered by electricity. She tripped on the broken sidewalk as they searched for room number seven. The motel was a two-story structure with painted wrought iron railings separating the rooms from the parking lot. They climbed an outdoor stairway to the upper balcony and passed an open door where a wrinkled man in a pair of overalls and a red and black flannel over-shirt emerged, spat off the balcony and eyed them through squinty slits. The thud as he closed his door behind him was a form of wordless contempt.

Their door stuck and Charlie shoved it with his shoulder. He was built a bit like a basketball player without the height of a center, with wide shoulders and a slim muscular torso. He'd tried before in the car. She'd always gone just as far as she knew she could stop. Charlie only once said how much pain he was in and put her hand on his hardened penis. I'm way beyond that, he had said. But she had stopped, echoes of the pledge wafting through and interfering. Not yet, she had said.

Grace touched everything, the drawstring that opened the curtains that were printed with potbelly stoves and lanterns like the ones outside. The heat control, the TV, a St Joseph's bible just next to it, the clock radio set for 12 AM and blinking. She pulled the plug from the wall. Then, she stuffed the St. Joseph's bible into the bureau's top drawer. Shouldn't it be a St. James bible? What was St. Joseph doing here? She pushed her just recited pledge from her mind and pulled the bedspread down while Charlie went out for food. The carpet had a scent of mildew and the fibers were worn. At least the sheets smelled fresh. The room phone rang, blaring so loud she jumped. Who would know…she lifted it. "Room service." It was Charlie. "Would you like fries with your burger, ma'am?"

"Yes, fries." She giggled.

"When I bang, let me in. I forgot the key."

The skin on Charlie's back was smooth and covered with tiny silken hairs. The redness of his complexion ended at his collar. Grace ran her hands up under his shirt while he started by lifting her face between his hands and kissing her, slow, long, deep, familiar, but more insistent than he'd ever been in the car. She responded, wiggling out of her jeans while he pulled her blouse off and let it fall on the bed behind her. Her breasts were even with his mouth and his tongue set off a series of contractions in a place she'd never felt before, then in his hands, she heard a crinkling while he fumbled with the condom. A pause, his finger, then his tongue, his hands reaching for hers while she cried out. Then his turn to gasp and thrust until he let out a groan and then a laugh. It was the laugh that drew Grace to open her eyes. He was over her, gazing into her eyes with a grin.

"Hey, this is the first time you're this close without your glasses?"

Grace shut her eyes.

"No, don't. Look at me."

"Hand me my glasses."

Charlie rolled sideways. "Don't Grace. This is perfect, don't."

"Don't what?"

"Hide."

"I want to."

"You're beautiful. You are."

Grace couldn't control a sudden surge of giggles surging up from deep, so deep and washing over her again and again until she rolled with peals of laughter.

He threw a pillow. She slapped his bare ass.

"Ouch."

"What time is it?"

"Want to again?"

"Yes, this time with my eyes open."

"Open?" Charlie asked. "For the whole time?"

"I want to see your face when you, you know."

"It's more romantic with them closed," he said. There was a drop in his voice. Grace heard it. So subtle. She reached up and touched his cheek where the welt had turned purple earlier. She felt the rough surface on his forehead where a series of tiny red bumps stood out above a blue vein across his left eyebrow. She stroked there with her fingers. "Close your eyes," he said.

She heard the drop again in his voice. Now she knew he'd been right. She knew more about him now, not just how he loved, but how he hurt. She lifted her lips to his.

"Okay, one more time, with my eyes closed, for you," Grace said.

Through her closed eyes she felt his burn into hers and she kept them closed so that he could feel as beautiful and perfect as he made her feel.

Grace found Ellen's blouse on the floor with her jeans and slid it over her head. Charlie dressed and together they pulled the covers over the mattress to neatly make the bed. Then, laughing, Grace crumbled the sheets and tossed them up toward the headboard near the pillows.

They left the key on the dresser and just before the door shut and locked them back into the world of before, Grace said, "Wait!"

"What?" Charlie asked.

She didn't answer. She lifted her hand and removed her glasses. She pulled at an earpiece until it snapped at the hinge. Then she tucked both pieces into her purse. "Okay. Take me home."

"Why'd you do that?"

"Now, Mom'll be so upset about my glasses she'll forget to ask about anything else." Grace grinned a wicked grin. "And I won't have to lie." Charlie held the door open and waited. She slid open the bureau drawer, lifted the St. Joseph's bible back to its spot next to the television, whispering a thank-you as she did, glanced in the mirror as her eye wandered wildly, then turned to go.

Charade

"We weren't trying actually," said my wife, pulling a grape seed from her mouth and dropping it on her dinner plate. "It just happened."

Kate was delighted with our news as any potential grandmother would be, but I would have preferred a little warning. We hadn't agreed to announce this pregnancy just yet, the two and a half months new one, despite how thrilled we were. Lila accepted my under the table kick by ignoring me and folding her legs up under her. Then she dropped a bomb.

"It's my second pregnancy," Lila said.

She and I had never told anyone she'd been pregnant before, although her doctor knew, at least Lila told me the doctor knew, but certainly we had never agreed to tell her mother. Why she chose this moment to ambush me with this breach of our ancient secret, the one she most wanted kept from her mother for all these years was beyond me.

"Why didn't you tell me? I had three miscarriages, you know."

"Mom! You never told me that." Lila glanced at me for the first time.

"Oh, Lila," Kate said. "Why on earth would I tell you such things? What on earth would it do for you to know?"

"I always thought I was an only child because you only wanted one. Were they before me or after?" Lila gulped her water.

So, they both keep secrets from each other, I observed, gulping my beer to quell my rising anxiety over what either might say.

Kate sat up straighter and took a prim sip of her tea. Her silence lingered longer than a sip and swallow. When she took a biscuit and bit into it I knew she had no intention of answering Lila. I withheld my burst of questions. Kate was playing their usual game stepping to the edge of full disclosure then stepping away as though bringing an issue to full fruitful understanding threatened ruin. Their closeness, as mother and daughter, despite their infuriating cat and mouse game was something that ceaselessly astonished me.

"Mama," I said, not looking at Lila. "I rented some old movies. If we're going to watch we should start soon."

"Bring the teapot into the living room. And I'll take the biscuits." Kate stood and practically lunged toward the living room.

"I had a baby. When I was in high school," Lila said to Kate's disappearing back. I stopped dead in my tracks. My beer slipped from my hand.

Kate laughed. She said, "Why on earth are you talking about high school? Bob," she turned to me. "Did you play that game too? The one that health teacher played? You have to carry around an egg in a basket for weeks pretending it's a baby? I remember, Lila made up a little cushion for the egg, and a blanket…" She left the room before she finished, her back to Lila, the biscuit tin in her hand, expecting me to follow. Automatically, I picked up the bottle and followed Kate because I really was with her on this. I paused to glance at my wife and cast her a bewildered frown. She watched her mother's back, gestured impatience by raising her hands to the ceiling and re-crossing her arms. She stared at the bunch of grapes on the table and said nothing to me.

118

"Why now?" I asked.

"When then?" she answered.

"How about never?" I said.

All I heard behind me as I turned into the TV room was a heavy sigh of frustration that told me something big was working on her.

"Please, not now Lila," I begged. "Let's talk first?"

At fifteen, Lila had put such high stakes on keeping her pregnancy secret, warning me they didn't give basketball scholarships to teenage fathers, I didn't ask any questions. I just did what she told me to do and because of Lila's secrecy her mother never knew that we were sweethearts. Well, we weren't actually, not then.

Kate settled in front of the TV, pasted on an exaggerated smile and sipped her tea.

My unease pounded away in my chest. Lila shot me back a scowl as she took a seat. I hit play and the credits rolled. Kate's hearing was not great, especially with background noise, so I sat down next to Lila and whispered, "Why now?"

"It's time," she hissed back.

"She's better off not knowing."

"Why?"

"This will change her forever. Don't hurt her."

"Don't hurt you, you mean?"

"Bob, can you turn up the sound?" Kate asked.

"I've got it Mama." I hit the volume button then went to the kitchen for her teapot and set it on the table alongside her. I noticed her hand was clutching the medal with the picture of the Virgin Mary she wore around her neck. Her thumb was absentmindedly rubbing the engraving.

"What's the movie?" she asked.

"*Charade* with Audrey Hepburn and Cary Grant."

I glanced at Lila when I said it. She grimaced but said nothing.

Kate tucked her feet under her. Lila took the same pose in a comfortable chair on the other side and I lay flat on the floor with a cushion under my head. Apparently my diversion was more comfortable for both of them, at least for now. But, I barely saw the movie myself. Would it hurt me for my mother-in-law to know I had impregnated her daughter when we were fifteen? That we had put one over on her? Kate thought I was a perfect son-in-law. I did not want that to change. I doubted Lila wanted change either. But why did she want her to know? Now, of all times? Or, was there something else in this, for me perhaps, for us, now that we were to be a family. Why now and why to Kate before she and I had a chance to talk it out first? That was Lila, at least, that was the Lila I first knew; she acted first and later brought me in for exactly the part she needed from me. I watched the movie but that question gnawed at me. I'd have to wait until Kate went home before Lila and I could hash this one out.

● ● ● ● ●

That long ago September I had just returned from a Nike basketball camp with guys who averaged three years older than me. The college recruiters had noticed me. Full scholarship potential, they said. I was fifteen and the groupies found me too, the girls who offered their services to all the up and coming NCAA stars at camp. More than my shooting ability was sharpened. Back home, Harry, my best friend, said rumor had it Yvonne Beiber, the girl who serviced all the varsity players was hoping to add me as a notch to her belt. Maybe if she'd gotten to me I'd have left Lila alone and nothing would now lay between her and her mother except a devoted husband, great cook and movie fan prone on the floor tipping a beer awkwardly into my mouth.

Lila, at fifteen, was the girl with the camera at all the school events. She had caught my game winning three-pointer the prior season and on the first day back to school I stared at the board to avoid eye contact with Yvonne Bieber. I saw the photo on the bulletin board in front of the principal's office. If not for Yvonne, perhaps I would not have seen that photo or the little cardboard sign "Photos by Lila Cass".

120

Lila ran between the art crowd and the jocks. Harry, who played point guard on Junior Varsity and forgave me for my superior talent because he was my best friend, never let me forget I had a crush on her in kindergarten. He pestered me to tell him my current Lila fantasies until I shoved him at a row of lockers. She was beautiful and too smart to pay much attention to someone like me, especially after Harry's foolishness in the halls, which I was sure, hadn't escaped her.

I asked her. I waited after school for her and stumbled alongside her for a block or two noticing fallen leaves clinging to the laces of my sneakers. She walked beside me, her long hair swinging behind her, her hips swaying as her low-slung jeans dragged on the pavement. Her tee shirt just met her waistline and revealed a sliver of skin as she moved.

Her eyes, behind cobalt blue frames, took me in and then looked around. She seemed to expect someone to be with me. But I had eluded Harry for this. I noticed her breasts heave at a deep breath. I saw her hand push her glasses up her nose and toss her hair over her shoulder. Her eyes were picking up the details, purposeful and so was her voice which sounded strong after my feeble "Uh, hi Lila…"

"What's up?"

"I found this at school." I held out her photo of my winning shot.

"That's mine. Thanks." She reached for it and stuck it inside a notebook. "Where'd you find it?"

"In the hall."

"You could've just stuck it back on the wall."

"It was on the wall." I paused. "I was going to ask you if you have more."

"Copies?"

"Copies, or other shots, of the team, or, uh, me…"

"Yes, I have lots of them. Not just you, the whole team…the whole season."

"Could I see them?"

"Sure. When? Now?"

This directness was the only thing Lila shared with the girls at summer camp but I didn't learn that about her until much later. They picked out their men, or boys, because that's what we were even though we all pretended otherwise; they hunted and consumed us, hands and mouth and sliding zippers and tongues against pulsing skin and it'd be a rare thing if the same girl came looking for you a second time. Girls who later watched NCAA games and counted the notches on their belt. Coach always warned us against them. Lila's purposefulness brought that out of the past summer and into the present and despite the accompanying physical sensation, I had to answer her question and tell myself this was not a prelude to something else.

"Now? Sure if it's okay with you."

"I'm not allowed to have visitors in the house after school. You'll have to look at them outside."

That brought me back down to earth. Lila turned up her driveway reciting what she called the ten commandments of living with Kate Taylor, divorced mother, religiously pious, insistent that Lila not date until she was seventeen, equally suspicious of men, cigarettes smokers, boys in cars, dirty movies, swearing, atheists, Jews, gays, lesbians and, God forbid Lila pierced her ears before the age of nineteen. I should have fled. But, Harry was right. I still had a crush on Lila and still believed, despite the sharpening pain in the tightness of my jeans, that my intentions were honorable. I followed, stopped at the steps to the back door and leaned on the railing. She disappeared into the house; I turned my face from the direct sun and studied the house and yard. A row of shrubs surrounded the small lawn. A single ancient oak occupied the center of the yard and a stone bench anchored it in place. Facing me, near the fence I saw one of those things we called "Mary on a half-shell".

Lila came down the steps carrying an accordion file in one hand and two cans of Coke in the other. She sat down next to me and flipped back the ends of her hair. I could smell the sunlight in it. She handed me a Coke and when she saw me staring at the statue of Mary, she said, "My mother prays out here every morning. She's very holy. And extremely old-fashioned."

"Catholic?" I asked.

"Yes," Lila said. "That's why she's alone. Doesn't believe in divorce, even though my dad's been gone since I was seven."

I pulled the flip cap up. The can erupted and overflowed. She just laughed and flicked hers open. "That must be the one I dropped in the kitchen."

She shifted toward me on the bench and pulled out a sheet of contact prints. Her hands were almost as long as mine, but slender, almost pointed at the fingertips.

She pulled out a small magnifying glass and held it over the sheet of prints. I stopped looking at her hands and leaned close.

I always feel paralysis when Lila asks me to look at her work. I say, "I love all your work. I'm not a good critic." And then I kiss her mouth, hoping she'll forgive me. Back on that first day I was simply mute until she pointed to a few action shots she said she could print and give to me the next day. I stood up and tossed my soda can into the recycling bin next to her garage. Nice clean shot with not even a bounce on the rim. I thought about leaving until she said, "Can I practice on you? I'm working on portraits for class."

"I guess so," I said. "You sure?"

Lila studied me. "Maybe the newspaper could use a head shot of you. "

She wanted to know if the paper would use black and white or color. And while I went to the kitchen to dial the newspaper office she disappeared into her basement.

I hung up and followed her. She was leaning over a drawer that squealed open. Her darkroom doubled as a laundry room. The windows were covered with black paper taped to the frames with masking tape. Two bulbs dangled from the ceiling and a line of string with rolls of film dangling crossed the center of the room. There was a crude counter made of boards across two old metal file cabinets and a slop sink where a bucket sat, fed by a rubber hose making a trickling sound as water dripped through a hole in its side. A sharp odor of chemicals attacked the lining of my nose when I stepped across a small puddle to enter.

"You should wait outside."

"Really?" I turned toward the steps.

"My mom would have a fit," she said. "She doesn't trust men since forever." She pushed her glasses up the bridge of her nose and went on.

"I'll go then," I said. "She home?"

"No," Lila glanced at me then down at the camera in her hand. "Stay. She'll never know."

She turned her back to me, slid the drawer shut and switched off the bulb. The story from my mother was that I could never sleep in the dark, that night blindness was an inherited trait. She never explained the panic that went with it though. I felt as though the floor had vanished into darkness. It occurred to me that Lila needed the dark to load the film in the camera. I couldn't tell her to turn it back on. I could only stand still and fight to keep my balance until she was finished. I stretched out my hands to grab at anything, to stop myself from keeling over. Then it was light again and Lila turned toward the door with the camera in her hand. I didn't move until she turned.

"What's wrong? You okay?"

"I'm okay. Just thought I heard your mother," I lied.

"Well, she's scary but I don't think anybody broke out in a sweat because they heard her coming before." She looked amused.

"Well, you just gave me all that on her. Who wouldn't be intimidated? Sounds like she hates everyone."

"She never recovered from my father leaving. I think that's what makes her like that. Come on."

Lila took my picture in the yard. And I asked her. Just like it was supposed to happen. I just said it. "Would you like to see a movie or something?"

124

"I knew you were here for more than a picture." She smiled.

I flushed deep red, betting Harry's quips had got back to her. She said she'd have to talk at school or sneak a call because her mother wouldn't let her talk on the phone to boys or date. "Not until seventeen," she said. "Can you wait two years?" She laughed.

She didn't call that night, or the next. She ignored me at school except for one second in the hallway between classes a week later when she handed me an envelope and a note. Inside were copies of the team photos in 5 X 7 size. The note said I should stop by after school to see the portraits. I had figured when I didn't hear from her, that she decided to obey her mother's rules about dating. Now, since she was breaking the rule about having me over, I figured she just didn't want to call me. She didn't like me, but I figured I'd give it another try. I ducked around back instead of using the front door. The Mary on a half-shell frowned at me.

"Hi, do you want a soda?" Lila opened the refrigerator and handed me a can. She put her own up to her mouth and sipped. Lipstick smeared the top of her can, pink and shiny around where her mouth had been. Her throat moved up and down as she swallowed and licked her lips. She had combed her hair. I knew because the static raised a few hairs.

"Your mom's not home?"

"She's working late. Otherwise you wouldn't be here." Her tone said that should be obvious.

"Thanks for the pictures."

I waited for her to say something about going outside because of her mother's rule.

"I think you'll like the head shots too. Come downstairs."

It made me uncomfortable, like there was some notion I was missing that anyone else would understand without having to ask. Her silences are familiar now, but back then they were blanks I filled with my own assumptions. It was cool in the basement. I followed her down and through the door. She shut it behind me and turned to pull the contact prints off the string across the center of the room. At the makeshift counter we used the same tiny magnifying glass to study the prints. She stood close enough that strands of her hair clung to my arm. I touched it. And I smoothed it back away from her face. She was intent on the prints so seemed to hardly notice.

She said, "I like this one."

She straightened up and held the glass for me. I bent over and as I squinted I felt her hand on my back. It was a long way down for me to get my eye on that tiny glass if I bent from the waist, so I knelt on the cold concrete floor while I looked. Her hand was still on my back.

"What do you think?"

"I like it. It's good. But this one is better."

"Why?"

"In that my eyes look squinty." Really it was because the panic from the dark was still on my face in it.

Our heads were close. Her hair hung down and draped over my hand while we took turns and made judgments on the prints, about which was better and why.

"This one." She held the glass and I looked.

"Why this one?" I asked.

"That one works. You look sort of, uh, serious, but there's something else in your eyes." Her eyes flickered at me like she was embarrassed to say it. Her face was inches from mine and I could feel heat from her body in the coolness of that room. She had a pink gloss at the corner of her mouth. I touched it with my finger. I accidentally touched the tip of her tongue. Then my mouth wanted to feel it too. I kissed her. Her hands came up and her fingers were in my hair and she was widening her mouth and using her tongue to respond. Then she shivered so I pulled her closer, down on top of me. I now sat on the cold floor with her kneeling over me, bending toward me to prolong this kiss that I could feel rocketing through me. It was there then, knowing she was accepting and coming with me. Her hands were pulling at my shirt and mine were on her and slipping into her jeans and she was wiggling out of them and my hand touched where she was warm and wet and she moaned. And somehow I'd freed myself and found her and thrust inside with her panting and clinging to me while I moved and pushed into her until she gasped and rocked and I moaned with her and we both were limp and sweaty in the cold air of her darkroom.

"Lila," I said her name because it was the only thing I could think of to say. She stood and shoved herself back into her jeans and covered her breasts with her tee shirt.

"Please," she said. "Go, before I'm so in trouble."

"Lila," I started again.

"Just go," she said.

"I don't want to go," I said. "Listen, I just…"

"No," she said. "Don't say anything. Just go before my mom comes home or something. Please."

"Can I call you tonight?"

"No," she said. "You can't call me."

There was no reading her face. No clue of what to say or do except walk out. As though all of it hadn't really happened.

"Lila," I said, turning, "I'm sorry. Did I hurt you?"

"No. You didn't hurt me."

I walked away. The next day and many following days she looked through me. She would not lift her eyes to meet mine, not in homeroom, not in the hallways, not at the beginning of the basketball season when she once again covered the action from the sidelines and hung the photos in the usual place and published them in the school newspaper, as though that afternoon was non-existent. I watched her. I listened for her voice. I played us over and over again whenever I was idle for a two second interval. I woke at night to memory. And then one day in late December she was waiting for me between lunch and study hall.

"Bobby," Lila said, just my name in a low deadpan voice.

"Lila," I answered. "How've you been?"

"How've I been?"

"Yeah. I thought you would call me."

She stared at me.

"I was hoping we could…I wanted to talk to you. I…"

"It shouldn't have happened." She looked down.

"Can I say something?"

"No." Now she was looking around, past me, on all sides.

"Please, Lila. You have to hear this. I need to say it so you can hear it."

I wanted to have all the conversations I'd played over in my head in the past few months. I wanted to explain myself, to ask her, to tell her that I hadn't wanted it to just be what it was, that I didn't intend to do what I did. To tell her I didn't know whether I should be sorry or not. I didn't get a chance to say any of it.

"Come over here." She beckoned me to a side hallway leading toward the stairs.

I followed. She turned and dropped her books to the ground. She turned her body to profile. She put her hands on her hips. "Look at me."

I looked at her face.

"No," she said. "Look where you like to look."

She watched my eyes drop to her breasts and her waist. The blood below her skin around her eyes turned to black ink and her fingers curled into fists. I didn't know what part of her she wanted me to see, why she stood without a hint of self-consciousness and said, "Finished?"

She folded her arms across her middle and her shoulders slouched forward, a position I would see her in for the rest of the school year, because it hid the secret. She turned and whispered in a biting spit. "I'm pregnant. Get it? I'm pregnant."

I stepped away from her and slammed into the radiator hanging on the wall behind me. I hit my head. Blood pumped like thunder in my ears. Lila turned and glanced up the hall emptying now of students.

"And," she added, "if you do everything I say and I mean exactly what I say, nobody will know about it and…and you won't in trouble. Teenaged fathers don't get basketball scholarships."

I nodded. "But what are you going to do? I mean…get an abortion? What? I can help… you know…"

"No," she said. "You can't ask questions. I'll decide what."

"Lila, I'm sorry…"

"No, Bobby, I'm sorry. Just wait and I'll tell you what to do." She turned and left me.

I had to look at her. I watched her constantly for a signal. I took to staring at other girls too so Harry's eagle eyes wouldn't pickup my unrelenting attention to her face. That was the beginning of my lifelong habit. I am still always waiting for Lila to tell me what to do, but pretending not to, reading her eyes until I know without any conscious thought what she wants. She still is the only woman who can keep my attention.

Lila handed me a note that said if I saw her look straight back at me I should go to her house after school and knock on her back door. Only twice that entire year did I catch her signal. The first time was just before Harry and I found the homeless man. I didn't go. I had practice. After an hour of suicides, defensive drills and a shower I stepped out the gym door with Harry for the walk home, knowing I'd been too scared to go, knowing she'd been waiting, and knowing it was too late and dark now and her mother was already home from work.

Pizza Oven across the street from school was frying garlic and my stomach rumbled so I pointed and Harry followed me inside. Harry with his eagle eyes didn't pick up on my altered state, or if he did he didn't let on.

Forty minutes later having consumed a half a pizza each and limitless cokes, we turned left and there, two stores from Pizza Oven, in front of the narrow alley with trash and recycling bins lining the concrete strip between the stationery store and the post office, we kicked at a black plastic bag left in the center of the sidewalk and heard a moan. Nelson was his name. He hung out near school at the bus stop shelter unless the police prodded him to move. Rumor had it he slept in the basement of the Shamrock, a shot and beer joint in town where proof of age wasn't needed if you wanted a case of beer for a party. We called him NO for short. No Oxygen because you had to hold your breath if you walked past him on the street. Mingled with the usual urine and body odor was the sharp clean vapor of gin.

Harry grunted and stepped away. We'd gone two paces when we heard a gurgling sound and a raspy cough and the black lump moved. I turned and Nelson's hand was slowly stretching toward our ankles, fingers red with scaly patches of dried white skin and long nails jagged at the edges.

"Hey, Nelson old man," Harry said. "Get up man."

Sounds, human but unintelligible, followed. His hand and arm went limp. I felt a slow panic in my own chest. All the mocking of this man we'd done weighed on me. We could just step around and go. Lila was waiting for me although I knew it was late and her mother might be home. I couldn't go to her even though I knew I should, even though she was expecting me. I was not doing the right thing and I knew it. I could do something here, for Nelson, instead.

"Harry," I said, "He's not right. I think he can't get up."

"I'm not touching him," Harry answered. "Don't even think about asking me to."

"Go back to Pizza Oven. Call 911." I dropped my gym bag on the sidewalk and Harry did the same.

"He's drunk, man. That's all."

"Yeah, he is. But go call anyway."

Harry sprinted down the street. I held my breath and stooped down. Nelson was on his stomach, face turned to the left, away from me. I pulled an eyelid opened and in the beam of a passing car I caught blue pupils and blood red veins filling up the whites of the rest of his eye. I pulled off my glove and felt for his neck, which was hidden among layers of clothing, looking for his pulse. Then I went around and used the wrist of his outstretched hand. I couldn't feel a beat at all. I heaved him over onto his back and arranged his body flat. Drool oozed from the corner of his lips caked with dried white sweat. I tore away the black garbage bag he wore for warmth and found it impossible to tell if his chest moved at all, if he was breathing, because of all the clothes he wore. Without the plastic, his stench filled up my nostrils and mouth and I held my breath again. Was it worth it? Should I try to save this guy? Maybe he wants to die. Maybe that's why he's a homeless bum and a drunk. Maybe it's a slow death wish and he's getting what he wants if Harry and I just leave him alone. Harry came back puffing steam from his mouth. There was nothing of the same leaving Nelson.

"They're on the way," Harry said.

I inhaled and stretched my mouth over his and pinched his nostrils shut. I blew and pulled my mouth off, listened for movement in his chest and tasted the foul dried spit now on my lips too. I did it again. In minutes I saw a flashing red light and felt a hand on my shoulder. The EMT's took over and I fell back into a sit on the sidewalk and watched. I belched and tasted pizza mingled with everything else. They got out the defibrillators and cut his clothes and jolted him there on the sidewalk. His body thrashed and I remember thinking they should put something under his head. Nelson didn't die. They put him on a stretcher and took him to St. Ann's where he spent a week in a soft bed. The local paper overdid the write-up about Harry and me saving his life so the principal gave us a morning off to go pay him a visit.

"Don't let him try to kiss you again," Harry said under his breath so only I could hear.

He was under the spell of one of the drugs they'd given him for his heart, or there was something else going on, because he kept trying to take off his hospital gown. The photographer took our picture, Harry on one side of the bed, me on the other, Nelson propped to a sitting position with the wrist tethers the nurse managed to use to subdue his hands hidden under the blanket.

Nelson fixed his eyes on Harry and worked his tongue in his mouth.

"I seen you boys at the Shamrock. Right?"

"Not us, Nelson. Somebody who looks like us maybe. But not us." Harry said straight-faced.

"Have you got a drink on you, boy?"

Harry kept the corners of his mouth pointed downward although I watched his eyes struggle to remain serious.

"William," Harry said, reading his chart. "May I call you by your first name, sir?"

"Who told you my name?"

"It's here on the chart."

"I go by Nelson, if you don't mind."

"So may I call you that? Rather than Mr. Nelson?"

"Who are you and why have you come to see me?"

Harry pointed to me. "See that tall guy there?"

Nelson turned toward me. "Him?"

Harry explained. "This guy kept you breathing til the right people got there."

I moved and Nelson looked right at me.

"Have you got a drink, boy?"

"No."

"Then why did you come?" His voice was a growl. "Why did you bother? Should've left me there. I'd be better off."

I felt as though he expected me to apologize. Then I understood why I hadn't gone to Lila's that night or any night since she'd given me her silent signal. I'd offered help to her without knowing what kind of help she would want. When I left Nelson's hospital room, I knew I had to go to her house. If they could keep Nelson, a homeless drunk alive, we could keep this baby alive no matter what it meant to either of us. I needed to hear what she would say to this thought.

She almost didn't let me in. I knocked at the back door. She saw me through the curtained window and swung the door open.

I said, "You asked me to come, remember?"

She stood back to let me pass then shut the door. "I'll probably deliver in May," she said. "I can hide it until then."

"Lila," I asked, "do you want to have an abortion? I know you don't want this baby." I looked at her. She was wrapped in a thick hooded sweatshirt with a huge pocket in the front. It hung down to her hips. Her jeans were loose in the thigh, an unusual fit for her. Her eyes had a soft radiance, more gentle than her clear-eyed sharpness that intimidated me the day of the first photos.

"There are places you can take newborns," she said. "No questions asked. They take them and find homes for them."

I nodded.

"You can be the one to take the baby there. Right after I deliver it. That's what you have to do for me."

No abortion. This eased my fear, but in the next second a new one rose.

"But how are you going to deliver it? What hospital?"

"I can't go to a hospital. It costs a lot to have a baby."

"My mother's a nurse," I said. "Let me ask her for help. Let's think this through. How are you going to do this without someone who knows something about it?"

"I can't keep it from my own mother and tell yours. Babies are born all the time. It's a natural thing. We can do it at a hotel or something."

"Lila, we can't do that. What if things go wrong? That happens. Women die giving birth."

"I won't die. Stop making it sound worse than it is. You're just scared. If we plan it right, nobody will know. My life won't change. Your life won't change. It'll be back to normal when it's finished."

She sat up straighter and her hand went to her stomach. She put her second hand under the sweatshirt and breathed sharply. "It moves." She said. "All the time. I lie in bed at night and watch my stomach rumble. There are little kicks and things, like it's swimming. Want to feel?"

She took my hand and slid it up under the sweatshirt. I stiffened;

surprised that she'd want me to touch her. Her skin was warm and smooth and taut across the rounded mound near her navel. Just under my palm I felt a push, twice, then nothing. Lila pushed my hand away too soon.

"I have those pictures. Do you still want them?" she asked.

"I thought after, you know, uh, that day, you'd throw them away or something."

"I never throw anything away."

I think this was the moment I knew I didn't just have a crush but that I loved her. She handed me the pictures. "Don't let anyone look at these."

"Why? They're just pictures."

"I don't want people to see them. They might know they're mine."

"Why don't you keep them then?"

"I don't want them here. My mother might find them."

"Where is she? Is she here?"

"No, she's at the supermarket. You shouldn't stay."

"Then just throw them away."

"No. They're too good to just throw away."

"If I can't use them why should I keep them? Giving them to me is just as good as tossing them in the garbage dump."

"Is that what you're going to do with them?"

"What do you want me to do with them?"

"Bobby, they're a gift for Christ's sake. I did them for you. You could at least keep them."

"I don't get it. You're giving me a present but you won't even talk to me most days."

"My mother can't know. Nobody can know. If anyone sees us together they'll start gossiping and it could get back to her. "

"Is she really that bad?"

"She's not bad, Bobby, she's just...fragile. If she found out I had sex she'd be praying over me, she'd send me to a convent."

She looked down at her abdomen and back up at me. She shoved her hands into her pockets. "I couldn't stand her knowing. She'd take it so personally, like I did it to her, like I was deliberately trying to hurt her, you know, destroy her life or something. She's like that. Like, oh, it's too difficult to explain her. She's afraid of the world. She's even more afraid of sin, for herself or for me. That's why her rules are so strict. She prays all the time. And on top of that, she pretends things are not what they are. She still pretends my father's coming back, as though that helps me cope with his not being here. It's for herself she pretends. It would be a living hell to be in this house with her knowing this secret." She took a deep breath and looked away. "And yours too. Are you going to show up when it counts?"

"Yes. I am. I already promised you."

"Well it took you two weeks to show up here."

I was a coward and she knew it.

"I'll do anything you want. Just tell me. Are you really going to forget all about this when the baby is gone? Are you expecting me to erase it too?"

She answered me with a blank stare.

The storyboard idea came to me in my film class the next day. I reminded myself that there were two stories, hers and mine. There were only a few places where the two intersected. I had to keep blazing a path toward a basketball scholarship. Lila's eye was set somewhere else; photography school was my guess. This secret could derail both of us if it got out. In the months of waiting I converted to her way of thinking, that the world could continue to function exactly the way it always had. I understood what Lila was saying about her mother. It was better for me at home than if I'd asked my mother for help. But I didn't have a growing bump in my middle to hide.

The second time I got Lila's 'meet me' signal, Lila gave me the address of the place called "Chapter Home". I checked names of motels out on the highway and saved money to pay for a room. The phone rang like an ordinary call but at six am on a Tuesday morning in early May. I knew it had to be her. I leaped to the phone in the bedroom before my mother could reach the extension in the kitchen where she was drinking coffee and reading the paper.

"It's starting," Lila said. "It's going to be today."

"So I'll meet you across from school. Can you get there? Wait across the street by the post office. We can call a cab."

"Maybe I should do this by myself."

A split second of hesitation passed. Today could be the first of Lila's promised back-to-normal days for me. The kind she had predicted we'd have when it was over. She was releasing me. But she wasn't. She was testing me.

"No, you shouldn't. Stick to the plan."

"The side of the post office facing away from school. So nobody will see us, okay?"

"All right."

Lila had her hair tied up in the back and held in place with a baseball cap and over her shoulder she carried her camera bag. When I approached from behind her I saw little evidence of our secret. There were no people in sight and the windows of the high school were gray as though they too were in on the secret. She turned toward me and gave a weak smile. Her jeans were wet between her legs. She saw me look and her cheeks turned pink. "I think we'd better hurry."

I called the cab company, hoping as I did the driver wouldn't recognize my face from the sports page. I'd made all state again. I prayed silently that the gym really wasn't open this morning and that Harry or any other teammates wouldn't arrive across the street and spot us. I took Lila's bag from her shoulder and leaned against the brick wall knowing it would make me look shorter and less conspicuous. She leaned on one shoulder facing me.

"My water broke," she whispered. "I knew what it was. We covered it in health class."

The Lantern Motel had black shutters on white aluminum siding and red outside doors to the rooms. But for the bright neon light close to the highway's shoulder, it seemed a peaceful place with its fake gas lamps and oil lanterns hanging from hooks around the portico to the manager's office. The proprietor, a thin wrinkled woman with hands that shook so hard I had to place the cash in her drawer myself, didn't look either of us in the eye.

Room 17 was half way back on the right side. Lila headed straight to the bathroom and shut the door. I stood and looked around at the tiny room with pine paneling and a brown shag rug. There were two double beds, a dresser with a mirror and a TV on a wheeler cart. Curtains with clipper ships and anchors were pulled across the wide window. I heard the toilet flush and the water running before Lila emerged carrying her jeans in her arms and a towel wrapped like a skirt low, under her belly to hide herself. She'd taken off her sweat-shirt and on top wore only a tee shirt. She sat on one of the beds and covered herself with blankets. I switched on the TV and played with the channels until I found a station running an old Honeymooners episode. I could fix my eyes there and not have to look at her.

"Oh, Bobby," she said, "for Christ's sake, you've seen me before."

I eventually had to look away from the TV. Slowly, as the morning wore on, she stalked around the room, leaning over, breathing with her hands on her stomach until I was drawn into it. I swabbed her forehead with cool washcloths. I rubbed her back and shoulders. Whatever she asked me for, I did. That had been my promise. Still the cold truth that I was of little use to her kept my throat dry, my palms cold and wet and my mind numb with fear. I ticked away the hours according to the sequence of half or full hour TV programs. We'd watched enough to bring us to the evening news.

Finally, the light got dim and we switched on the lamp beside the bed. I went outside to the soda machine and got some more water bottles. She left a message for her mother that she would be home late, that she was at the library doing a paper.

If I had been inside Lila, in her skin, I wonder if I could have felt more of what I witnessed in her face that day. If I thought she was silent with her long pauses and her resolve all those long months when she pretended I was non-existent, what I knew about her after that day dissolved the barrier between what she showed the rest of the world and what was her private inner world. I knew that this day would never be over, not really, for either of us, no matter how much she pretended otherwise.

Lila squatted on the mattress on top of sheets already wet from her own sweat and the other liquids that I now know come with child-birth. The baby was covered in a foamy white substance, her skin wrinkled and prunish to the touch and in color. The cord attached to Lila pulsed and Lila knew she should clear the baby's mouth of mucus. In my single moment of inspired thought, I found a bath towel for Lila to wrap her in.

"Get the scissors," she said.

Lila did it herself. Cut the baby from her and made a knot in the cord close to the baby's skin. She held the baby out to me. I stood there helplessly watching as blood gushed from between Lila's legs and Lila didn't seem to notice it was there. The baby was so light in my arms. Lila put her hands on her own stomach and pushed. She crunched her face up and I smelled a metallic blood smell. It looked like Lila was going to bleed to death. I turned to find somewhere safe and lay the baby in the middle of the clean bed. "I'm calling 911," I said.

"It's just the placenta." Lila's voice was a whisper. "This is normal. It's okay. Bring her to me."

She pulled up her tee shirt and exposed her breast. She pulled the baby close and cradled her while the baby opened her little mouth and suckled.

"What should I do?"

"Nothing. Just don't do anything. Just let me do this and then we'll get her ready to take."

I didn't really want to look at them. This pair soothing each other and Lila's face tensing. "I'm still contracting," she said. "It gets more intense when she sucks."

"You're bleeding more."

The stain spread and wet the blanket she used to cover herself.

"Lila, you have to do something. Or I have to. There's too much blood. You're chalk white. I'm calling."

"You can't Bobby. Don't. I'm fine. Bleeding is normal. It'll stop." She was pleading. "I'm okay. Here, hold her. I'll take a shower and you can go."

I called the cab company. I was so afraid someone would discover what happened here, I lay the baby down on the clean bed and yanked at the dirty sheets. I rolled the bloodiest sheet into a ball and carefully wrapped others around it so that the outer layer of fabric had no visible stains. This I could do for Lila, the least of the acts of deception performed by either of us that day.

It was night and aside from a few dim lights the parking lot was dark. I took the key and carried the bedding to the back of the lot where a dumpster sat like a black hulking entrance to hell. I lifted the lid and tossed the bundle in. It barely made a sound as it found it's resting spot in the stench. The cover thumped down and a pair of blinding headlights hit me in the eyes as I turned back to climb the stairs to room 17 to flip the mattress over.

A small sound, like a sigh came from the bed so I sat down and picked up the baby. She was moving her mouth and her hands were tucked under her chin. The light from the lamp crossed the baby's face so I reached over and flipped it off. The light from the bathroom was enough for me to look at her face and see her mouth moving still. I walked around, rocking her lightly, staring at her face, thinking about Lila's face and looking for signs of it or mine in her.

Then Lila pulled the door shut and the light went out. I reached out to steady myself and banged my left hand on the corner of the dresser. My other arm tightened around the baby as my throbbing hand groped further in the dark. I called toward the bathroom door. "Lila, open the door."

The exhaust fan hummed and she didn't answer. And as seconds ticked around me the dark stood still and the gentle wet sound of the girl's breathing, barely audible, hardly there at all, steadied me. There was no terror like I felt in the darkroom that first day with Lila, no falling, no disappearing floor, but minutes passed and still no light. My heart maintained its rhythm. I waited, I knew there was no place in this room for my own demons. This baby had chased away any demons that may have haunted me in the past. The light streamed around her as Lila emerged in a cloud of steam and stood watching me. She was dressed in a clean tee shirt and sweatpants. Her wet hair clung to her neck. I handed her the baby and she sat, serenely cooing. I saw her face flush red when on one, then the other of her heavy breasts a circle of wetness soaked through her tee, and she just glanced down, then at me and said, "Ready?"

I was silent this time. I didn't tell her about my night blindness and that I'd conquered it at last because she looked just so incredibly strong and beautiful.

I saw the cab through the window. Lila wrapped her in another blanket and I left after one last glimpse of her when she said, "I'm fine. Go." I only left because this was the promise I made to Lila. I would be the one to take her. If not for that promise, I could not have left her sitting there in that room, alone, beautiful, tired, and for all I knew, still bleeding. I went because it was the only act of love Lila would accept from me.

It was as she told me it would be. I wondered if she'd seen the place. It was a large old home in need of repair. An extremely red faced woman with large breasts and even larger buttocks, wearing stretch pants and a sweatshirt, took the baby from me. She left me standing in the entrance hall, with empty arms, staring at a row of doors shut tight against all the secrets brought and left here. When I went back to the motel Lila was gone.

• • • • •

My romance with Lila, once it actually started, after about a year and a half of pretending to be our two separate selves again, after her body went back to its old shape, was no surprise to Harry. He just nodded and said, "Since kindergarten, buddy."

She spent the summer in art school and I went back and did the Nike thing again, including the groupies, which I welcomed with great relief. I even let Yvonne do me the following fall. If she bragged about it, it never reached my ears. I was using Yvonne so I could stop thinking about Lila for a few minutes here and there. I got a phone call from her in December, at the start of basketball season. She said she wanted to add more sport shots to her portfolio and needed a practice subject. My insides turned white as I listened to her voice. My own came out weak but I said yes on one condition. She was silent, waiting for me to finish.

"You have to meet me for a soda, or a movie."

"Bobby," she answered. "What movie?"

"Does that mean yes?"

"I'm allowed to date now."

"Does that mean yes?"

"Why?" she asked.

"What do you mean, why?"

"I just figured you'd want that chapter closed. I just figured you'd say yes about the pictures because you could use the pictures for your clippings folder."

"Never mind then," I said. "You're right. Just take some pictures."

"Maybe I should just ask somebody else."

"Do what you want." I hung up. Harry told me a few days later that she'd called him. He was finally first string point guard. He told her no. Told her that she should call me. Then he looked me straight in the eye and said, "Don't let one mistake trip you up buddy."

"What mistake?" My stomach dropped like lead.

"Bobby," he glared at me like I was an idiot. "Don't ever say no to that girl again."

Harry had it wrong. She'd never asked me for anything I'd had to refuse. It was Lila who said no to me.

I called her back. Her mother answered and I almost hung up.

"Is Lila home?"

"Oh, yes. Hold on please." She sounded pleasant enough through the phone. I remembered Lila said she wasn't bad, just fragile. I listened for a click that told me her mother had hung up after Lila picked up an extension. There was no click.

"Hi Bobby."

"Hi Lila."

I heard a sigh. I couldn't tell who it was, Lila or her mother.

"Harry told me you still need some action shots."

"Yes, I do. Thanks. How about tomorrow?"

"After school?"

"Sounds good. In the gym. I'll see you then."

Lila squatted on the floor with a huge lens, like the pros do at pro games, shooting upward then hunkering down under the backstop to capture me in midair while I stuffed the ball. She shot a full roll and paused to reload. I stopped to catch my breath. "Did you tell Harry I said no?" I didn't want to sound like I was accusing her, so I whispered it.

"Well, you kind of did." Her eyes were on the film, not me.

"No, Lila. You said no to me."

"Well, I didn't want to get into anything with you, like, well, you and Yvonne have been at it, haven't you?" Her cheeks turned pink.

"Lila, I said something about a talk. It doesn't mean anything else."

"But it would, wouldn't it? Mean more."

"It wouldn't have to. It would be whatever you want it to be."

"Oh. Really."

"Yeah, really."

She was silent.

"After Harry told me you called him, he told me I should never say no to you again." I was sweating more than when I was in motion. "And I realized, later, I never said no to you. I did everything you asked. You didn't ask me to do much. I'll admit that. You asked me to stay away and I did. I did what you wanted with the baby. I kept the secret. I did everything you wanted."

"Yes, you did Bobby."

"And," my heart was pounding in my chest as I said it, "I would've stopped if you'd asked me to. That day in the darkroom. If you'd wanted me to pull away, I would have."

"Yes," she whispered. "I know that."

"So I'm sorry I didn't know what you wanted. I'm sorry. That's all I ever wanted you to know."

"I never let you say it, did I?" she asked.

"No. I wanted you to call and at least say something."

"I couldn't call…"

"Yeah, I know, the whole thing with your mother and her rules. I guess I get it now."

"No. You don't get it now." She looked away from me. "I couldn't look at you." She looked back. "And I couldn't call you."

I waited for her to keep going. I was afraid she'd just get silent and leave me wondering again.

"I knew I couldn't say no to you, Bobby. That's why I stayed away. I knew after that day that I'd never say no to you. And after all this, after you did everything right, just what I wanted, I knew neither of us would."

"What?"

"Neither of us would ever say no to each other again."

I look at Harry's picture sometimes and speculate that if he had moved away in first grade instead of after college I might not have ever looked at Lila. Maybe it was Harry who'd had the early crush on her. Who knows? He probably knows more than he lets on. I speculate that what I share now with Lila isn't because of destiny, or because of that sense of fate I felt that first September afternoon sitting on that bench under her ancient oak tree; it's because of Harry and his teasing. I guess I owe him, big time.

• • • • •

"Will you be present at the birth?" Kate asked me when the movie was over. I pushed eject and retrieved my beer bottle from the floor. She carried her teacup and the empty box of biscuit cookies into the kitchen.

"Yes," I said, "of course."

"My generation started doing it that way, with the father present at the birth," she said, "My mother's generation made the men wait outside."

"Men can't stand the sight of blood," Lila said. I caught her scorn.

"Oh, that's not it." Kate laughed at me. "Women are vain about so many other things. I don't think they really want their men seeing them in the middle of labor. I don't know why it's changed. We women keep nothing to ourselves anymore."

"Come on," I said. "I'll drive you home." Neither of these two women made any effort to continue the conversation Lila had tried to start after dinner. It was as though only I had heard Lila's words. Lila took her keys off the hook near the back door.

"I'll drive her," Lila said. "You go to bed."

I forgot Harry's warning about the word 'no' and Lila. I said firmly, "You stay home and rest." I kissed her.

"Lila," Kate said as she planted a kiss on her daughter's cheek, "Everything happens for a reason. You're both ready now. And you'll love this baby more for having lost one. Believe me."

In the car, Kate was silent. At her apartment I parked the car and opened the door for her.

"Come in for a minute," she said.

I opened her door and flipped on the first light.

"Thank you."

"You're welcome."

"I have something to tell you." Kate stood under the glow of the bulb on her front step.

I waited.

"I've always known."

"Known?"

"Lila had a baby in high school."

I opened my mouth to speak. Kate held up her hand.

"Just listen. She doesn't know I know. I don't want her to ever know that I knew. So don't ever let her try to tell me again, please."

"Kate…"

"Bobby, mother's keep track of their teen age daughters. At least I did. Lila missed her period for an entire year. There were no tampons or pads in the trash for a year. No cramps. No missed gym days. I knew. And she switched to baggy clothes to hide it."

"So you knew? You didn't let her know you knew?"

I listened to Kate tell me how she didn't want to create unpleasantness between herself and her daughter. "She's all I had at the time." And, she said if Lila wanted an abortion Kate would not have been able to help her. "I'm a devout Catholic, as you know. I wanted no part of her sin if she did." Kate dropped her purse inside the apartment door and crossed her arms. "I worried. I kept an eye on her. She's always been a strong girl. I followed her around some days to see if I could name the boy. I couldn't, until the day of the birth."

I stood mute before this. Then I heard her next revelation.

" I know what you did too. I saw you drop it in the dumpster. I was sitting in my car in the parking lot of that motel. All day, I waited."

The day came back to me again, as it had while we watched *Charade* earlier. "Mama, how did you know where we were?"

"I followed her. I didn't know you were the father until that morning when you showed up at the high school, right there across the street. I followed the cab from the corner where she met you. You have no idea how grateful I am to you…to this day…you took care of her… When she brought you home, God, it was almost two years later, your first real date, I almost cried I was so glad. I prayed you'd marry her. You took such good care of her that day. I knew you were a good soul. I saw the article about the homeless man and how you saved him. I knew my Lila was safe with you." She wiped a tear from the corner of her eye while I stood mute. "I sat outside The Lantern. And I saw you throw it in the dumpster."

"Kate, I brought the baby to the Chapter Home. It was what Lila wanted."

"So that's what you told her?" She seemed relieved.

"Because that's what I did. What are you saying?"

"To you it was just like having an abortion, wasn't it?" Kate's eyes widened. Her teeth glowed in the slanted light from above. "Only later."

"She didn't have an abortion."

"That's what I'm thanking you for. She didn't have to live with a mark on her soul remembering her unborn child."

"Kate, you've got it wrong."

"That's what I always appreciated about you Bob." She continued with utter confidence in her deep voice. "You believed in her, helped her be what she wanted to be. You know her better than I could ever hope a son-in-law could know my daughter. She had the baby. She did the right thing. And now that you tell me she doesn't know the rest I love you even more. You saved my daughter's soul. By sacrificing your own. It was your sin, not hers. I'll always be grateful to you for that."

"Kate, you've got it wrong." I said, trying to dispel the unthinkable. She wouldn't listen. All these years we thought our secret was safe. All these years Kate had deceived us right back. And with a blink, as the outdoor light went out, I remembered the headlights hitting me in the eyes in the parking lot of The Lantern, when I turned from the dumpster; my fear of discovery made me toss those bloody sheets in there. The final evidence of that secret birth. And she thought I killed our baby?

"Bob, this is our secret now. Lord knows, I've kept it from the two of you all these years. Promise me you'll keep it from Lila now." With that, Kate leaned over and landed a kiss on my cheek. She smiled. She turned and disappeared into the house and shut the door firmly.

I heard the lock slide into place. I lifted my hand, but I didn't knock. I left. I didn't drive straight home to Lila. I turned and rode past the high school. Pizza Kitchen was still there. Even the Shamrock was still in business. The Lantern Motel was gone, replaced by a new Courtyard by Marriott. Chapter Home was gone. Or, maybe I just couldn't find it. I remembered I'd been in a cab with the baby. Yes, I could still feel the weight of her in my arms. For the first time the thought that the cab driver had to know what I was doing hit me. With that came comfort, someone else had seen me do it, carry the baby safely there. Not that I had any doubts. Still, I was throbbing with humiliation that my mother-in-law thought she held this terrible knowledge. The thought that she could decide, suddenly, for no reason at all, to share what she thought was the truth with Lila made me ill. My thoughts turned to Lila and her admission after dinner.

What was Lila thinking to suddenly try to tell all? My route took me down past the Shamrock again and while I waited for the traffic light, I heard a rap on the window. "Can you spare a few bucks?" a voice muttered, muffled by the window. I refused to roll it down. It belonged to a wrinkled brown face under a wool cap, whiskered and coated with gray dirt, or was it just that the whiskers were gray. The light refused to change color. I stared straight ahead, but he rapped again. "Buy me a drink?" I relented. I pulled a five from my wallet and cracked the window. His stench reached me, body odor, urine and the stringent sharpness of gin on his breath. He took the bill and bowed slightly. "God Bless," he said and retreated toward the curb. It wasn't Nelson, old No Oxygen, too young to be him, yet he brought the old guy back, his body prone on the concrete sidewalk, his head snapping from the defibrillators that night I was too scared to go see Lila. I rolled my window all the way down. "Ever see old Nelson anymore?" I asked. "He still around?"

The homeless man turned. "Old No? Moved south about ten years ago." He turned again, this time away from me and disappeared inside the bar. The light was turning red again as I looked forward.

Three cars had passed while I let the old panhandler take my money.

I imagined a scene where Kate told Lila what she just told me. How could I ever prove to my wife that she was right in trusting me? That I'd done exactly what she'd wanted and that bundle Kate saw me toss in the dumpster was only the dirty bedding, the smallest gesture of concealment from either of us. I didn't think Lila would believe Kate over me but just the idea of doubt entering the trust between us disturbed me.

I remembered she'd been gone when I returned to the Lantern. What did she do with all of that day? Had she really left it in the past? We hadn't let ourselves dwell on her, on our baby. We didn't speak of her; except for that day every year we might have wished her a happy birthday. Lila's request. Lila's desire to let our trouble remain in the past. I knew now that Lila's earlier attempt to tell Kate was a signal. That it was not only in the past, it was with her every day, and she just pretended otherwise. If what Kate believed were true, it would simply be something from our past. But Kate was wrong. Was it my pride or was it a longing harbored for ten years in my own heart that drove me to do what I did next?

Lila was asleep when I got home. I lay down in bed beside her. She curled toward me.

"Lila," I whispered.

"Hmmm?"

"I want to find her," my voice came out low and soft.

"Our baby?" she asked. Her head came up off the pillow. "Really?"

"You okay with that?" I asked. I kissed her hair and waited with thudding heart for her answer.

Muffled Voices

I heard muffled voices in the walls. Not indiscernible, they were clear enough if I paid close attention. It was the woman who lives in the next apartment. Her daughter's voice followed hers, or led hers. I don't know which. Their voices had interrupted my solitude before. I tried to continue reading undisturbed, but with my hand absently stroking the stubble on my chin that I did not shave this morning, I was compelled to fine-tune my ear to their words in spite of myself.

In my mind I saw her as the child in the morning going to school. She is ten or eleven with dark brown hair, thick as rope and straight. It shines in the sunlight when she walks to the car. Her body is thick, solid, and she walks with purposeful steps. She tucks her chin in toward her chest, eyes straight ahead, so she appears to be peering up and out of herself. Her mouth is turned downward on each side, firmly closed over her teeth.

At the car door, she hesitates. I see her working her facial muscles. Her mother is standing next to the driver's side door, hand on the handle, waiting, not patiently. The daughter turns and starts back toward the steps that would lead her back to the safety of their apartment if mother did not sharply call, "Come on, get in the car. We'll be late."

The daughter, grimacing, turns and sighs. With a slight jerk she is back at the car. Her backpack lands on the seat followed by her stout body. The door slams shut. The mother then turns and slips into the driver's seat and they pull away from the curb. As they pass my window I see the daughter, lips moving, eyes darkly frowning. There is a wet look about them. They have not noticed me watching.

In the early evening, the muffled voices started and stopped, and came to me as I read my book and drank my tea. I diverted my eyes from the page and, instead, listened to the scene on the other side of the wall.

"There was an argument during gym class."

"What about?"

"Two team captains were choosing up sides."

"Why the fight?"

"Both girls wanted Amy. Neither wanted me. So they fought."

"Teacher solve it?"

"Yes, she chose who got Amy and who got me."

"Did you play?"

"I didn't want to play with the girls who called me fat yesterday."

"Did you explain it to the teacher?"

"No."

"Why not?"

"She was busy refereeing the game."

"Where was Sarah?"

"On the other team. She was the second girl picked. She couldn't pick me to be with her. She wasn't the team captain today."

"You sat out the whole class?"

"Yes."

"Annie, what will that do to your grade?"

"I don't know. I don't really care."

"Well, I care. School is important. Good grades are too."

"But I hate it there. The girls all laugh and talk about me."

"What do they say?"

"I don't know. I can't hear them. But they're always standing together and talking and laughing."

"Maybe they're just having a good time."

I swallowed a mouthful of tea and closed my abandoned book. With their noise they filled the barren landscape of my apartment with a semblance of life, which, however troubled, improved on the naked silence in which I lived most days. I was aware that they were not aware of me. It was safe. Not being noticed, they could ask nothing of me. I felt secure in my anonymity.

That struggle was always there. Medication eased the intensity of my despair, but it gave me no courage to end my loneliness. It only felt like a burden, meeting people, speaking to them, listening to things people said to me and mustering a response. The panic and pain always returned, and drinking myself to unconsciousness, the therapists cautioned, would put me back in the hospital. Best that books filled my mind and heart and only tea and my rigidly adhered to menu of healthy foods fill my stomach.

The daughter's voice again, louder this time. "I spend my day with enemies. They're all mean. Nobody even looks at me, except the teacher. When they do, they just see my ugly face and my fat, disgusting body and they don't say anything."

Mother's voice, calm, invited calm. "You are not ugly. And you are not disgusting. They don't see what you think they see."

Daughter's voice, rising with pain. "You just say that because you're my mother. You didn't say I was not fat. Just now. You just said I'm not ugly and disgusting. But you always look at me when I'm eating. You make that cluck sound in your throat."

The mother again. "Please. Keep your voice down. Our neighbors will hear you."

I felt my heart skip. I picked up my book again but did not read.

Someone walked across the room. The daughter said, "Get away from me. You are so ugly. Look at the face you're making."

I was covert, listening to the voices but not seeing the language of their bodies or their faces, only recalling them from the morning scene by the car. That scene had repeated more than once since they'd moved here. I sensed heat rising in the room beyond my walls. I could feel it in my chest. I imagined faces flush with red. I saw that they were bound in a repeating pattern of conflict. All that talk, and, it seemed, neither mother nor daughter really listened.

The voices on the other side of the wall were mingled with other sounds now, tears and pleading, some loud, some whispered urgently, insisting that the shouting stop. I wished she'd stop telling her daughter to lower her voice. Each time, she'd whisper for a second or two, which interfered with my ability to make out what she was saying, then she'd raise her voice enough to spur her mother on to more intense levels of pleading.

I dropped my book again and reflected on my recollection of intermittent scenes I observed through my window. The mother, who looked to be close to my age, maybe mid-thirties, liked things to look good. She arranged what little my proximity allowed me to see, in neat orderly rows. Flowers in her window boxes matched in alternating patterns, red, white, red, white, her own body clothed with a carefully planned, uncluttered flair, her hair curly, but dutifully subdued by meticulous grooming. No flaws, no crack in her veneer of perfection. What drew me to watch them was her eyes. They darted. And like mine, they were unlit and dull. They felt familiar.

There too, was her daughter. Not ugly, as the child's outcry insisted, but gently ordinary as one who hasn't yet, at this young age, recognized her own beauty. The daughter was the subject of her mother's efforts, however. One couldn't help noticing the polished shoes, the well-fitting knee socks that never landed around the ankles, the care taken with that long curtain of hair that glinted in the morning sun. Under the hair, that face, made imperfect by the struggle that turned the corners of the mouth downward, was the only thing not managed by the mother's hand.

Back through the wall, the mother's voice became decreasingly solicitous of her daughter. Patience gave way to annoyance then irritability.

"I don't think you are fat."

"Then why don't you let me eat ice cream? I love ice cream!"

"Ice cream has a lot of fat and sugar in it. It's not a healthy snack."

"So what. I don't want to eat a lot of it, just a little bit once in a while."

"All right. I'll buy you some ice cream."

I silently celebrated the child's victory.

"I like chocolate chip mint the best."

" You can get a cone after school."

"Oh, Mommy, thank-you."

Silence.

My cup was empty. I walked softly to my kitchen and re-lit the flame under the kettle. Was this whole conversation simply a ruse to get the mother to relent on the issue of ice cream? The talking was done, the heat gone, the television the only sound now coming through the wall. It was over, but the early parts of their exchange lingered, stubbornly nagging me. I took up my book and replenished tea cup and returned to my seat, expecting to get immersed in someone else's world, eavesdropping now on the lives of the characters that existed only on printed page after printed page.

Their television comforted the stark silence of my apartment. My book filled the room with characters. When my eyes drooped, I closed it, left my half empty cup of cold tea and retired to my bedroom, too tired and ready for sleep to anticipate the emptiness I felt in my soft warm bed. I detoured into the bathroom and dutifully brushed my teeth, inspected my now shadowy face that would be clean and smooth after a morning shave. I noticed early glints of gray and some lines around my eyes.

I slept well and rose to a new day, if not with eager anticipation, then, at least with no dread in my heart for what might face me. Susan's picture stared at me from the bedroom dresser. It still sent a pang of hurt through my chest. I shaved, forcing a smile to my lips and willing it to gain enough energy to reach my eyes. The effort failed. I saw her face but could not muster the feeling she exuded so perfectly, that joy, still so tangible in a simple two dimensional frame, Susan at sixteen. It was taken nineteen years ago, a week before the doctors named her illness and a year before she died. My sallow face, which had once bravely smiled and given her hope of recovery, now empty of all that love which failed so miserably to change the course of her short life, now stared blankly back at me. I took a bottle from the chest, filled the bathroom glass with water and sensing my own dutifulness, swallowed my daily prescription.

Voices again through the wall. I heard the mother screaming. The daughter was crying and shouting.

"No, I can't do it, I can't go back there."

"It's Friday, the last day of the week. Just go today and you will have a two day break."

"No. I hate it there. I won't. You can't make me."

"You have to go to school."

"No I don't. I won't. I won't. I won't." It began to sound like a chant.

"Get dressed. NOW. Do it!"

I was naked but for a towel around my waist. I wasn't trying to listen but their voices were urgent, loud. Accompanying the voices, drawers and doors scraped open then slammed shut.

"You'll make us both late. We can't keep being late. We look like lazy people. Too stupid to get to work on time. I could get fired for constantly being late, you know that? You want that? GET DRESSED!"

"NO! I CAN'T!" Pause. "Get away from me. Don't touch me. Oh, I hate you. You're horrible. I'll dress myself if you'll just get away, get out and leave me alone."

"I'm standing here until you are completely dressed. Now move. Do it."

"Turn your back. I can't stand your face."

Silence from the mother.

"Are you finished? I'm turning around."

"No, don't turn around."

"Well, hurry up. I don't want to stand here all day."

"There, I'm finished."

"Good. Now come eat some breakfast."

Silence. Only crying, no words. I listened for words of comfort and heard only silence.

I dressed. My breakfast was a glass of orange juice and a breakfast bar at my front window watching them leave. The mother looked pretty, dressed in a dark blue suit with low shoes, white blouse and a scarf. She walked next to her daughter, in school uniform, polished shoes and neat cardigan sweater.

Side by silent side, they reached the car and the mother held the rear passenger side door for her daughter. She stood expecting that the daughter would simply toss the backpack in and sit down. Her presence in this position and not at the driver's door, sent a clear signal. Her daughter meekly obeyed. Mother shut the door and walked primly around to the driver's side door and opened it.

Some sudden motion in the back seat drew my eyes off the mother. The daughter was tapping her flat palms on the window, tapping, then banging. And I heard her voice.

"Save me." She pleaded. Her eyes were desperate. Mother started the engine and then the daughter rolled down the window. Mother's head turned slightly, then the window jerked up, then down again, then up.

"No," yelled the daughter. "No! Open it. I'm getting out." She turned and stretched her hands out the window and then her shoulders and her head. The mother stopped trying to close the window. "Save me. SAVE ME!" the daughter screamed. She was looking at me in the window. Her eyes pleading, her voice loud, shrill, piercing the morning stillness.

I froze. Caught at the window. Save her from what?

The mother opened her door and got out. She opened the rear door and sat down in the back seat with her daughter. I saw hands and arms reaching around to envelope the daughter. It was a firm motion, but gentle. It pinned the girls' hands and arms and I watched her withdraw back in to the car. With her mother's grip engulfing her, the daughter tried thrashing but quickly gave up.

Through my window, I could hear nothing now. The screaming had stopped. The mother was holding her daughter, gently stroking her hair, trying to soothe her. It took twenty minutes at least. Finally, the mother returned to the driver's seat and the car pulled away. The girl sat still and silent, hands in her lap, head facing forward, eyes staring. I stood, not certain if the girl had seen me when she cried out or if she was just pleading with anyone, real or imagined. Calm and serenity again reigned on the street. I moved away from my window.

I cleaned the teacup from last night. I cleaned the glass I had used this morning. I made the bed. I read the newspaper. By noon, the air was warm and the sun was bright through my window. It was enough to inspire me to a walk. I clipped a fistful of roses from a bush that hung over the fence near the dumpster. The thorns prickled my hand and I carried them gingerly the short blocks to the old stone church and through the wrought iron fence surrounding the graveyard. I found it peaceful there.

In among the new and ancient, I found Susan's stone and gently placed the flowers. I stood back and read the words. Susan Stokes. 1956-1973. The peaceful feeling vanished and tears came. I didn't stay long. That's what Jane, my caseworker, advised, a quick visit then find something each day to be thankful for. I'll eat lunch out, I thought.

I strode along, watching the traffic lights controlling the cars and the pedestrians. At the signal, I crossed the street and sat on the steps of the library. My book was at home. My only recourse was to watch the characters that passed by, mothers with babes in strollers, joggers taking advantage of the lunchtime sun, businessmen striding along with purpose. I felt detached, but I felt no regret, only safe in my invisible solitude.

My stomach growled. I stood and wandered, summoning my resolve to find a restaurant with a healthy menu, where I could find a seat near a window. I walked purposefully down the street, my face masking my wariness, willing myself to walk in, read a menu and order, but my nerve failed me. I approached a hot dog vendor and took one with mustard and a can of soda. Not healthy, but filling. This was easy and it tasted good. I found an empty bench in the park, and sat to eat. I sat there a long time.

A team was playing in the field. Lacrosse. Blue and white uniforms and helmets with stripes of yellow. Two players collided. One fell to the ground and didn't move. A familiar combination of colors and action. He wasn't getting up. The food in my stomach churned and it started-- the slow increase in my heart rate. I recognized the sensation and felt it intensify. Oh no, I'd better get home before something happens. My chest felt tight. My breath came rapidly, keeping up with my heart which was pounding against my ribcage. I wiped my sweaty palms on my trousers. The scar on my back, just over my right hip, began to throb. Before I could leave I had to bend low to allow blood to flow back to my head to eliminate the dizziness. I could not faint here, alone, in the park among all these strangers. I had to get home. The boy was still on the ground. The adult, must be the coach, was kneeling over him.

I was there. I was there once. It was football though. A big kid from St. Michael's High School hit me from behind. I remembered the ambulance, the sirens, my mother crying, and the cold of the recovery room where the nurse kept taking my blood pressure. And the news.

"They took your kidney. It ruptured. They took your spleen too. No more football for you."

That was two years before Susan died. Later my mother said that's when I started to withdraw. "The big change happened when you couldn't play sports anymore. You started hanging around with those other boys. They were no good for you. Then you met Susan and I thought that would change your life for the better. You two were so sweet together. I know you loved her. I know," she said, "I know why you can't let anything before her or after her feel significant." She says the same thing each time she visits me, time not lessening her remorse for her son's abdication in the aftermath of lost hope.

The afternoon sun was beginning to slant, casting longer shadows. My legs carried me toward the opening in the fence which led to the street. I tried to stay calm. Through my panic, I was surprised to recognize the young daughter, my neighbor, Annie, sitting on the last bench just at the edge of the park. She was dressed in her school uniform. She had carelessly tossed her backpack on the grass next to her. She held a cone with two round green balls of ice cream speckled with chocolate. Her tongue flecked out and daintily licked the cold refreshment. Was her mother nearby? I scanned the park.

"No wonder you're so fat."

The girl stopped licking and used a crumbled napkin to wipe her lips.

"One of those a day will keep you nice and round and ugly."

A short blond girl, hair tied tightly back in a French braid which reached the middle of her back stood between me and my neighbor. Her backpack rode high on her shoulders and she had both hands on her hips with the left jutting out toward the side, her foot tapping impatiently on the paved path. She was staring at my neighbor who was staring back. I felt the hot dog and soda churn in my gut.

In two minutes time three other girls joined the blond with the braid.

"Now we know why you are so fat. Look at that, is it a double?"

A high cackle emanated from one of the girls, the others tittered.

"Give me some."

"NO, leave me alone." She spoke firmly and pulled the cone closer to her body. The corners of her eyes and mouth turned instantly downward. Her cheeks flushed.

"Too piggish to share?"

A group of five girls, all in the same uniform, approached from the opposite direction. They were slowing down near the bench where she sat. Quickly, all the uniformed backs and knee-socked legs made a wall around the front of the bench. I could no longer see her.

"Piggy, piggy." A chant began. It reached a fevered pitch and the wall seemed to close in around her.

"Leave me alone."

There were laughs, wicked ones, now. In one instant the laughs changed to single syllables.

"Fight! Fight! Fight! Fight!"

My feet moved of their own volition. I found myself grabbing the backpack of the blond with the braid and pulling her backward.

"Hey…"

She turned and scowled at me. I set my eyes steadily on Annie's face. She returned my stare.

"Annie, let's go. Let her through, girls."

Silence. No more chanting. The wall separated and made a door for her to walk through. And she did, right toward me. I saw the ice cream colored streak down the front of her blouse. She brushed angrily at it with the napkin.

"Go to Daddy!" Someone muttered as she passed.

"He's not my father."

She picked up her backpack and stalked off, not turning her head, not acknowledging me. I glanced back at the girls, all of them whispering to each other, with former smirks dissolving into stone faces of fear, their eyes on my face. I could think of no words. I scowled and turned to follow her home. I was twenty paces behind her. She did not slow down. I sped up but that thirty second encounter was enough interaction for me for one day. I changed my pace and hung back until I watched her climb the five steps to our foyer and disappear behind the door. Only then did I climb the stone porch and use my key to enter the building. I slipped my key in my apartment door and I heard a faint cough.

I turned. She stood in her doorway, the corners of her eyes and the corners of her mouth still down-turned. She looked into my eyes. Soundlessly, she mouthed "Thank-you." Then abruptly shut her door.

The mailman had come. I found my federal disability check among some junk mail and placed it deliberately in the middle of my table so that I would remember to go to the bank. I took up my book. Eventually, in my cocoon of four walls, I heard voices again. Or, more accurately, I heard one voice.

The girl was speaking in a conversational tone. There were pauses in the conversation as though someone would answer her. Of course, maybe she was on the telephone. But, I didn't think so. There is an inflection in the voice when it is expecting to be sent over a wire. This was missing. So, who was she talking to? A favorite stuffed animal? Herself?

It was pleasant, as though acting in a play, taking on a character other than her own, so foreign to the usual agitation, pleading and misery I had become accustomed to. I tried to imagine her face. I imagined it cracking from the unnatural position of upturned mouth corners, her eyes hurting from the squinting that results from all the skin and muscles pushing upward. I imagined warmth transmitting itself, cell by cell, through her skin, bone, muscle, and nerve, toward her brain, where, with a little catalyst, it would spread well-being to all parts of her, until it lifted her off the ground with weightlessness. Perhaps, someday, it would create a laugh. Then, the laugh would exorcise the pain and transform her.

I faded back into my book. Time passed. I ate and slept, exhausted from my venture.

Heat again was rising. This time in my apartment. I felt it in my head. My ears felt strange, stuffy. Sound was absent. The neighbors were asleep. It was three am. No traffic sounds came from the street. I found some fever medication and took two pills with a glass of water. In a few short minutes I fell back asleep.

At seven I awoke, my ears still strangely annoying. I took an old glass thermometer and stuck it under my tongue. 101 degrees. I'd have to go to the doctor and the bank today, I thought. What a bother. I felt awful. I shouldn't have gone to the park. Being near those girls, I probably caught a germ.

The Chinese doctor didn't ask me to say much and he said little. He only read the form the desk nurse had handed me. Surgical history. I hadn't finished the form when they called me in. I didn't tell him I wasn't finished and he didn't ask. I should have told him about my kidney and spleen but I didn't think something that long ago was still important.

"An ear infection. Take these drops and the antibiotic. That should take care of it."

I now had to go the drug store. Bank first, before it closed. It was Saturday. Drug store second. I was feeling awful. I was grateful not to have to get on a bus or in a car. My eyes felt strange. I was dizzy. Motion made it worse.

"Ear infections can affect your balance." The doctor had told me to be careful.

My hands were trembling when I reached the comfort of my apartment after the morning ordeal. First the doctor, then the bank, all those eyes staring at me at the drug store. I closed the door on the world and ran the tap to make the water cold. I took two of the tablets and lay my head sideways on the kitchen table. Two drops in each ear with a wad of cotton. My fever made me shiver. I was exhausted. I passed my chair and my book and fell into my bed fully clothed. The blanket up to my chin, I slept.

The room was still dimly lit by sunlight. I was no longer cold so I kicked the blanket down toward the foot of the bed. I stripped my socks off and threw them on the floor. My shirt was soaked with sweat. The sheet was too. I took off all my clothes and stood to make my way to the shower. I could not stay upright. The room spun. I shut my eyes. It stopped spinning. I crawled toward the bathroom. The tiles were hard and cold under the bones in my knees. I couldn't turn the tap. My hands were too weak. The cotton in my ear slipped out. I could hear a little better, but a rattling feeling, like something else was in there was sending my finger probing toward my ear canal.

I gave up on the shower. I crawled back to the bedroom and pulled open a drawer of tee-shirts. It made a loud thud as it landed on the floor. I put on a white tee-shirt. The underwear drawer was higher. I knelt and yanked it. It too toppled out of its place. It landed on the tee-shirt drawer. I crawled back to my bed and lay on top of the blanket. Just before I passed out I shoved the window open so cool air would flow over my hot body.

The television. The sound of television. So loud. Turn it off. I struggled to my feet. This was a bad fever. And my ears. The sound was hollow, and far away. I staggered toward the television. It didn't seem to be on. But I heard it. There was no picture. I reached the set and lost my balance, falling onto the set and watching it, in slow motion, crash to the floor. It was still emitting sound. I pulled the electric cord. Voices still came to me. I could not turn them off.

"Shut that off!" I only whispered it. I could not make my voice work. And the dim light in the room slowly faded to black as I fell again to unconsciousness.

She heard the thud. It surprised her. She sat up straighter in her chair where pen in hand, she took notes from a book for a school assignment. She moved closer to the wall. Another thud. She put her ear against the wall. It was almost indiscernible now, the noise. She turned down the volume on her television set. She only had it on for company while Mom was out. Mom would never let her have it on during homework. She returned to the wall and listened again. Mom would tell her to mind her own business too. For a few moments there was only silence, then the loud crash. Like a bang. Her ear picked up the smallest voice, a whisper.

She ran to her television and shut it off. She heard nothing else. She walked out to the hall and knocked on his door, ignoring the echoes of her mother's imagined admonishment. No answer. Knock again. Still nothing. She wondered if she could see inside the window. Not from the front, she couldn't reach over the railing. She opened the window in her bedroom and threw her leg over the sill to the fire escape. From there she saw his open window but she couldn't look inside.

A sense of urgency crept over her. She could not later say why her instincts compelled her to dial 911 and tell the police she heard strange noises from the apartment next door. She just knew, she said, that he was alone. She figured she'd risk being wrong if it was nothing, but she was afraid someone was robbing him.

My eyes were shut against what I knew to be bright light beyond them. Yet I could not see the light, I only knew it was there. It was cold. My arms were too heavy to lift to grope for covers. My eyelids felt just as heavy. Voices came to me.

"Jack?"

I opened my mouth. I closed it again. Someone reached for my hand.

"Squeeze my hand if you can hear me."

I squeezed with all my strength.

"He can hear."

"Jack. You are a very lucky man. Did you know that?"

I squeezed the hand again.

"You made enough noise in your apartment that your neighbor heard you. She called 911 and saved your life."

I squeezed the hand again. I tried to push my breath past my vocal chords. It didn't work. I flicked my eyelid open, the right one, against the bright light, and quickly closed it again. I saw a face. It all faded away again.

It felt like moments later when I opened both eyes. A woman, a nurse, stood calling my name.

"Try to stay awake. Jack. Next time you're sick, tell the doctor you have no spleen. You should've been on an IV. Would've saved us all this trouble." The voice softened. "Can you hear me? Listen…Try to stay awake for a minute."

I did. Then I didn't. Darkness again.

A familiar voice broke through the mist in my head.

"Jack?"

"Susan?" That was the sound of my own voice.

"It's me. Annie. Can you hear me?"

"Ummmm."

"Mom brought me down to see you."

I opened them again. She stood there, her long rope of hair pulled back from her face in a neat hair band. She was wearing jeans and a sweatshirt. Her eyes were downturned. Not from sadness, from worry. I could see the difference. That little girl face. Her mouth was set but there was a bit of light gleaming in her eyes that reminded me of Susan. I made a feeble attempt to smile. It was too hard. But then I saw her gleam grow and I saw the mouth and eyes change shape. An upward turn of the corners of both began. Through the mist of my clouded shroud of barely attained wakefulness I felt something important happening and I watched as her face reflected the smile I could not muster.

Mother of the Bride

Darla switched from domestic goddess in a flour dusted apron to mother of Claire. Her roles were one big deck of cards from which she selected for whatever was listed on her calendar for that moment, each with its associated facial expression, or mask, as Jason preferred to call it. He and Claire were introducing a new card, mother of the bride. He watched a dark sense of irritability rise in Darla's tightened jaw, then turn to a bright eyed smile.

She set the oven timer for the latest batch of cookies. Jason waited for it, but she hardly glanced at him. He sensed her struggle as the news swiftly dislodged all her other definitions of self: hostess; member of the acapella group that sang at nursing homes; Irish-American wife of former VP at the company; decorator; aunt; mother; daughter; consumer.

Here was her only daughter, Claire, in her kitchen just before Christmas, interrupting an afternoon of cookie baking. It was as though she couldn't deal with this, something she had not set it in motion herself. And that alone caused her to flinch, to resist. A slip of the mask because she didn't have one for this role.

"I thought he was tying his shoe," Claire said. "That's how he proposed. Down on one knee. But then he said it. We were right there at the mall, in the crowds all around the Santa station where all the little kids and their parents were in line." She touched Jason's shoulder and leaned her head toward him. "I can't think of a better Christmas present. He had this all planned out. Jason you know how much I love Christmas and surprises. What a perfect way to propose...to me... maybe somebody else would prefer the candlelight and the romantic dinner, but it was perfect."

Jason smiled and just held Claire's hand. Claire glowed. She held out her left hand, which glimmered with a solitaire diamond in a gold setting. Simple, beautiful, understated. Darla did not reach out to lift Claire's hand for a closer look. Instead, she held out her own left hand and displayed her sapphire circled with tiny diamonds and repeated a story she'd told often over family dinners, how she'd had hers remade to imitate the Royal's, Charles and Diana's famous ring. She had married the same year, and that was what she wanted, and her Richard hadn't objected but had gone back to the jewelers with a photograph and a few weeks later Darla had the one she wanted.

Jason watched the mask slip revealing Darla's disappointment with Claire's ring. Jason was an engineer, a civilian at the Navy Shipyards in Newport News. He was precise and purposeful in his mental habits and deliberate in his decisions. His future mother-in-law appreciated him because he was so very good for Claire, but she didn't wholly approve of him. He was overweight, a bit dumpy and he didn't measure up to the fiancés of the daughters of the wives of the executives from the company. At least that's how Darla made him feel most days.

"Nice," Darla said. "Very classic." She hugged Claire and lit her face up with another wide smile. Then Darla put her arms around Jason for a quick embrace. "Weren't you both shopping this afternoon? Did you pick it out together?"

Claire's voice was lilting and full of excitement. "We were at the mall. It's all decorated for Christmas. Pine branches everywhere, so many trees, snowflakes and the ice rink…well we thought a bit about skating, but the line was so long, so we watched."

Jason continued the story. "I saw this big draping mistletoe display, lots of it all hanging down from the ceiling, so I lured Claire over."

"For a kiss," Claire said. "And then he did the kneeling thing and gave me this little green box with a gold ribbon. It's in the car. I should have brought it in. Early present, he said. And then, he said it, 'Will you be my wife?' I was so surprised!"

"She started to cry," Jason continued. "I was like, oh no, she doesn't want to."

"But then I just kind of shouted YES!"

"I thought he was tying his shoe," Claire repeated. "Is Dad home?"

Darla opened the door to the basement and shouted for Richard. She then turned and said, as a way of explaining why he was down in the basement when there were three televisions in the family room on the main level, "It's a football day".

Richard appeared, ducking his head as he took the last step into the kitchen. He was a tall six foot four. "Claire, Jason. Hi." Richard's eyes immediately went to Claire's hand.

Jason saw immediately that Darla was pissed that Richard was in on it and she was just finding out now. She couldn't help it, not really. Jason felt a tinge of pity for his future mother-in-law. She reached into the glass-fronted wine cooler under the counter and pulled out a bottle of sparkling cider. "Let's have a toast."

"Mom, we shouldn't drink. We're driving to Richmond. We've got to see Jason's family."

Darla peeled the metallic wrap and set to unwinding the wire from the cork. Richard took it from her as though to help, but at Claire's words just placed the bottle on the counter out of her reach.

Just then, the oven timer buzzed. Darla turned to take out a batch of cookies. The scent filled the room. So did an awkward silence. Darla took a spatula and one by one placed the cookies on the cooling rack. Jason's mouth watered. "Chocolate chips? Toll house?"

"We could call your parents," Darla said. Claire and Jason exchanged a glance. "We could even do a Zoom call. " They exchanged another silent glance.

Claire said, "Mom, would you have liked me to tell you on a Zoom call?"

Jason and Claire had met at Villanova. Claire was a nursing student, Jason in the electrical engineering school. He'd seen all of Claire's struggles. Her leave of absence, her medication fails, the difference in her when she was finally on the right one at the right dosage, living in the dorm, away from home. A deep dark abyss inside her slowly filling with light with the love he gave her. She was exactly what he wanted in a girlfriend, in a wife, in a mother for his future children. She would have been an excellent nurse.

She didn't finish Villanova, but they fell in love and she began to live and actually enjoy life. He knew what she needed. She knew what he needed. Maybe her mother did too, but the way Darla went about it infuriated him.

Claire was not the perfect daughter. Darla would never forgive her daughter for that. The abyss, between the ideal Darla wanted for a daughter that embodied all of the best parts of herself, and the reality of Claire's difficulty, was long and wide and deep. She didn't know how to handle it. She had never seen a therapist although she insisted Claire do so. Jason sensed all this and remained silent. How he knew he couldn't say, but he'd been around his future mother-in-law enough. He read the subtext of her words. Her pity for her child. Her disdain at her weight. Her major fail – dropping out of the school she'd been so proud had accepted her daughter. He knew Darla loved Claire. He didn't think she knew how to love her.

Richard might be said to be a different kind of parent. Jason had already asked Richard, as tradition goes in his Greek culture, for permission to marry Claire. He had shown him the ring, essentially signaling to Richard that the engagement was already going forward as far as he was concerned. He'd done that as a challenge almost, daring him to create any obstacles to his daughter's happiness, unconsciously or deliberately. To Jason's great relief, Richard hadn't consulted with his wife before giving consent. Richard had given his blessings, shook Jason's hand and offered him a drink.

A metallurgical engineer with Exxon Mobil, and an electrical engineer, Richard's and Jason's educations were the one thing they had in common, aside from their love for Claire. And, they both understood Claire's mother although that was only expressed in mutual silence. Jason had learned also, by Richard's role playing, how to best navigate this family, keep the peace, find a way to passively assert his and Claire's desires. It mainly meant smiling politely, staying silent, and getting away as fast as possible.

In the kitchen, Darla asked, "Did you get the ring today?

"Mom, I just told you the story…"

Jason answered the question. "It was my grandmother's ring. It's very old. I had it resized for Claire. It's an heirloom."

And here it comes, thought Jason. The put down disguised as a philosophical question. The pattern was so consistent. It made his stomach lurch.

"I'm only asking because just like a marriage, a ring is something you wear forever, so you'd better like how it looks on your hand." She held out her own left hand. "I had mine resized. My fingers are fatter than they were when I was twenty-one."

"My fingers are already fat," Claire said, with a short abrupt laugh.

"Jason showed me the ring," Richard's head was stooped, his eyes boring deep into his wife's, "when he asked me permission to marry Claire. We talked a long time about family traditions, about continuity, about how linking generations is good for a family."

"Dad, well I'm glad you said yes. And, I'm very glad you like my ring. I love it." Claire gave her dad a hug.

Richard shook Jason's hand. "Welcome to our family Jason."

Darla nodded. She didn't offer a cookie to Claire or Jason, but she didn't bat away Richard's hand when he went for one.

Jason came from a very large extended Greek family. His father was in a wheelchair and Jason was devoted to him. His mother relied on him when it came time for visits, doctor appointments, other occasions. He and Claire were always running down to Richmond from Fairfax. Claire helped his mother with other non-physical tasks associated with his care. Darla respected their effort. Secretly, she felt like her daughter's innate kindness was a bit taken advantage of by Jason's mother, but she realized the same could be said for Jason who sometimes cancelled plans with Claire's family when they summoned him home.

"How's your dad these days?" Darla asked. She looked at Claire. "We should definitely call your grandmother. She'll be thrilled there's an engagement in the family. Maybe get a trip up to New Jersey to pop the news in person."

Richard pulled out his phone. "Let's get a picture of the happy couple."

Jason wrapped an arm around Claire. Claire turned toward him, encircling his waist with her arms, tilting her head slightly toward his shoulder, smiling. Darla snapped a few shots. "These are good," she said. "Put out your hand." And she snapped a photo of Claire's with the ring.

Jason looked. The photo showed them only from the neck up — disembodied heads. "Do another one with our whole selves? Here, use my phone." He pointedly handed his to Richard. "These look like the selfie I took at the mall."

He flashed forward imagining Claire in a wedding dress. Then he realized it was going to be a tough world to navigate, selecting a dress, with Darla overseeing Claire's choices. He sometimes wondered if he himself were the only choice in Claire's world that had not been made by Darla. How he knew all these things, he could not say, maybe it was just that Claire spoke to her mother every day, ran everything past her, waited for her approval on every choice she made. On the surface, it looked like closeness. Jason thought it was a culmination of a lifetime of control. He reminded himself that he hadn't been there and couldn't possibly judge their past, but yet he did.

It was just the way he felt Darla judged him for some fantasy of hers he didn't live up to. He always felt he fell short. He imagined Claire living with that for her entire life. No wonder she'd broken down at Villanova when she was finally away from home. She'd showed him photos of her theatre roles in high school, the community theatre productions she'd done. She brought down the house once according to a news clip of a review. A budding character actor, it had said. Claire, upon his questioning, had said, "I need to have a skill I can rely on. A job. You can always find a job if you're a nurse." In that response, he heard the voice of Darla, but Jason read it as discouragement disguised as good advice. Darla had auditioned at the same community theatre company Claire had. She'd been offered roles Claire might have been selected for, while Claire sang in the chorus. It made Jason sick. Acting was good for Darla, but it wasn't good for her daughter? Darla, he knew, had met Richard when she was 21 and working as a secretary at the company. She had not followed the advice she now gave her daughter about training for a career that would last a lifetime. Jason knew that without Richard's success, Darla would have nothing, hadn't earned a salary since the birth of Claire's elder brother. Nursing was a field of study imposed on Claire. No wonder she had a crisis and dropped out. She was working as a teaching assistant at a Catholic school right now. She loved the kids and had been offered a classroom of her own for next school year.

"We'll host a party in New Jersey too," Darla said, returning to the conversation about engagement celebrations. "At the shore house. All your cousins will want to come."

Jason looked at Claire and said, "That sound like something you want to do?"

"Mom, let's take things slow. We don't have to plan everything right now."

To Jason that showed a new strength.

"Let's see that picture," Jason said. Richard handed him his phone.

Too much back light. They looked like two mounds of gray against rays of sunlight. His own fault, but still, what struck him again was the control, it was in the very air in this house. Darla's will had permeated Richard's after how many years of marriage? No wonder Richard was in the basement. It was his man cave where he went to avoid his wife. Jason couldn't help it. He blamed Darla for Richard' drinking too. Yes, it was irrational. And, he feared the longer he allowed himself to be in her presence, the stronger her assertion of her will would be over him. He strained against being rude, strained to keep the surface level exchange with her light and pleasant. He knew what the flip side of her polite adherence to social protocol yielded. Jason forgave Richard and gave up on the idea of a full body photograph at this house. He'd ask his own mother in Richmond later.

"Claire," he said. "Do you want to drive, or should I?"

"Yes, we should get going."

"We didn't have a toast," Darla said.

"Mom," Claire said.

Richard went to the counter and popped the sparking cider. "Darla, you want some cider? Here." He tipped the bottle and the cider foamed into a flouted stemmed glass, one of four she'd placed on the table. He poured one for himself.

He lifted a glass. Handed her the other. "Here's to the happy couple." He drank. He lifted his eyebrows at Jason and lifted the bottle. Jason shook his head. Claire sighed when he gave her the same silent question. She nodded. He poured. She took a sip. She placed the glass down.

"I'm going to use the bathroom," Jason said. He left the room.

He passed the foyer and turned toward the room where there were three large screen televisions mounted on the walls to face the bar across from a billiards table covered with a felt cloth. The main floor bathroom was just to the right through a door in a wall adorned with baseball memorabilia.

His face felt hot. In the mirror he saw how red in the face he was.

His heart rate was slightly elevated. The bathroom too, was baseball themed. Darla had managed to bid and win two stadium seats from old Yankee stadium when it was torn down and replaced by the new one. He passed those on his way to the toilet. Her tradition. Her values. God knows how much money she'd spent. It was cool, yes, to love a baseball team, to be a fan, to attend games and root for your players. He'd enjoyed his trips to the new stadium with them. The magnitude of her displaced nostalgia and respect for the past roared at him while he relieved himself in her toilet and washed his hands and dried them on pin-striped paper towels. Her rejection of the inherited ring rang hollow and hurtful.

When he returned to the kitchen, he sat on the stool near the counter. "My grandmother was fifteen when she arrived from Greece. She came by herself. She had two things waiting for her, a room in the apartment of a woman from her island and a job at a diner making pastries. She carried two things with her that had value. One was the ring I just gave Claire." He looked at Richard. "You can tell her the rest of the story." He looked at Darla. "I told him the whole history."

Claire looked at her hand. "I feel like I'm carrying your family's history on my finger."

"It's our family history," he said. "Once we're married."

Darla said, "Claire's grandmother lost her diamond. I remember that. I was a kid and my mom looked down at her ring one morning and the setting was empty. I remember she had all of us down on our hands and knees going through the house, the laundry, our bedrooms, the trash cans in the bathrooms. I remember sneezing while she dumped the vacuum cleaner bag on the kitchen table and went through it inch by inch." Darla said all this with a hard edge to her voice and a steely cold in her eyes. "She and my dad had gone bowling the night before so she called the bowling alley to see if they could do anything. They couldn't. It was a small perfect blue-white diamond. My mother cried for hours."

"That's so sad," Claire said. "I'm going to be so careful with this one." She took it off. "I think maybe I'll keep it in the box for now."

"It's safer on your finger," said Jason. "We'll be sure to take it to the jeweler once in a while to make sure the setting is tight." He looked at Darla. "Thanks for telling us that. It would be awful to lose the diamond that way."

"The diamond she lost had been her grandmother's," Darla said.

"A few years ago, I bought my Mom a ring like this one," Darla said, holding out her own hand. The blue glinted in the overhead light. "When she dies I'll get it back. Then I'll give it to Claire."

Jason felt it, the incipient drip, insertion of herself into the intimacy of this moment. This was a sad story. Today wasn't the day for sadness. He stood up. Claire returned.

"In my family," he said. "It would go to a son and the son would give it to his fiancé. Claire has a ring. Surely Karl or Matt will get married some day. That would be such a welcome to whoever it is, to the family, to honor her the way my family's ring does that for Claire."

He shook Richard's hand. He turned and shook Darla's too. She leaned in as though to land a kiss on his cheek but he ducked it. She embraced Claire. While they shrugged into their coats and made their way to the front door, Darla followed. "Here," she said, sticking the cork back into the bottle of sparkling cider. "Take this. It'd be a shame to waste it."

Claire's eyes dropped at the corners as did her mouth. Silently, she took the bottle. She said one last 'good-bye' and slid through the door while Jason held it. Then he shut it firmly behind him. The fresh December air filled his lungs and he heard Claire's sigh as he exhaled. He drove. She sat in silence for a bit. As they approached the commercial road that led to the highway south, she said, "Stop at the 711? Right there?"

"Do you need something?"

"No." She got out as he stopped. She took the bottle of cider, tossed it in the trash receptacle near the door. She didn't go into the store. She just got back in, "We've got everything we need."

At the Pool

It was right to do it there, at the pool, under the oak where she spent so much time pondering this final act, the visual exercise, in her mind, of watching the skin open and the red line appear, just there, between the blue highways that carried life up and down from wrist to elbow. And then to overflow, just the way pain overflowed, whenever she watched freer souls take paths that led away, not towards her heart, the blood in her arteries.

Silently and secretly, like her lover when he left her and reminded her, chiding her for the very indulgence he'd allowed between them, that family, her family should be the most important thing in her life, not him. How right, she knew his words should be, but how to make them so? It hurt so much. Love. Love him, she anguished, then stop when he says so. Go back to your husband. He doesn't deserve to lose you. The children don't. Not to me. And then she watched his receding back cast a cold shadow in her direction.

The pool was in its final season, sold to a real estate developer to be torn down, buried and forgotten as eleven new homes, each with an acre of land, took their place on the landscape; she and her last place on earth vanishing almost simultaneously. They both would be vaguely recalled, perhaps, by the later inhabitants of this soon to be artificial habitat, trees placed just so to conjure an image of domestic paradise.

Domestic. That's what she'd done these past few years. Exclusively. Such a wide span between her former self, blue suited, well-heeled, (she was still well heeled thanks to her wickedly lucky investments and those of her husband) she'd managed to out earn the expectations she'd left college with, a useless degree, she heard her father whisper, and the woman who inhabited that same body, same physical self, now. Business had embraced her cold steely wit, her grounded sense of practicality and what was seen as irrepressible creativity. Such a combination, one boss had written, made for executive potential. But she chose this. Children, three of them, in three short years, needed her far more than the executive boardroom ever would. Until it seemed, their preferences were no longer for her company. Camps and school and sports relegated her to chief keeper of the clock and the files, files filled only with socks, underwear, homework, and that last piece of the chess game that always disappeared mysteriously.

It could be done, she'd known, looking around at members of the club on a sunny afternoon earlier in August. A flock of geese signaled the coming end of summer's tranquility as their formation held steady across the sky and nature's imprint took them south. Nobody would see.

She read a book under a shade tree. Yes, well, she had stopped to talk of idle things with other club members, the weather and vacations planned or just past, handing coins to children who pleaded again for a snack or money for a turn at the ancient PAC man game in the clubhouse. The community of women whose children were still the main reason for their presence here had long exhausted her with their intimations of privilege, of an implied sharing of fate, with eyes behind dark glasses, laughing hollowly at golf addicted husbands whose faces she couldn't recall. Their brand of comfort she could not share, a new

hair color, a manicure, a furniture acquisition for once again reno-
vated houses she'd never see, not well enough acquainted to be invited
to their homes. Her books took her away from the shallow end of the
pool and into the rich shade of the aged oaks.

What else mattered? She took in so much as she read. Her heart
melted or leaped or cringed with the joy or pain on the page. So much
more exciting to ride these emotional waves than to sit and paste a
smile and stifle a yawn closer to the pool's edge.

She did it quietly, back in the picnic area, behind the hedge, while
her husband took the three children and his wallet to the snack bar
for ice cream. She did it with deliberate timing, knowing the youngest
always bought an Italian ice, taking at least twenty minutes to thaw
enough to eat with the little wooden paddle that served as a spoon.
After consuming the ice cream, she knew, the girls would use the
bathroom, which took twenty minutes due to the irresistible allure of
playing in the lockers, swim for another fifteen minutes, then come in
search of a warm beach towel. Her husband would return to his chair
long before they did. There would be enough time, for him to keep
them from discovering her.

The male members of the club had finished reading their Sunday
Times and had let their heads fall back against the slope of their lounge
chairs, their mouths drooping with stolen naps while their wives chat-
ted poolside. What would these husbands say if they stayed awake?
Her own husband's mouth was slightly open, a soft snore escaping
every few seconds. What would he say if he stayed awake? A good
conversation might make sleep feel so very wasteful on this glorious
sunny day with scant clouds, the scent of coconut oil faintly rising
from browning skin. Paper folded and worldly news consumed and
digested, the distant world was so much more vital, she feared, than his
once intimate companion.

How do I find my way back? With no apparent awareness that
she'd even been gone for these last twelve months, her every waking
thought dwelling on someone else in the place near her heart where

she'd always assumed he'd live, her husband, her partner, the father of the three children who consumed every moment of her days, at least, this past year, every moment she'd not been with the man who in a fit of conscience no longer wanted to be a distraction to her from her family.

She compared his sleeping with the endless hours a few years past of tagging along behind toddling children, so intent on missing nothing, the children were; the swing, the water fountain, the wading pool, four responsible eyes, hers and his, not leaving them for a second, so to not catch sight too late of the curious halfway up the ladder to the high dive. Those days, happy, silly, filled with sudden laughter at the ice cream cone dripping down past the wrist of an enthusiastic but slow eater. Diapers filled with pool water and the plastic membrane of protection burst, and urine and chlorine-soaked gel from the diapers' core scattered on the cement pool platform like birdseed for the pigeons. There had been joy in all that toil. Laughter. There had been no time to talk.

Reach further back in time, she silently beseeched her dozing husband. When we lay on the white sand of a beach, a towel under us with just a bottle of lotion and a book lying near our heads, and eyes behind dark sunglasses lingering over taut skin and lean muscle, touching, fingers brushing lightly with the ache and longing. Had there been words exchanged?

That was far enough. Earlier, she'd known, was best left behind. His silence was familiar. The same silence echoed between her father and mother. She remembered. One day, at breakfast, they'd simply stopped talking. She was a channel after that.

"Ann, ask your father to pass the sugar bowl please."

"Daddy, pass the sugar bowl please."

"Ann, tell your mother I'll be late from work again tonight."

"Mommy, Daddy will be late tonight again."

At age nine, it began. And ended, how horribly it ended. Father's gray eyes, with red lines, so watery but not spilling over, and so she could not allow hers to cry. And still, after she was dead, her dear mother, it was not for him to say a single word.

Not today. There had been no good attempts. "Depressing," her husband commented when she'd convinced him, once, to share a bit in her selection of short stories. He'd spent twenty minutes with "Good Country People" and the girl Hulga who was left without her prosthesis in the barn by a boy she'd felt sameness with, fleeting sameness. Lucky her, she thought, Hulga had only wasted an afternoon losing her soul. Her husband gave her back the book and retreated to his safe place behind the sports page.

Here they were, the girls, the three of them, so beautiful, wet and glossy from head to foot, towels over shoulders, teeth visible between shivering lips, laughing at drips flying off the ends of their hair as they twisted their heads from side to side. "Can we get an ice cream?" said in almost perfect unison.

She nodded. There, proof that he'd once been close to her. These three lively girls. Eyes behind sunglasses, she drank their laughter and turned to watch their father take the same pleasure from the sight of them. His eyes remained shut. His breathing still rhythmic but no sound escaping from his throat now, he remained motionless. She sat in a stubborn pause. So far today his presence had changed nothing in the routine of coming to the pool except that she packed an extra towel for him in the beach bag. She felt his expectation that she'd tend to the children's needs while he, after a hard week at work, relaxed with his newspaper or dozed in the sun.

"Dad will take you for an ice cream."

He sighed and reached for his wallet. He swung his feet over and pulled himself to a stand, tugging primly at the waist of his swim trunks, sucking in his stomach and running his hand self-consciously over his chest, which was covered with gray hair. She said thanks when he departed in bare feet, with a trail of three children behind him, children unaware that their dad was not smiling. He did not offer to bring her an ice cream.

Moving away, forever moving away, their receding backs to her, shadows cast backwards, in her direction, she kept her eyes on their steady progress. Like him, they would run out of need for her. Already, they'd left her to her books under the trees while they indulged in sunlight and blue water, only beckoning her to join them when some urgent task was imagined impossible without her help.

She fingered the final pages of chapter eleven in *To The Lighthouse*. She kept reading until they were gone to the other side of the long hedge that lined the boundary between the picnic area and the pool deck, then, with her eyes still hidden behind dark sunglasses, she surveyed the nearby space and felt satisfaction that nobody took notice of her. She laid the book flat on its pages, spine up, saving her place as though she'd soon get back to it. She moved the cooler bag, which was empty now of soft drinks but still contained the ice packs she placed there to create cold, to the chair just vacated by her husband.

She had a small cosmetic case with her swimming goggles in her handbag. Everything neat. The surface of her life showed not a ripple, although her heartbeat felt oddly strong against her sternum. It had been at a slow resting rate. It quickened and she felt blood in her ears, the pounding like a whispered echo.

The sound of voices had hammered against weathered rock a few short weeks ago, when she and her children skidded down the falls in rafts between the chasm's walls, on the river, on vacation. While he was working, she took the children alone, feeling wonder at the traveling water that wore the repeating layers of granite and limestone into two walls until, it seemed, there was never anything but the abyss, so beautiful, so inspiring of awe in it's stark height. That her children could be happily alive within the confines of that canyon, and still feel the softness of the sun's light filtering down from above, with the color and texture of the leaves and the bark of trees so vividly illuminated, drove her to turmoil. Even the water sparkled with life. She could not reflect the light from that sky. She knew daylight hours shifted and opposing walls of cold stone would block the warm rays.

She pulled out a Swiss army knife with a blade so sharp she forbade her children to touch the thing even when closed. She bent the blade and in two deliberately swift motions, so quick and natural that if someone's peripheral vision caught the motion they might think she was chasing away a mosquito, she slashed her arm from elbow to wrist. She folded the knife and put it back in the case and the case in the bag.

He had sent her back to this man. This absent man. Physical presence mattered little. It might only be his work that filled his thoughts as he existed by her side, it could be a woman. Wherever his heart took him, she only knew that it was not her that resided inside his consciousness. He simply didn't see her. She was so present, so constant, so assumed, always available, and, like oversupplied goods in the marketplace, so diminished in value. He hadn't even noticed she'd been away. Hadn't noticed the silent glow in her eyes before she'd sanctimoniously returned to him, or the dark circles there now.

Still he said he loved her. Insisted, regularly, over the telephone wire from distant cities where business took him. Why did talk come so readily over that long distance? Why did he never touch her when he was home, next to her? She was, she knew, still invisible. So invisible that only by departing could she make him see her. Her chasm, her abyss, would be left here with him, forever filling all the vacated space. There, the only tangible proof that he'd ever been close to her, the three children, would remember, she hoped, how she loved them. How she loved them.

She realized that her blood did not spurt recklessly over her chair or the book at her feet. It flowed thickly and evenly, getting a redder, then bluer tinge as it emptied and began to drip to the ground. She calmly acknowledged there was no pain. She could still move her hand, but it was starting to look white and the fingers were getting numb. She imagined her heart trying to pump with less and less in her veins. She groped for the two pink beach towels she and her husband used after swimming. She rolled them and placed one over each arm and smiled at the tie-dyed effect the red made as it seeped into the threads, obliterating the Cannon label and wondered if the pink would all turn red before she closed her eyes against the sweet weakness that came over her.

She felt the air stir against her skin, and shivered. She could not move to cover herself for warmth and so she closed her eyes and willed her trembling to cease. Her lungs were in spastic panic, still sucking in air, still thinking the heart was waiting for it, the heart waiting too long now. This would bring him home, his presence would be essential now, his blood had mingled and created life, those three beautiful lives, he would have to be present now to sustain them.

He reappeared from behind the hedge, walked across the clearing to take his seat next to her. Briefly she knew if he looked at the red towels he might think their color a bit too flashy. Her eyes were closed but the rustling of the pages of the Times told her he had resumed his reading. Her brain shut down and she faded into unconsciousness and the rest closed down and she plunged unobserved into the dark and went silently still.

But, light again, and cold shivering, a brittle taste and the scent of urine, and blood, metallic. A beeping, a siren in the distance, she was flat on white sheets and someone shouted her name. Then darkness again. She felt wet and warm, then the sun was in her eyes. Red lights flashed and she was lifted up. She dared not move. Where were they? The girls? Where was he? There, at her feet, touching her arch with a soft finger. Rubbing. "Feel that?" She could. She flinched her foot away from what felt like electric current, hard and brutish. It was her hand she couldn't feel. The other was tightly grasping something. She was strapped and rolled into a wagon. Faint shame singed what was left in her. Better had it been complete. A bag on a pole, a tube in her good arm, three small faces through the window. The sobs, shouts of "Mommy". Better it was not complete. Better she was still here. No, no, no, I'm sorry, she whispered. The stranger's voice soothed her. "You stopped your heart. We got it going again. We'll take you where it's safe," he said. She tried to move her head, open her mouth, correct him, but it was dry inside, she could not part her lips. Tears are hot, she thought. Someone enveloped her in a warm blanket. She closed her eyes against the motion, breathed because she still could. "Don't let him in," she said. "My husband. In this car, don't." The stranger leaned close. She said, "He's dead now. He's dead and dark and done." "No," the stranger said. "You're alive, he is with your daughters."

And her heart pumped because blood was flowing through a tube into her arm. There were words but she could not find them. She lay in silence, listening to her breath, feeling her heart's rhythm, and waited. Someone was driving and talking. A radio was playing. Was it a male voice? Was it her own? No, it was only words in her head, repeating, to her, like a mantra, to which she must listen. But she couldn't be sure, of what she thought she heard…something about how there needs to be an ending before there can be a beginning…and there were many kinds of ending and that she had chosen the wrong one, shutting off her heart was no way to heal it. Someone's love had healed it and now life's rhythm would begin anew.

Voice Rest

"You can't live this close to the ocean and not have a boat."

They converted the shore house to a year-round home with central heating, then, counting what was left in their newly combined checking account, they made a down payment to Squan Marina Boat Sales. It was their singular indulgence, a sixteen-foot Wellcraft with an inboard motor, which they moored every spring off the pile-on just behind their small backyard. Most nights, after work, from May through late October, they enjoyed a sunset cruise. Donny stood at the controls, Janet sat toward the stern with a cocktail in hand, a smile pasted below her very large sunglasses, waving to neighbors on patios or decks in backyards as Donny motored slowly through narrow channels toward open water.

Once out on open water, Donny yelled, "Hold tight," and gunned the engine, leaving not only a huge frothy V-shaped wake behind them but if she wasn't prepared, Janet's half-empty glass as well, right out of her hand into the swell.

She preferred vodka, with a splash of Ocean Spray cranberry juice, and kept the bar in their stilted contemporary home well stocked with Smirnoff's. She only drank one per cruise. She only lost a dozen or so glasses per summer. She also lost a few plates, an ice cream bowl, a copy of Jules Verne's *Ten Thousand Leagues Under the Sea*, which she re-read because one of her seventh grade students had finally shown some interest in books after reading it this past spring. She planned to talk to him about it when school resumed in the fall.

Donny drank Jack Daniels when he drank which was certainly not on the boat, not anymore, not since his encounter with the Coast Guard patrol boat two summers ago. The boat went unused the second half of that summer, Donny's boating license revoked, the Wellcraft relegated to dry-dock after Janet's attempt at captain. Donny said her handling of the boat made him too nervous. He never approved of her taste in vodka either. He didn't like her hair color, now a henna enhanced dark brown, her newly straight hair, now that poodle-like perms had gone out of style, or her choice in bikinis, crocheted beige held with just a tiny bow over her round hips and what he called her worst feature, her navel.

Last Sunday evening, in front of the Del Veccio's who lived across the street and joined them for a barbecue in the yard, he had made a suggestion about her cooking.

Last night, he arrived home from Betts and Stanford, the whole-sale distributor he worked for these past eight years, carrying a carton of sample size bottles of moisturizer from Neutrogena and said, "Try this on your skin. You're looking your age lately." She was only thirty-one; she tried it to please him.

This evening, Janet lifted her cocktail in front of her, stepped over the side of the Wellcraft and settled into her usual seat. She lifted her chin toward the red sunset, savored remnants of the afternoon's rays on her skin and sniffed the sea air. Donny lifted anchor, throttled the engine and slowly motored through the labyrinthine channel past white pebble lawns, market umbrellas and redwood patio sets. Her ice cubes rattled against the solid sides of the glass in her hand, a square design, by a company from Denmark, one of three left in the set of twelve she purchased this past spring. She didn't like Donny's suggestion that she use Dixie cups on the boat just because Betts and Stanford could get unlimited Dixie cups for free.

Three more cruises, she plotted, just three more glasses to send to the depths and I can buy that new Mikasa set I saw on sale at Macy's. The mermaids can have the last of these, she thought, gazing at the glassy calm, trying to look beyond the surface, imagining the silent world of sea creatures below. Lovely glasses, those Mikasas, traditional European cut crystal, very old fashioned for a change. She pictured them on the dinner table next to her best china, the table set for eight. She pictured all her lost glasses turning to sea glass and washing up on the shore for children to collect with their shells. Or, maybe there really are mermaids and mermen and they're down there, like the fairy-tale, collecting all things human and storing them in a cave. She sat in the boat wishing for a peek at their serene lives.

"Your party is in a few weeks," she said, watching as he squinted forward, his hands on the wheel. The bridge was up. Janet knew he was thinking if he could pick up a bit of speed, he could get under it and out toward the bay and past the inlet to open water, something that wasn't possible every night, especially during the height of the tourist season. But tonight was a slow Tuesday and no boats had lined up for passage under the narrow bridge. She lifted her glass to her lips for a final gulp and rested it on the back of the boat near the outboard motor. Donny preferred large parties, with live music, kegs of beer and something to celebrate, like the Superbowl, New Years, or his birthday. She preferred to see a few friends at a time, but his birthday was in a few weeks and the plans had been set according to his taste.

"Don't serve that beef dish from last party. Jesus Christ, it was cold by the time it got on our plates. You've got to figure out how to time the cooking so it all hits the table at once." His voice was ragged.

She sipped. "Doc says don't talk."

She lifted her eyes to the underside of the bridge as they passed through. It amazed her that something so large could be raised and lowered so easily when small things in life were often so difficult to budge. She waved to the bridge operator and watched Donny smile up at him.

Donny was on voice rest. It was the third time Dr. Bob had put him on voice rest in the last year. This time he meant it. Dr. Bob had called Janet at her job. She was a school social worker and the call came in mid-morning while she was bribing a middle-school student. Everyday he showed up and stayed at school all day, she would give him a Hershey bar. At the end of every fully attended month, she promised him a present. She sent this boy on his way, candy in hand, and picked up the phone.

"He's got to rest his larynx," Dr. Bob said. "The vocal chords are going to tear and he'll have no voice at all if that happens."

Janet asked him what he suggested she do to keep him from speaking.

Dr. Bob said, "You know him better than I do. Can't you think of something?"

"Donny talks for a living," she said. "He talks to clients, suppliers, truckers, accounts receivable people all day long. How is he going to stop?"

"If he doesn't," Dr. Bob said. "He'll need an artificial larynx in three years like his dad."

He is putting the responsibility for this on me, she thought, hanging up. How do I get Donny to stop talking? He's too old for bribery.

Donny's left hand palmed the wheel and his right jerked the throttle. The boat jumped and Janet's glass flew. With a half smile on her face, she fluttered her fingers to bid it goodbye. It hit the water and sank in the churning white wake, the ice cubes landing just a second behind it. The mermaids are following us, she imagined, and they'll find this one too.

"Mama should know better," he said. He called Janet Mama, even though she wasn't yet a Mama and wasn't sure she'd ever be one. Once, his phone slipped off the deck. He swore Janet had left it out on purpose while he jetted across the inlet, water-skier in tow. Who had been out on the skis, she searched her memory. That was just last month. Donny was still complaining about it, when his voice worked properly.

Donny sold everything to supermarkets that didn't fit the food category. Fuji film, Dixie paper goods, Johnson & Johnson lotions, Cover Girl cosmetics, Pampers for babies and Depends for old people. He talked all day. Evenings he entertained customers and suppliers, at restaurants, sporting events, bars to make them happy, get them to say yes to an order, a contract. Janet was right when she told Dr. Bob he talked for a living. His work strained his voice. His voice also suffered from his need, in his off-hours, to talk over the music he played too loud, and his habit, when he and Janet went out, of getting up with any band at any bar and belting out his personal rendition of his own rock favorites. Just last week at The Stone Pony, where it was rumored Bruce Springsteen might show up, he'd sung Glory Days with his buddy Al whose band had performed at their wedding. Dr. Bob was right. Donny's throat needed a rest.

Now, on a calm sea, the curtain of night beginning to darken the eastern sky, Janet held on as the bow lifted up over the wake of a fishing boat and pounded into the drop that followed. She wished the engine could run without sound. Janet loved the silence out on the sea. Voice rest, she thought. It's so nice when he's not suggesting things to me.

First time he was on doctor's orders she savored his silence for two days. Two peaceful days of soft words, no shouts, no suggestions. Janet had given him warm tea with honey and lemon to sooth his throat. She cooked his favorite homemade clam chowder, remembering his exacting suggestions for the right combination of cream and butter with clams and not too many potatoes. She had Eileen and Gerry over for a quiet dinner, just the four of them, no music playing, and they had sat on the deck overlooking the river drinking Kahlua flavored shakes with vanilla ice cream for dessert. Donny seemed content.

The morning after this sedate gathering, because he couldn't make himself understood that she had only thought she had dusted the living room furniture but in fact, it was still dirty, he had stuck the can of Pledge in her hand and wrote in the thin layer of residue on the coffee table "clean me". She had used her own finger to write, "do it yourself". That had gotten her a black eye. She decided, applying an ice pack to her eye and wearing her sunglasses to work, telling her boss she'd been to the eye doctor and had drops that dilated her pupils, things were better when he could talk, much better, despite how Janet loved quiet, except, the sex after he apologized was better than it ever had been. So good that she cancelled the appointment with her lawyer her therapist suggested. The therapist had said, "Just explore divorce, as an option. You don't have to file."

A school of dolphins passed far out toward the horizon. Janet played with the idea of a party under the sea and imagined her cocktail glasses sitting on tables in front of mermaids and mermen, their long tails glittering in flickers of sunlight filtering down from above, all of them sitting and sipping. She imagined little Nicole's doll, her niece had lost it off the boat earlier this summer, wearing a tail, held in the arms of a young mermaid, enjoying a silent life under the sea. Donny's lost phone would keep any young merboy happy, waterlogged or not. A Frisbee, caught by the wind and sunk in the wake last week, was a platter for their little morsels of seaweed.

A silent party, she thought. That's what I'll do. If Donny can't talk, well, hey, they'd have a party where nobody can talk. And, it'll be his kind of party, not hers. He'll love it. She laughed out loud and glanced at Donny who was intent on carving wide figure eights across the open ocean. All I need are post-it notes and a bunch of pens. She stood up next to Donny. An all-night fishing vessel chugged past followed by seagulls diving to steal from its long trail of chum. She said, "Hey, a party where nobody can talk. We'll put everybody on voice rest. What do you say?"

Donny shook his head. He rasped over the wind, "Won't work.

Five minutes and they'll all revert. Except me."

"Let's try it. It's your party. If you can't talk, then nobody can. Whatever we say goes."

Donny frowned. His voice came out in a whisper. "They need to talk. What are you crazy?"

Janet nodded. "Everyone will write down everything on post-its. You've got so many free samples from work. Remember that book by John Irving? The Ellen Jamesians? They cut out their tongues and had to write everything down. We'll call it an Ellen Jamesian party...Yup. Don't argue with me. You'll strain your voice."

He mouthed, "It'll be dull."

Janet went on, "Or, we'll call it a mermaid party...or an under the sea party. I'll even decorate."

Donny shook his head.

He'll see, Janet told herself. He can make a joke out of it instead of being embarrassed about his malady.

Eileen, her best pal out of all of Donny's gang, and Gerry had just bought a puppy. "I can't leave little Rex alone. Can I bring him in his crate and let him sleep in your kitchen for the night?"

Janet said yes. "Donny loves dogs. And, would you bring a salad?"

Janet handed her guests a pad of post-its and a pen as they arrived. Eileen and Gerry were the first. Eileen laughed. "This will be really funny," she said. Gerry frowned. "Come on," Eileen said, elbowing him in the chest. "Go along for Donny's sake."

Eileen and Gerry let Rex run around the yard for a bit. He was not little Rex. He had already grown to full size. "Let his energy out," Eileen said. "Otherwise he'll be miserable in his crate."

Gerry threw Rex a rubber toy, a floppy dark blue rubber squeaky toy shaped like a bird. "He loves this thing," Gerry said. "Watch."

Rex bounded across the pebbled yard, stones flying, grabbed the toy and galloped back to Gerry to drop it at his feet, his tail wagging, tongue hanging. Janet watched through the window where she was lining up her new Mikasa glasses on a tray to carry to the bar. More guests arrived so Eileen settled Rex in the kitchen. Rex was enormous. Janet found a serving spoon and fork for the salad, and Eileen said, "Gerry's got a small motor skill problem."

Janet set a bowl of water inside Rex's crate and after scratching his ears and shutting the gate, said, "Then we'll teach him sign language." She pulled out a card the size of the palm of her hand. "Give this to him. He'll learn it fast."

The house filled quickly. The party was not as silent as Janet anticipated. Because nobody talked, Donny turned the stereo up so loud Janet needed to stuff cotton in her ears. Janet, who was accustomed to children with learning disabilities at school watched as Gerry became frustrated trying to write on the tiny squares of paper. He could not move his fingers to shape the sign language letters either. By ten o'clock, Gerry was drunk and angry at Eileen. Janet's head was pounding. In the kitchen downing a Tylenol, she saw Rex in his crate. He looked miserable. Soon the floor in the TV and living room was littered with spent post-its and everybody was talking as usual. Donny didn't turn down the music so everyone shouted at each other, including him. Eileen and Gerry left at midnight whispering hoarsely to Janet that poor Rex may have hearing damage. Gerry grumbled that he certainly did and stumbled to their car. Eileen carried Rex's crate and Janet led Rex to the back seat and gave him a quick scratch behind the ears before Eileen drove off, Gerry with his head back, eyes closed and his mouth open.

Dr. Bob was among the guests and shook his finger at his favorite patient when Donny got up with a microphone and sang along with the Huey Lewis's "I'm So Happy to Be Stuck With You" pointing at Janet, grinning wildly, his eyes glazed from too much Jack Daniels. With the mike he was loud enough, but raspier than Rod Stewart on a bad day. By two AM, he could barely let out a sound and was forced to turn down the music so he could thank everyone for coming and say good-bye.

Donny had a lot of suggestions once their guests left. He suggested

Janet get down on her knees and pick up all the post-it notes. He suggested she stop spending money on expensive glasses. He croaked at her, his voice spent. The whisky he drank all night hadn't helped. Donny hit the off button on the stereo and went to bed. His voice was shot.

Next morning, Eileen called and said, in a voice barely above a whisper. "Janet, please don't ever do that again. I don't think Donny liked it at all. And Gerry was embarrassed."

Janet said in a hoarse croak, "I think you're right. It was a total failure." She pressed an ice pack to the bruise where her elbow had hit the edge of the coffee table on her way to the living room floor. She hung up on Eileen and went back to their bedroom to slip under the covers. Donny's apology was non-verbal but thorough. They stayed in bed until noon, Donny's hands and his kisses moving over her body, warming her, erasing the mistakes of the last twelve hours, then sleeping, his arm wrapped around her, his body spooning hers in a cradle of comfort.

Back at work, Janet stopped explaining her dark glasses. The boy she bribed all last year with candy bars came to her office the third week of school and said, "Mrs. Galante, you don't need to buy me candy bars anymore. I'm coming to school because I like it now." When she gave him a present, two days later, a bound set of Mark Twain classics, she couldn't take off her glasses to wipe her tears.

Janet signed up for a CPR class, a request from her supervisor. She learned from the instructor that in an emergency the rescuer's first duty was to keep herself out of harm's way. She wrote in her notebook, first inspect the site of the incident; ensure there is no danger to you in helping the victim. Then, check for pulse and respiration and call 911. Only after professional help is summoned should you begin rescue breathing and CPR.

Donny's voice was so bad it was November before he could make himself heard over a telephone. By December, because there were so many opportunities for apology, the non-verbal kind, Janet missed her period and bought a home pregnancy test. She wasn't sure what kind of suggestions he would make when he heard the news so she put off telling.

The boat sat in a corner of the yard on a trailer, covered in rubberized canvas and tied down against the Nor'easters that blew strong along the shore. White-capped waves roughed up the sides of the river and weakened the stanchions that held back the churning water. Their neighbors, who occupied their stilted homes only in summer, left and the neighborhood took on the winter season's isolation. Janet and Donny broke the eerie desolation of their abandoned neighborhood with parties, very large cocktail parties for New Years, Valentine's Day and St. Patrick's Day. There were fewer things for Donny to criticize because Janet let him plan the party details. The only thing down side was their sex life. It waned when he could talk again.

Donny built fires in their fieldstone fireplace after he got home from work. Each night, he sat next to the flame with a whisky on the rocks waiting for Janet to come home from her late meeting with parents or the child study team, or, on Wednesday nights, her CPR class. When she arrived home, Janet cooked dinner while he listened to music and drank, and they ate from trays in front of the fire.

"You're gaining weight," Donny said one night in a rasping whisper.

Janet sat up straight and pulled her sweater down over the tiny bulge in her abdomen. "No, I'm not," she said quickly.

He took her plate and scraped it into the trashcan. "I think you need to cut back on calories."

"You need to go on voice rest," Janet said. Tears welled up and the muscles of her uterus tighten. "You're voice is cracking again."

"Look at you," he said, standing her in front of the hall mirror, "you're droopy and pale." He went on and on. By the time he suggested that she join a health club, that she join Weight Watchers, he talked himself hoarse and she ran into the bedroom and locked him out. Janet was right. The next morning Dr. Bob put him on voice rest again.

Because of the pregnancy, Janet begged forgiveness for any transgression Donny invented. She no longer cared about the great sex as apology, no matter how good; she was afraid her intense orgasms would bring on premature labor. Janet called Dr. Bob from her office at school. "Can't he have surgery to correct this voice problem?"

Dr. Bob said, "He's too young. I hate to attempt such a risky procedure and leave him mute for the rest of his life."

Janet remembered how she loved the silence of the sea. She thought about her cocktail glasses in the mermaid world. She imagined herself and her baby joining them, bubbles the only sound under the open water of the Atlantic. She remembered Dr. Bob's suggestion that she knew Donny better than anybody and could certainly think of some way to get his problem under control permanently. Surely there was something. She combed through her social work textbooks. She tried whispering to Donny all the time. That only made him talk louder.

Eileen asked her to keep Rex while she and Gerry took vacation in Mexico. Knowing Donny would do anything for Gerry, remembering how he seemed to like Rex, she agreed. Eileen brought Rex over the following Saturday with several pounds of dry dog food, a large dog bed, a water bowl and that toy that looked like a dead duck.

"Rex loves when you throw it. But only do it outdoors. He'll knock over your furniture. And," she added, in a flat emotionless tone, "Rex responds to voice commands. We have never hit him."

Borrowing Eileen's even tone, Janet said, "Of course not."

Janet combed Rex's long golden hair and vacuumed up the fibers before Donny could comment on the dirt. Against Eileen's instructions, she fed him table scraps, chicken and lamb. Rex licked her hand. Janet walked Rex for the first few days until Donny offered to take over. At first, he seemed to enjoy a nightly walk but soon complained in his damaged whisper how Rex yanked his arm, wouldn't walk calmly and chased everything that moved, from a squirrel to a bird to a piece of trash blowing across the yard.

Five days into dog sitting, a blizzard hit and two feet of snow fell. The river grew a layer of ice and in just a few days it was frozen solid and covered with drifting snow. School closed and Janet felt like a hibernating whale. Donny wrote on post-it notes, suggesting daily that Janet call public works to complain and demand they plow their road. "Our road is last priority," she reported after reaching the town manager's office, "they do the more populated areas first. And we are the only year round house here."

She still hid the baby from Donny, under an old gray hooded sweatshirt and sweatpants with an elastic waist. She was terrified of how he might respond, this baby not being his idea, not her idea either, but he might not understand that.

A gull swooped down and landed on the frozen river one gray morning. It stayed there, not flying but hopping across the ice. Janet wondered why it was still around when most of the others sought garbage dumps further inland in the winter. Rex went wild for it, and one day dragged Donny, who used the leash for the morning walk, across the yard to the edge of the river. Donny smacked him with an old rolled up newspaper and Rex cowered and slinked into the house. Donny took him out again the following night and carried the newspaper with him. "I'm doing Gerry and Eileen a favor. They'll come home to a nice tamed Rex." She stirred a pot of homemade soup on the stove and said nothing. She saw the gull lying on the icy river. The thing was dead. Being cooped up inside was not good for the pup and the rolled up newspaper was making the poor dog wild. He was trying to escape Donny, all the way down the driveway and across the yard. The wind, still gusting from the recent storm, howled. The dead gull lay motionless then suddenly moved as the wind whistled under the hulk of the Wellcraft in its trailer. Rex bounded toward the river. Donny lost his footing. The leash was around his wrist so Rex with the retrieval instinct of his breed crossed the slippery snow that had crusted with a layer of ice, leaped down the embankment dragging Donny with him onto the frozen river. Janet watched in horror. A howl of wind blew. All the lights in the house went out. Janet saw an electric wire snake across the backyard and stop against the hulk of the Wellcraft, anchored in its trailer. Sparks flashed. Donny was on the river, then, Donny was gone. A light from a house across the channel flickered on Rex backing away with the dead bird in his mouth. The ice did not break under Rex. Janet ran to the phone. She lifted it. The line was dead. Of course. She ran back to the window. Rex had somehow managed to leap up the embankment. He was free of Donny, the leash dragging along behind him. She ran from the window and flung open the back door. The wire crackled across the yard. Rex leaped over it and ran to her carrying the dead bird. He dropped it at her feet and sat on his haunches, proud of himself, his eyes pleading with her to throw it. She lifted it. She stared at Rex. She peered into the darkness toward the river. She could see and hear nothing but the howling wind and the snaking wire. The wind died for a moment. She heard total, utter silence in the cold night. She felt her baby kick her in the ribs and took in a sharp breath in response, lifting her hand to the spot. Then, from the side of the house, she heard a tinkling sound as an icicle dropped from the gutter and hit the picnic table on the patio. She bent down and picked up the dead bird and the loop at the end of Rex's leash. She stepped back through the door, stood aside for Rex and gently closed the door.

Rex lapped at his water dish then sat, motionless, staring expectantly at her. An odor of decay from the dead bird reached her nostrils. She wrapped the bird in a black trash bag and dumped it in the receptacle under the kitchen sink. The slap of the cabinet door on its frame was the last sound. She stood near the window, just stood in the dark and silent house, for how long she couldn't say. Snow, like cresting waves in the blue moonlight surrounded her as though she were on a boat on the sea, and underneath, the mermaids who followed the boat all summer, watched her, curious to see what she would do. The mermaids will keep him; they'll take him away, and set me free. She groped for a flashlight. She found her galoshes, her parka, a scarf, mittens, and a wool hat. She would have to walk out. She'd have to get to the police station. But, she knew, their help would be too late. By the time she returned, Donny would be frozen, dead, waterlogged. Silent. Should she go? Yes, of course. She shut off the flame under her pot of soup. She grabbed the flashlight and her house keys. She paused to savor the quiet. There will be no need for voice rest anymore. No bruises. No sunglasses to hide her eyes at work. No sneers from Eileen. She will be free.

Life lay before her, empty and glorious. Her baby would never know her secret. Would never accuse her, like Eileen did, of hiding the truth. A burst of wind rattled the windows and a branch from a leafless shrub tapped on the glass. Janet stepped toward the front door. The branch tapped again. The howl of wind died but she still heard tapping. Then, she heard banging, loud, fierce banging. Rex growled deep in his throat but as though he knew, he did not pull.

Janet stepped through the front door while the banging went on. She locked the door behind her, tucked the dark flashlight into the pocket of her parka and felt not a twinge of regret. She lifted her knees high, stepping through the deep snow toward the street, looking furtively over her shoulder. She marched toward town. Behind her, the banging on the locked back door went on, and as the distance between her and the stilted house grew, wind moved through barren tree limbs overhead and she mistook its siren sound for a mermaid's song.

Have Fun, Stay Fertile

He wants my uterus. My OB/GYN wants me to give it up. "You have no need for it anymore, do you?" It was acceptable for him to say that. I've known him for twenty five years, since he saved me from his knife happy colleague who told me at the age of twenty one that he needed me to sign a release form giving him permission to remove "everything" in the event he "went in" and found cancer while exploring the reason the ultrasound had shown one of my ovaries "six times the normal size". Dr. Gold, my hero, re-did the ultrasound and three weeks later called and said, "You have nothing wrong with you. He must have measured your bowel."

On one hand, he was right. I had three children. Mid-forties. The likelihood of my having any more children, although I suppose biologically I could, circumstantially I probably would not, was not high. It was hard enough to pay for the three I had. And it would be even harder to find someone who might want to father a child with me, provided I had the urge for further procreation, or time to even dwell on the thought. My husband, always plunging forward, had gone on to a new woman five years ago. Within months I had acknowledged the flood of relief that replaced my hurt. We really were having no fun, not even with the parenting thing. He was too tense and self-absorbed to feel the pleasure of the children's presence after the diapers, midnight crying, and restless toddler stages were over. The girls got used to seeing us separately even before he'd left, since he routinely came home from work just after bedtime and earlier only when I had somewhere outside the house to go. Weekends we took turns living separate lives, pursuing the interests we had individually, and giving time to the kids, but never together. He'd said to me once, after my first was born, when I left the house on a Saturday afternoon to shop and go to the library. "Is this how it's going to be? Weekends? I come home. You go out?"

"I'm here all week with the baby," I replied. "I need to do something beside change diapers and clean up spit-up. I only want a couple of hours."

"I thought women liked to do those things."

"Like changing diapers? I do it out of love. Who would get pleasure from cleaning up a poopy bottom?"

His face took on a sour expression. I wondered if he knew what I meant by love. Doing something for love. Five years later, after he'd left, I knew he hadn't the slightest idea.

"We'll snip and suck it out vaginally," Dr. Gold explained. "That's the easy way. But if we wait too long, the fibroids will grow and we'd need to do an abdominal incision."

"Isn't there another way?" I asked. I was skittish.

"Not really. At your age, the hysterectomy has little impact on your life, quick recovery, and reduces the chances down to zero that you could develop uterine cancer."

"I just don't want the pains anymore."

They came over me at random, pressing on my pubic bone, my lower back and rectum, causing me to gasp and clutch my abdomen and slowly breathe until they passed. In a few seconds, they were gone. No predictability. They could come in the middle of teaching journalism at the junior college, in the middle of a consultation with the writers whose work I edited for the medical publisher I worked for. It was embarrassing. My sister completed the Iron Man Triathlon while she was menstruating. She didn't even need, after a hundred mile bike ride, to change her tampon. I spend the greater part of every fourth week in the bathroom changing tampons and pads every hour on the hour for three full days. A hysterectomy would end all that. That was a definite benefit.

"I'll think about it."

At home, after I fed my darlings dinner, I coaxed them into their bedrooms where they read themselves to sleepiness and I visited each of them for a few moments of precious talk. Downstairs, I flipped on the computer and searched online for "Fibroids" and "Hysterectomy".

"First 20 of 13,000 matches" greeted me. How thorough does my research have to be? I asked myself. I was an editor for a medical journal. I hadn't had to research a topic for personal health reasons yet. But I knew how to find what I needed.

Fibroids are harmless. Unless your symptoms become severe, (define severe, I begged) there is no medical reason for removing them.

Some new procedures for blocking the veins that sent blood to the fibroids by inserting little pebble like objects, also were being tested on women with severe symptoms (define severe, I begged again). What if the little suckers slipped? I wondered. What if they travel to the brain, the heart, the lungs? My pain wasn't worth the risk, or was it? Practical reasons, good reasons, to have the surgery were definitely there. Yet, something about losing that organ which was the source of life saddened me.

There were references to countless books on women's health, whole body, whole life approaches to maladies suffered by women. I printed a list and vowed to visit the bookstore at lunch the next day. I went to bed.

A man stood quietly in the doorway to my office next morning at nine. I was writing in the margin of someone's manuscript when he coughed, causing me to look up.

"Maureen O'Boyle?"

"Yes?

He stepped across the threshold. "I'm Jim McKeown. I'm working on that series on colon cancer?"

"Yes." I remembered he was coming in to dissect his first submission to the journal with me this morning. "Come in."

He wore small wire glasses, gun-metal, with bifocal lenses that enlarged his eyes. Brown. Brown eyes and silver hair, a full head of it. His face was smooth skinned. He must have been close in age to my own. He was not tall. Not short. About 5 foot 10 inches, I'd say. He was dressed in neat khaki's and a blazer. He sat down and shoved his glasses back up his nose with his finger. His nose was long, I noticed. Just the right length.

"Our deadline is two weeks from today. We can make changes until then."

He was easy to work with, took my criticism well and nodded at every comment and suggestion. "Um, yes, that would help…"

I spend most of the morning with my head down, not much eye contact with him. I was focused, business like, efficient, working toward lunch-time when I would throw him out and go to lunch at Barnes and Noble and read through some of those women's health books.

"Jim, your work is very precise. I like your writing style. It's technical, but not dry."

"Thank-you."

He left stating he'd email the next draft with the suggested additions in a few days. I glanced at my calendar. No meetings 'til three o'clock.

The bookstore always looks like a library. Quiet, classic, but missing the dust that would authenticate the place as a home for books. The place was, after all, not the final home for the leaves that inhabited its shelves. I breathed in, hoping to get a whiff of binding glue and paper. All I smelled was coffee.

The women's health aisle was not busy. It was crowded with titles, though. I felt the burden of my overlarge purse on my shoulder as I bent low to peruse the latest trends in medical advice. Women's Bodies, Women's Lives, hmmm. I carried it to the café and ordered a cappuccino and selected a croissant, a chocolate one, from the display case. I dumped the book on a table and folded a piece of napkin several times and wedged it under the leg of the wobbly table. When I struggled back up, I heard a familiar sound.

"Maureen?"

I looked up. There was this morning's writer, I searched my memory for his name, the one who knew all about colon's, standing there with a cup of coffee. Damn, I won't have time to read if I have to talk to someone… Jim is his name… Jim McKeown…Now I'll have to actually buy the book and take it home. It cost thirty-seven ninety-five. I smoothed my skirt down and straightened. I placed the extra napkin over the title and smiled.

"What a coincidence! Do you spend your lunch-hour here often?" he asked.

"No. Usually I work through lunch so I can get home to my kids. I just had to look up something." I left it there, not wanting to arouse his curiosity about my subject matter. "Do you?"

"Yes. I like the quiet. And I have a heavy coffee habit."

"I do too."

"Do you mind if I sit here? The place is pretty crowded."

There were no other empty tables; I already knew that, having sought an alternative before my repair job on the rocking leg.

"Not at all. Please, sit down."

He did.

I retrieved my coffee from the bar and self-consciously took a bite from my croissant. He was rail thin. I noticed when he took off his blazer. I wasn't. Thin. He was having only coffee. I could do without it, the croissant, but habit bade me eat something at the noon hour. I'd be famished at 4:00 if I skipped.

I usually didn't dwell on the size of my body unless I was eating in front of someone who was not eating. Today, I felt terribly self-conscious of my food choice, considering the topic of the book that sat there on my table with the title hidden under a napkin. It's only 15 extra pounds, I told myself. It's not like I'm fat.

"What are you reading?"

"I'm researching some women's health issues."

"I'm still on the colon subject." He held up a volume entitled, *Foods For A Clean Exit.*

I nodded, wanting to roll my eyes, but resisting the urge. After all, he was a professional acquaintance.

"What do you read for pleasure?" he asked. My mind drew a complete blank at the question. Pleasure? What was that?

I explained, "I don't have much time for reading. I have three children. I read to them."

"Oh. What do they like?"

"Right now I'm reading A Wrinkle in Time to my younger daughters. My oldest is reading the Chronicles of Narnia series."

"Good choices."

"They read their share of junk, too. What about you? Who's work do you read for pleasure?"

"Murakami lately, King, Barbara Kingsolver…"

"Barbara Kingsolver? I thought only women read her stuff."

"I like to keep my mind open."

I was singularly impressed. I still, however, wished to be left alone but hid that fact from him. He was too polite to dismiss out of hand. I looked closer at him as he spoke. His gaze when he asked a question was penetrating. It wasn't just the glasses that did that. He did it. Genuine interest. It felt good. I allowed the tension in my shoulders to flow out of me.

"What other publications do you freelance for?"

"Oh, I did some for The Medical Exchange, ghost wrote some for the AMA Journal." He was modest about that.

"Do you specialize? In other than colon's I mean."

"Not really. I'm a quick study. I started medical school but quit. I found writing to be the preferred way to make my living. Can't take the close-up view of reality and pain, I'm afraid."

"It's not for everyone."

"What about you? Always in journalism?"

"Yes."

I recited my employment history. I'd been with this journal for five years.

"How old are your children?"

"Thirteen and ten - twins."

"You're raising them alone?"

"Not really." His penetrating eyes could read my aloneness? How? "Their father lives nearby. We share custody."

"Is that awkward?"

"Not anymore. When we were married, toward the end, it was much worse."

Why am I allowing him to ask me all these personal questions? I should tell him it's none of his business. Yet, he was so off-hand, so light, so imploring, I found myself welcoming his interest.

"It's amazing what unspoken expectations can do inside relationships."

"Marriage does imply certain expectations. Yes. I think you're right."

"Are you married?"

I was not as intuitive as he.

"No. Never been. I came close a few times but never went through with it."

"Are you the leave 'em at the altar type?"

"Perhaps. But I never got that close actually."

We both sipped our coffees. His cup was soon empty.

"Well, I've got to go." He stood. "It was a pleasure. I'll call you in a few days time, when I'm finished with the work we did this morning."

"Sounds good." I murmured, unable to remember if I'd felt the same pleasure this morning and ignored it, or if the warmth was only from this chance occurrence.

I glanced at the clock. Only ten minutes left in my precious lunch hour. I carried my book to the cashier line, my half-empty coffee in my other hand. My purse slid off my shoulder and dragged my arm down, the arm with the hand that held the coffee. The impact propelled the cup from my hand to the floor. Coffee splashed on the counter, the floor and the back of the shoe on the woman in front of me in line. It missed me, and my book, thank God.

I paid with my credit card and signed quickly, anxious to get out of there, embarrassed at my fumbling. I turned to leave, my now empty coffee cup in my hand, seeking a trashcan.

"Need a refill?"

I froze in place. He just stood there. Hand outstretched.

"Take it. It's hot. Actually, it's burning my hand." He laughed and switched hands, shaking the hot one to cool it.

"You can't go back to the office without some caffeine in your system. If you're like me, you'll fall asleep over the boredom of colon's and other diseased body parts." He smiled shyly. "Admit it. It isn't all that thrilling, is it?"

I laughed at his honesty. "You're right. It's a real sleeper on some days."

I took the cup. He said, "Can I carry your books for you?"

I handed him my plastic bag confident the title would not show through the stylized portrait of James Joyce on the advertisement. He turned and matched my steps to my car.

"Do you think that woman knows she's got coffee stains on the back of her shoes?"

"She's my wife, I'll ask her when I get home."

"I thought you said…"

"Maureen, that was a joke."

"Well," I quickly matched his ironic tone. "Maybe she's used to it, considering the coffee habit you say you have."

"Actually, our entire house is coffee colored, just to hide the spills. I drink so much my hands shake. By the mid afternoon, I can barely hold the cup in my hand."

"Next article I hire you for will be about misdiagnosing Parkinson's disease because of coffee consumption."

"Or undiagnosed heart palpitations."

"Or the influence of caffeine in axe murders."

We reached my car. I stopped, turned and held out my hand for my package.

"Thank you. It was very kind of you to buy me a cup of coffee."

"You seemed to be in distress. I like rescuing distressed maidens."

"Maidens? Please…"

"Well, what then? What would you call yourself?"

"Well, certainly not a maiden…"

"I would."

"Thank you." I found myself saying thank you to him an awful lot. I was uneasy however. Was he following me? He seemed so intent on furthering our acquaintance. Or was it just because I had the power to hire him again for more work. Personal relationships are everything, I remembered, especially in business.

He stepped back and turned to leave.

"The pleasure was all mine. Talk to you in a few days."

He left. I climbed into my station wagon and tossed the book onto the seat. Before I pulled out into traffic, I scanned the parking lot, wondering what kind of car he drove and if he was behind me. He could be obsessive compulsive, I thought. He could be a kook. I didn't see him. Part of me felt disappointment. Part felt relief.

The afternoon held me glued to the screen of my computer making grammatical corrections on an article about hand surgery. The text was boring, stale. The writer came in at three and left at four. I'd rather read about colons in Jim's style. My mind drifted back to Jim and a picture in my mind of his hand waving across my vision when he handed me the hot coffee and when he took my books from me. His hand were strong, large and slender.

I settled down with my thirty-seven ninety-five copy of Women's Bodies, Women's Day's after I sent my children to bed. A cup of chamomile steamed in the cup on the saucer I'd placed on the small round table next to my chair.

"Animal protein induces the body to produce more estrogen than the body needs. Estrogen in excess will stimulate the growth of fibroids in the uterine wall. Women with severe fibroids may find they can reduce the size of fibroids by limiting their consumption of animal protein sources in their diet. Vegan diets, with no eggs, dairy or meat can help shrink fibroids and ease their symptoms."

I read on. The uterus is the creative center of a woman's body. Life begins there. Some believe fibroids are the symptoms of blocked creative energy. Once unblocked, the uterus can eliminate the growth of these usually benign tumors. Deep abdominal massage, stimulating the body to send more oxygen to the uterus has been shown to increase healthy blood circulation and again reduce the chance of abnormal growths in the female reproductive organs.

Channeling creative energy, particularly in women who fulfill nurturing roles in our society with decades of their lives, who have subjugated themselves to the demands of motherhood and domestic obligations, is the most important life change requirement for women suffering severe symptoms of fibroids. I read and yawned. This was worth trying. I called my health nut, triathlete sister and read it to her.

"Vegan," I moaned. "I've done vegetarian. I guess I can do vegan if it means avoiding surgery. Creative energy? How, with children and a demanding job would I have time for channeling creative energy?

"Exercise," my sister said. "Set a goal for yourself. And if you don't have time to create, read or do something that helps you appreciate creativity. At least to start."

Two months later I'd lost ten pounds. My week now included a few visits to the gym where I worked my way up to two miles on the treadmill at a slow jog. I used weights to firm my arms and abdomen. The jogging took care of the legs. I felt better. The kids adjusted to the changes in my diet as best they could. I stir-fried some tofu for myself while they ate chicken or lean beef.

After the kids were in bed I sank myself into a hot tub filled with aromatherapy crystals and read novels for pleasure. My fibroid symptoms didn't change but I didn't expect them to so early. I shopped, not just for books on lunch hour when I wasn't at the gym, but for new clothes.

My beverage of choice was now green tea. I missed the flavor of coffee, but substituting soymilk for half and half put the brown hot liquid in the category of puke. There would be no compromises, I thought. Vegan, or surgery.

Six months later I visited Dr. Gold. Time for an ultrasound, to check the size of those fibroids. Disappointment. They were still there. They were still growing. And, in spite of my glowing health, my heavy periods still left me anemic.

"I'm on a vegan diet."

He didn't exactly frown. "Make sure you take your iron supplements."

I pulled out the women's health book again that night while I soaked my tired muscles in aromatic bubbles. Increased circulation to the uterus can encourage better oxygen flow to the muscular walls of the uterus creating healthier function. How do I increase circulation to the uterus? Exercise increases oxygen flow to the muscles. How do you exercise your uterus?

Slowly, the idea crept up on me. I denied it at first. Then laughed at it. Secretly, I thought about posting the question on a women's health website but wrote the idea off as ludicrous. But, still the idea stayed with me and grew until I could no longer ignore it. Orgasm. I was now using every muscle in my body, except those tiny muscle fibers in the wall of my uterus, the ones that through sheer force of nature had contracted with violent strength to push my children out through the birth canal. Could they be brought out of their current state of deterioration with a little exercise? I lay there in the tub as the water grew cold and the bubbles disappeared. That's what was missing. I needed a man in my life. I stood up and dried myself.

Some giggling was emanating from the bedroom across the hall. Then I heard footsteps creeping down the hall and down the stairs. My daughter's were up. Sneaking out of the house? I crept behind and followed them.

"Shhh, Mom will hear you."

"She's asleep. She won't hear."

They were crossing the front porch. I waited just inside the front door, pushing the curtain on the window aside to watch them. It was 11:45. They reached the front lawn and disappeared. I opened the door and followed them, hidden by the rhododendrons that lined the railing. They giggled and whispered.

"It's not midnight yet."

"It's close enough. Give me the hairbrush."

"Didn't you bring your own? Mommy doesn't like us to share hairbrushes."

"Just give it to me."

My eldest daughter sat under the holly tree and brushed her hair. Then she handed her sisters the brush and they did the same.

"Hurry. Just a stroke or two is all you need."

They crept out from under the holly tree and I stepped toward the stairs and silently confronted them.

"Mom!"

"What are you doing out here in the middle of the night?"

"We're playing."

"Obviously. What's with the hairbrushes?"

"I just read a book. It said if you brush your hair under a holly tree at midnight the first man you meet the next day is the man you're going to marry."

"Really?"

"Yeah, want to try it?"

"Maybe she'll see Dad early tomorrow. Is he driving us to school?" Her voice was hopeful.

"No. He's in Utah."

"Oh."

They looked disappointed.

"Go back to bed. It's late. And you're to young to be wishing for husbands."

"Mom, it was just for fun."

"I know. Go ahead, back to bed."

I kissed each of them and nudged them toward the door. With them safely tucked back into bed I returned gratefully to mine and turned off the light. I lay there thinking of the silly game. What about me? Would it work for me? Just for fun I climbed back out of bed and put on my bathrobe. I took a comb from my bathroom and crept downstairs and out to the front yard. It was 12:10 AM. Hopefully no one was out roaming the neighborhood at this hour. I sat on the ground under the holly tree next to my front porch. Just a partner, for the purpose of my reproductive health. I took three quick strokes with the comb through my short wavy hair. I stood up, brushed the cedar chips from my bathrobe and went back to bed feeling foolish.

At the office the next morning I opened my planner and read. Nine AM, Jim KcKeown. I felt my face flush.

I brewed a pot of coffee in the Xerox room and breathed in the aroma. Ahhh. I washed out two porcelain mugs. He announced himself in his unassuming way, peering through his glasses slowly, shyly, waiting for me to acknowledge his right to be there. I motioned him in and stood to greet him.

"Would you like a cup of coffee?"

"I'd love one."

I retrieved the mugs and filled them, carrying them carefully back to my office where he moved papers aside to make room on the desk. I sat down.

"You look different."

"I'm on a health kick."

"It shows."

"Thank you." I felt my face blushing again. Wondered if he noticed.

"You have good color too."

He did notice. Oh God.

He was submitting a new series of articles on diabetes. This morning I lifted my eyes from the page to address him. He was wearing a dark denim blue shirt with khaki's and a hunter green cable knit sweater. His eyes looked large through his lenses and I wondered how they looked naked. I wondered how the rest of him looked naked. Then forced myself back to the subject. Then I wondered what he would think of me naked. That was excruciating. I made a mental note that if and when, we would definitely have the lights out. Back to diabetes. He was thin, but I couldn't tell how fit he was under his clothes. At least I'm fit, now, I thought.

The final page of the diabetes article was in need of only a few re-writes. We made quick business of it and each exhaled with relief.

"More coffee?"

He stood with his cup. "I'll come with you. You shouldn't wait on me. I'm the subordinate here, aren't I?" He took mine from my hand and followed me. The pot was empty.

"Can you wait?"

"Yes. "

I washed the pot in the sink and filled it from the tap. He took the filter from the basket and replaced it with a fresh one. He opened the cabinet and found a silver packet of pre-measured coffee. He tore it open and filled the filter. I poured the water in the top and we listened to the hiss and spits of the water hitting hot metal. The drip flowed slowly into the pot and we stood, he looking at the pot, me stealing glances at him, from his hair down to his toes, making judgments on his every garment and each obvious body part.

"Are you reading anything?"

"I just picked up Cold Mountain. It's the Book of the Year pick from a few years ago…"

"Yes. How is it?"

"I'm finding the details amazing. The man is incredibly perceptive."

"I'll have to try it."

"I'll loan you my copy when I'm finished. What are you reading now?"

"The House of Earth."

He looked up questioning.

"Pearl Buck. A collection of four of her novels."

"China?"

I nodded. Then I plunged into action. "Do you ever do book discussion groups?"

"Once in a while. Do you?"

"Yes. I started one a few months ago. Everyone is too busy to come all the time. We meet at Starbucks." I smiled at the coffee link. "Sometimes in people's homes. I'm hosting one next Tuesday. Would you be interested in coming?" I felt my innards freeze waiting for his response.

"I'd like that."

"We're doing Angela's Ashes."

"I've read it. Good."

"We do movies too sometimes."

"Now that's a great idea."

"We've done a few. Most recently we did Russian stories. Comparing them."

"Which movies?"

"Reds."

"Warren Beatty's? Great movie. All those old wrinkly faces talking about the past."

" Dr. Zhivago too."

"Another old favorite of mine." He paused. "I'll try it out."

"Okay, it's a very laid back group. You come when you can." What am I talking about? Laid? Come? I should just shut up. I would have giggled, but he'd think I'd lost my mind. Did he notice my choice of words? I think not.

The coffee dripped silently now. The pot was almost full. He took each cup and filled it and wiped the hot plate where the pot sat on the coffee maker with a paper towel. I poured half and half into each cup. Vegan, smegan, I thought. This is for the greater good of science and my health.

We sipped and returned to my office.

"Most of the copy for this month journal is already put to bed."

At the word bed my face flushed again. Damn, I wish I could control that.

He drank his coffee and left with directions to my house.

I threw myself back into work for the remainder of the day.

The eldest, Sarah, was beside herself. At dinner, her sister laughed at her anguish.

"Bob Marzulli. Sarah saw Bob Marzulli before anybody else this morning."

"He's gross. He eats with his mouth open. He picks his nose and eats it."

"Please, Sarah, not at the dinner table!"

"It's true Mom. I saw him at school." Her younger sister had the end of her fork up her nose and her mouth open with green beans oozing through teeth parted in a wide grin.

"Mom, it's not funny. Tell her to stop."

"Who did you see first?" I asked.

"I saw Mr. Collins, my teacher."

I silently wondered if Mr. Collins was a child molester. My youngest daughter, in fourth grade, developed crushes on all older men, although her heart still belonged to her dad.

My secret visit to the holly tree was not fodder for this conversation, I vowed.

"Mom, you should do it. Comb your hair under the holly tree."

"Why?"

"Do it the day before Dad gets home, maybe he'll dump his girlfriend."

"Dad and I tried marriage already. The best thing that came out of it was one, two, three." I pointed at them and smiled.

"Don't you get lonely?"

"Not with you around. When you leave me to grow up and be independent, maybe then I'll get remarried."

"We'll never leave you, Mom. We'll always live with you."

"I hope so."

Tuesday night came. So did Jim. He brought them a gift. An audio taped version of Harry Potter and the Sorcerer's Stone. The ten year old shouted with glee. The older one, the skeptic, mumbled thanks, took the tapes and my Walkman and retired immediately to her room.

"Attitude about Dad?"

"Could be."

"Do you date?"

Why does my face take over when I hesitate over my words? Scarlet faced, I replied, "No. Who's got time?"

"Does your ex-husband?"

"He's seeing someone, yes."

"HMMMMM"

"What?"

"She's losing control of one parent. Now a man turns up in her house. She's feeling her world shake up a little."

"You're very intuitive, aren't you?"

"No more than anybody else."

"Actually, there have been men here for the book group before."

Now it was his turn to blush scarlet.

"Maureen, let's start. The kids are settled. Quick, before someone calls you upstairs to sing."

"There's a pot of coffee in the kitchen."

Jim stood. "Thanks."

While he helped himself we began. Sandy, a short round woman with dark brown skin, the designated leader of tonight's discussion, pulled out a sheet where she'd written some questions.

Sandy pointed out the humorous and highly lilting tone of the author's voice, even while telling a story of such poverty and tragedy. She was amazed, she said, at how his children still loved their father in spite of the devastation wreaked on the family because of his alcoholism.

"Did any of you have parents who drank?"

"I did. My father had a problem. He stopped. Got it under control when I was a teenager." Sandy explained. "When I was younger, it was tough."

"Our dad never drank, except on social occasions." I looked at Barb as she said this. We were lucky I guess.

Sandy led us through the questions. When we digressed, she brought us back around. At ten o'clock I eyed Sandy, and signaled her to wrap it up. By ten fifteen she was through the questions and throwing her purse over her shoulder. My sister looked at the time and left too.

Jim offered to carry the now empty platter to the kitchen. I took the bowl of hummus.

"You never answered the question about alcoholics. I was wondering. I hope Sandy didn't move too fast through her questions."

"No. She did great. Actually, it was the best book group meeting I've been to in a while."

"You didn't mind being the only male?"

"No. That happens a lot. When you're single and all your friends are married, you spend a lot of time with single friends. Most of my single friends are women."

"Are you dating anyone?"

He'd asked me that. I figured it was fair to do the same.

"No. No time."

"You're not gay though, are you?"

I held my breath waiting for his answer.

"No. But people ask me that a lot."

"Does it offend you?"

"No."

"It is unusual to be this age and never married."

"I know."

He fell silent for a short minute. I wasn't sure if I should say anything or not. So I waited.

"My father was an alcoholic. My parents divorced when I was fifteen. I think they soured me on the idea of marriage."

"That could do it I suppose."

"My sister drinks. We've, my brother and I, tried to help her. But I think my father's problem affected her more than the rest of us."

I leaned against the sink and returned his penetrating gaze. He looked away and said, "I'd better go. Work to do in the morning."

He reached the door and turned. "Thanks for inviting me. I really enjoyed it. See you in a few days."

• • • • •

"PWI."

"What's that?"

"Problems with intimacy. Children of alcoholics are notorious for avoiding intimacy. That's why he's single."

My sister always had the answers. It was Saturday morning. My girls were at soccer practice. She and I were at the gym, side by side on treadmills, the only way we could run together and each get a workout commensurate with our abilities and fitness levels. Mine was set at 10 minute miles, hers at 7:30's. I was sweating. She wasn't.

"But he's so nice. And seems so sensitive." I repeated what he'd noticed about Sarah at the book group meeting.

"He won't get any closer. Watch. And be careful. You sound like you like him."

"I don't. I do. But I'm not looking for lifelong intimacy. Just a casual relationship."

She gave me one of her "yeah right" looks and fell silent as she pushed her treadmill setting to a hill profile.

Next time I saw him I was returning to the office from lunchtime at the gym.

"Ah," he said. "Now you're my role model."

Role model. What every parent strives for.

"I'm still on my health kick."

"I should be on one. I quit smoking two years ago. Started running. But then I slacked off."

"You can run with me. On Saturday's. Having a running buddy helps. Keeps you motivated."

"I'm afraid I'll slow you down."

I laughed. "No, you won't."

"When?"

We chose the park with the hill and the rose garden. 9:00 AM? Saturday? He was thin, but he was, after all, an ex-smoker. I slowed down, marveling that I'd have to slow down for anybody. When we completed two miles we stopped at the water fountain. While I drank he said, "You are very kind. You welcome people easily into your life."

"Well look at you. Buying me that cup of coffee at the bookstore. I'm just responding to you. You're so easy going."

I breathed in and said nothing, not sure yet why he'd said what he'd said. He drank deeply at the fountain. As he straightened, he looked toward the horizon and the trees and said, "Would you have dinner with me tonight?"

He didn't look at me until I answered.

"I could. Yes. Thank-you." Did he detect the surprise in my voice? I answered quickly.

His eyes on my face, he just said, "Seven? I'll pick you up at seven?"

I nodded.

There was a self-conscious smile on his lips. "What as."

"What?"

"Remember that line from 'REDS'? Diane Keaton looks at Warren Beatty and says 'What as?' when he asks her to go to Moscow with him?"

"Yes, I do remember. She said, 'As your comrade? As your wife? As your lover'?"

"Don't you want to ask me?"

"Should I?"

He turned bright red.

"No. I'm not sure I can answer you."

"I feel nervous in the house without you Mom." Sarah objected to the idea of me on a date.

"Nonsense. I'll be in town. And you can reach me by cell phone if there is an emergency."

"Okay."

She hid in her room and did not emerge until well after Jim and I left the house. Five minutes into the car ride to the restaurant, my cell phone rang.

"Where is he taking you?"

"We're having Mexican at El Toro Loco."

"What's the number there?"

"You have my cell phone number, you don't need the restaurant number."

"What if you run out of power?"

"I won't run out of power unless you stay on the line or keep calling me for no reason."

"Don't stay out too late."

"Who's the mother here?"

"Nevermind. Bye."

I looked at Jim.

"Should have brought her another present."

He laughed.

I relaxed. There was nothing requiring description about our dinner. It suffices to say, it was fun. The conversation was lively. We laughed a lot. And we drank three margaritas each.

After coffee, of course, we took a walk through the park where the overhead lights created shadows that lengthened and shortened as we approached them along the path. In the deepest shadow of a tall tree he stopped and put his arm around me. I slipped my arm through his. His second arm encircled my other side and I let him pull me close. He just held me for a moment and I tightened my arms around him.

"You feel very familiar," he said. "Like I should recognize you from a long time ago. But you don't really look like anyone I ever met."

"Is that a good thing? I hope so."

"Actually, maybe you look like Mrs. Freezewhick, my fourth grade teacher."

I pushed him away to look into his face. He was laughing at my reaction.

"Great. How old was she?"

"How old are you?"

"Forty four. How old are you?"

"Forty five."

"How old was she?"

"Twenty nine."

I laughed now. When I closed my mouth and put my head back near his shoulder he pulled slightly away again and reached to kiss me. I closed my eyes and opened my lips slightly to accept his kiss. And as his lips touched mine and pulled gently, I felt a twinge deep down in my visceral self and responded slowly. I felt him shudder so very slightly. And felt myself just deciding to stay there. Just stay there as long as he wanted me to. That turned out to be a rather long time. He pulled away first. We walked through the dark park. Silently. Just breathing in the soft smell of grass and the faint moisture in the ground.

"I'll take you home, friend."

"You don't have to. It's early." That was me talking. It surprised me, those words, coming from my mouth.

"Yes I do. Your daughter has the police out searching for us."

"I guess you're right."

When he dropped me at home and I used my key to let myself through the barricade my daughter had created with the deadbolt and the doorknob lock. It started that night. That silly thing I called a glow. Quietly and completely it overcame me with such surprise that I marveled at how new yet familiar it felt. He wasn't the only one who'd found something familiar.

The following week Jim was sick. He called and offered to email his latest article to me. My printer was broken. So instead I offered to pick up a copy of the final at his apartment. He hesitated then gave me directions. I drove to his place but stopped first at a deli and bought him a quart-sized container of chicken soup. He answered the buzzer and mumbled "Come on up." His voice crackled and broke up in the static of the speaker next to the rows of buttons.

In gray sweatpants and a tee-shirt that said CAPE COD he greeted me and held the door aside for me to enter. His hand held a manila envelope as though he expected me to take it and make a quick exit.

"I have a sinus infection. I'm probably contagious."

"Here." I handed him the brown paper bag from the deli. "Soup."

I took his envelope and stuffed it into my purse.

"Thanks." We both said the same word simultaneously. Then after an awkward moment I turned toward the door.

"Do you need anything else?" I searched for words. "Food? Juice? A video?"

"No, thanks again. I'm sorry you had to come all the way over here."

He still had one hand on the doorknob, I noticed. He wants me to leave.

I left, feeling a bit let down. I left. And called my sister.

"I know you. You can't be casual about anybody. And it's even worse now because you're old and out of practice. When's the last time you even just liked someone?"

"It was Henry."

"See? Slow the emotions down. You're out of practice."

"You're right."

I hired him to do another series. He had to see me with the drafts. He was polite and distant. So was I. Underneath I was in turmoil. I wanted to be casual. I forced myself to be casual. He relaxed in response. What happened, I wondered. Did I say something stupid at dinner? I wanted to ask him. But I was afraid to bring it up. It was only dinner, after all.

"My sister has been sick," he said. "I've been a bit pre-occupied. She's in one of those dry-out clinics."

My heart stopped. It had nothing to do with me. It was about him and the rest of his life. The part I was not part of. I felt relief. How self absorbed I was, how stupid.

"Is there something I can do to help?"

"Maybe just distract me for a few minutes."

"I can do that."

"Want to go to lunch?"

"That would be great."

I picked up my purse and dropped my pen. He left his notes and draft on my desk. We walked to his car and in silence drove to his apartment. That was his pick. I said nothing.

Inside, I put my purse down on the floor. He dropped his keys on the table next to the lamp. His hand reached up and touched me on the cheek. The other hand felt for my hair. I lifted my arms around him and leaned to accept his kiss. Then, slowly, I pulled his hand from my hair and led him toward the couch. He followed. His long slender hand slid up under my skirt. I kicked my shoes off. His hand was warm. It found the part of my thigh just below the line of my panties, then he slid his fingers up and under them and I gasped. I unbuttoned my blouse and his hand undid the back of my bra and the straps slid down my arms and I dropped it on the floor. I stepped out of my skirt and he kneeled in front of me and took my panties down to my ankles.

I stepped out of them and stood before him in the daylight, naked, my nipples hard and the wetness between my legs warm and urgent. I knelt too. My hands went to work on his clothes. From top to bottom, I gently opened all the fasteners while his hands traveled over my skin and his mouth covered mine. His tongue lolled around mine and when I'd finished undressing him, his tongue moved to my left nipple and he sucked. My hands were in his hair now, guiding his head, my own head bowed to watch him taking pleasure from giving me such sensation. I groaned. His hand slid again between my legs and I leaned into it. I moved my hips. I lay back on the floor and he put his tongue where his hand had just been. I moaned again. And he made a sighing sound. I moved my legs apart and let his tongue stroke me, suck me, explore me. And I felt the spasms fill me from front to back, top to bottom, and reach up inside me until I was throbbing with pleasure. Then, he came on top of me and pushed into me. He filled me and I could feel the pulse of him inside and he matched the gyrating motion of my hips. We breathed hard, together, moving and feeling each other's pleasure. There was no giving and receiving, it all blended together and I felt my womb. I felt it pulsating and then releasing all the tension, all the tight-ness, dissolving into one final moment when we found the height of pleasure at the exact moment and collapsed from exhaustion, sweating and breathing. I was so wet still. It was him spilling from me. Getting cold in the air. But the warmth of his body still on top of me was such that I wanted him to stay there and crush me if it gave him pleasure. He rolled off and held me. I leaned over and kissed his mouth. My breasts, still hard, stroked against his chest. His hands caressed me and then quieted me and found their way around me and held me still, against him for a long silent time.

"Distraction enough?" I didn't look at him when I said it.

"Yes, thank-you." He sounded polite. Then he laughed. "Would you like some lunch?"

"I'm starving."

We dressed. He found a can of tuna and made two sandwiches.

We ate sitting at the counter in the kitchen. He was no longer silent.

"My sister is committing a slow suicide. It's driving me nuts that I can't find a way to help her."

"Some people don't want to be helped."

"I know. But I can't stand by and let her do this to herself."

"No you can't." I was at a loss. I could offer nothing substantial to help him.

"I wonder too, if it will happen to me."

"What?"

"The drinking. My father let it ruin his life. My sister is letting it ruin hers. Why isn't it happening to me?"

"Jim, what was your mother like? You have his genes. But you also have hers."

"She was patient. She kept waiting for him to stop. He never did."

"Why did she get a divorce? If she kept waiting for him. Did she love him?"

"Yes. But he was abusive. Not physically. Mentally."

"OH."

"She left him because I told her she should."

"How old were you?"

"Fifteen. I knew he was fooling around with his secretary. Sounds so cliched, doesn't it? But he was. And my mother knew. She just didn't want to break up the family. I told her we'd all survive. That she needed to survive too."

"Did she?"

"Yes. But she never remarried."

"Why are you afraid it will happen to you too?"

"Because he's my father. I'm his son. I feel him in me. There are things about me that are just like him. Sometimes they ambush me. I don't want to be like him. I don't want to ruin anybody else's life. Like he did my mother's."

"That's why you're still single."

"I suppose. I guess I'm carrying a lot of baggage, huh?"

"Must be. But you are so unlike what I imagine he was. You're intelligent. You're so sensitive." I blushed. "You're so nice."

"So was he."

"Really."

"He was a high school English teacher. He was good at it too. Then he left teaching to earn more money for the family. In business. That's when he fell apart. He took on too much. Three kids."

He looked at me. "How do you do it alone?"

"I don't. My ex-husband lives nearby. He takes the girls half the time."

"Why are you alone?"

"He and I just stopped wanting to be together. He met someone else."

My heart was racing. He watched me closely. My face reddened.

"His secretary?"

I laughed. "No. A girl from the gym."

"Were you still in love with him?"

"No. I was relieved when he left. He spent money like it was water. The girls love him because he still always buys them things. I'm the frugal one, saving for college. He won't. Someone has to take responsibility. I felt like he was the oldest child and I was the only parent."

"No wonder your daughter got nervous. The night I bought them the tape. It was just like Daddy, huh?"

"It was familiar behavior."

I looked at the time. "I have to get back to the office."

"I left my notes there. And my drafts."

"You have to drive me back. My car is there."

"Oh, you're right."

We threw our dishes in his sink. Back at my office, he became distant and cool. But, as he left with his papers, his penetrating eyes held mine.

"Dinner again?"

"Call me."

He nodded and left.

So much for lunchtime workouts. So much for my mental concentration. I was panicked. The experiment had begun. And I'd not used any birth control. I checked my calendar. Looking for the little star I put on the first day of my cycle so I could predict my next period. I sighed with relief. Tomorrow was day twenty-five. Slim chances of a sperm finding a live egg at this point. My period was due tomorrow.

I waited four days. Nothing happened. My period didn't come. I ran an extra mile at the gym and lifted heavier weights, hoping to see a little blotch of red on my underwear. Nothing. Two days later I bought an EPT test at the drug store. It indicated a negative. But it might be too early. I panicked. But the next morning, as I awoke from a dream which included water, lots of water, surrounding my house, stranding me and my three girls in a third story window, the same dream I had over and over again during my two pregnancies, I felt wetness and found, at last, I was bleeding. No baby. No way. Thank God.

It nagged at me. A diaphragm with spermicide was not a sure thing. I was too old to go on the Pill. Condoms weren't perfect either. I was consumed with fear of becoming pregnant. Yet I couldn't do it. The hysterectomy. Not yet. Not until I knew if the experiment would work. I wrote the lead sentence for the article I would compose. Women who lead satisfying sex lives do not suffer from fibroids. No, it is not creative energy that, when blocked, causes fibroids. It is not animal protein ladened diets. It is sexual energy, unused, that builds up the excess estrogen to encourage abnormal growths in the uterus. Sex. Lots and lots of sex. That is the answer. I would receive the Nobel prize for women's health issues. Yeah, right. There's no such thing.

Jim called and we had dinner at an Italian restaurant. Over dinner, he spoke of his sister and her determination, this time, to stay clean and sober. He relaxed. So did I. Afterwards, we made coffee at his apartment and sat on the couch. He held me and we kissed like two teenagers on a forbidden date. I was embarrassed. I told him we had to wait a few more days. Then he said, "A little bit of blood doesn't have to stop us."

Oh, so how do I answer that? Could I risk this? No, I had to do some explaining. I didn't want him to think I didn't want him. He was a medical writer. He had to listen and understand, didn't he? I breathed deeply and looked away. "What kind of doctor did you want to be…when you went to med school?"

He pointed. "If you look right there, you might guess."

I focused on his bookshelf on the other side of the room, letting titles distract me. Until I saw them. A full row of books on the female body, reproduction, childbirth, anatomy. Our romantic mood was broken. I didn't want to discuss my bleeding, my pain, my fibroids. Oh gees, how could I? I stood up and went to the shelf, pulling down a textbook on menstruation. "Did you read this?"

"Not entirely, but yes," he said.

I flipped through the volume, viewed the chapter headings; there was a full gallery of photographs and drawings midway through the pages. I used the index to find menses and flipped to the chapter.

"There," I said. "This is the mythology of a woman's period." He studied me. I read, "Women lose a few tablespoons of blood every month as the uterus sloughs off the endometrial lining if egg fertilization has not occurred." I slammed the book shut. "If only that were true."

He looked at me.

"Not exactly buckets," I said. "But enough that you would need a new couch if we had sex here tonight."

"Well, then, would you like a cup of tea? Or should we take a walk? Do you…"

"I'm out for at least five days," I said. "I'm sorry."

"Maybe not."

He took my hand. He pulled me up. He led me to the bathroom, shut off the light except for a small electric candle above the toilet. I watched as he ran the shower, checked the temperature, then slowly undressed. He got in first. I did what needed to be done with my tampon and pad, shed my clothes and stepped in. His gaze did not leave my face, but his hands explored, and I responded. The sensation of release when he entered me, the throbbing intensity, the warmth and the release came in wave after wave, the pain I expected was simply not there, not then, not after we smothered each other with soap and rinsed.

I dressed and joined him in the kitchen where he had poured two cups of tea.

"If I had a hysterectomy and that's what my doctor wants me to do, we would not have to…"

"Let's do that even without…"

"Can't get pregnant during your period." I said, "There are additional benefits too."

He smiled. "I think I witnessed that."

He pointed at a page in his book. I read out loud. "The uterus and the cervix play a strong role in a woman's orgasm. Women don't often know this before they make their decision to follow a doctor's advice but post hysterectomy sexual intercourse is less satisfying."

"We should talk about birth control," I said.

Then he said, "I've had a vasectomy. You don't have to worry about pregnancy. I have a feeling it's a good idea to preserve your fertility."

"I'm not sure I need my fertility," I said. "But I'd hate to give up the other."

"The fun, you mean?"

I nodded and felt my face flush scarlet.

"I would think it would be harder to give up than coffee."

"Yes," I said.

Grace and Ellen Reprise

A story in dialogue

Grace: God, it smells like a funeral parlor in here. I told you she likes chocolates. If you wanted to bring her something, you should have brought her chocolates.

Ellen: I figured you'd bring her chocolates. She loves flowers. And she can't exactly get down on her knees in the garden anymore.

Grace: Right. If I live near her, why should we both live near her? If I bring her meals and take her to the doctor when her arthritis gets bad why should you do it too?

Ellen: I'm just talking about flowers Grace.

Grace: I'm there for her and you're not.

Ellen: Grace, if it's getting too hard maybe it's time she went into assisted living. And you've got Lou to help, right?

Grace: Lou is very busy with the baby. And, for Mom, assisted living would be her first step toward the grave. She's not ready to die. She's only 80 for God's sake. You sound like you expect her to be dead soon.

Ellen: That's awful.

Grace: Well you do, don't you?

Ellen: I'm just thinking that if it's that difficult…

Grace: It's not difficult. Not for me.

Ellen: Then why are you complaining?

Grace: I'm not.

Ellen: You could have moved away. You and Charles. You loved PEI. Why didn't you move?

Grace: And leave her here all by herself? Go off, like you?

Ellen: No, I have responsibilities. I got a fellowship to do research.

Grace: Yes, Miss high and mighty got a fellowship to dig in the dirt in England. Should I call you Dr. Leakey?

Ellen: Why do you still do that Grace?

Grace: Do what?

Ellen: Make fun of what I do. You're still doing it.

Grace: What are you talking about?

Ellen: Oh, come on. We all know what went on when we were kids.

Grace: What? What went on?

Ellen: That's exactly it. You say you don't know. You're acting like my leaving home was a betrayal. I left because I couldn't take the ridicule anymore.

Grace: What ridicule? Ellen, please. I don't want to get into this. Get a shrink. Maybe I shouldn't have planned this party. You shouldn't have come home. You always bring up trouble and ruin things.

Ellen: No. You have to go and make some snide remark and set me off.

Grace: What snide remark? All I said was you should have brought her chocolates.

Ellen: Don't you ever wonder why you and I were never friends?

Grace: It's hard to be friends with someone so far away.

Ellen: I mean before I left.

Grace: Before you left?

Ellen: Yes. Like in high school.

Grace: I don't know what you're talking about.

Ellen: Oh, come on. You and MaryLou were always so close. And you and I never were. I never understood why... you treated me like I had leprosy in high school except when you needed to borrow clothes, or get me to iron your blouse, or chip in on a gift for Mom.

Grace: I think you're making this up.

Ellen: I am not making this up. And you know it.

Grace: I don't know it. And I can't believe you are bringing this up the night before Mom's party. No wonder I never wanted you to be my...

Ellen: See? You admit it. You just said it. Why? What did I ever do to make you hate me?

Grace: I didn't hate you. I just... I just wanted to kill the sister act. You know...

Ellen: You didn't kill the sister act with Lou. You and she did everything together.

Grace: See? That's what I don't get. You never wanted to hang with us. You always had other friends. You always put your friends ahead of either of us. Sandy, and what was that freckled girl's name, Jeryl Ann? You can't blame me for us not being friends.

Ellen: You forget. Don't you?

Grace: I guess I do. I'm going to call Mom and see how she is.

Ellen: This isn't finished. Sit down.

Grace: Yes, it is finished. You need a shrink, you know that? You make things up to justify your own behavior. Then you try to tell me you left the family because I didn't want to play the sister act with you anymore. You are the one who left.

Ellen: Do you know when it started?

Grace: When what started?

Ellen: You and Lou without me?

Grace: Yes, it was after you broke that Confirmation gift of mine.

Ellen: What?

Grace: That holy water font Aunt Barbara gave me. You were jealous. You broke it. That morning. You got out of bed and you reached up and hit it with your hand on purpose.

Ellen: That was an accident.

Grace: Yeah, that's what you said then.

Ellen: It was. I said I didn't see it.

Grace: How could you not see it? Your eyes were wide open.

Ellen: (sigh) Grace…Did you ever get up too fast and have everything go black on you?

Grace: Oh, please. You're not going to say that's what happened.

(a beat of silence passes)

Grace: Really?

Ellen: (nods) Low blood pressure. I didn't know. I was only 11. I thought that happened to everyone when they got out of bed.

Grace: You expect me to believe this?

Ellen: Yes, because it's true. So, is that really when you started to hate me?

Grace: I never hated you.

Ellen: Then why, when we were down at the beach that summer, you and Lou left and went down to the head shop and the village without me?

Grace: When?

Ellen: That next summer. It was the night I got my first period. I remember every last detail.

Grace: We, um, I don't know. Mom said we could go.

Ellen: She said you could go without me?

Grace: Yeah.

Ellen: Why did you?

Grace: I don't know. Maybe Lou and I just wanted to…maybe you were reading or something.

Ellen: Oh, come on. We were all always reading.

Grace: You got your period that night?

Ellen: Yes. That's why I remember. I cried all night. Then, I looked in my underwear and there was this stain. I went and showed it to Mom. And you know what she said? She said, 'No wonder you're crying.'

Grace: You were always crying when you got your period. It had nothing to do with us going without you.

Ellen: That's what drove me nuts. Mom blamed it on the hormones. She didn't understand how awful that was for me. You and Lou going off without me. I was so upset.

Grace: I really don't remember this as well as you do.

Ellen: That's because you didn't get your feelings hurt. That's the night you and Lou bought those love bead necklaces. I wanted to buy myself a set. I wanted to go and Mom said to me, I'll never forget this Grace…She said, let them go, they're different from you. They don't want you.

Grace: Do we really have to…

Ellen: Yes, we have to. I've been wanting this answered for ten years. Why? What was different about me? Why couldn't I go with you? We were always three kids together in the family. We always did everything together.

Grace: We did not. You and Lou were best friends when we were little.

Ellen: Yeah, because you never played with us. You were always down the street with Mary Curran.

Grace: She was my age, I guess.

Ellen: You still didn't answer my question. What was so different about me?

Grace: Well, look at you now. You're so different from me.

234

Ellen: Not now. THEN! And the thing that really was awful was that Mom LET you do that.

Grace: Then maybe you should go ask Mom. See if she can answer this ten year old question for you about one night ten years ago when you had a crying fit.

Ellen: It wasn't just one night Grace. It lasted until now.

Grace: Maybe for you it did. This is awful. You come home, and you step back into this world you left as though it is still the same. We've all changed. We've moved on. You're stuck in the past.

Ellen: Do you want me to ask Mom? Really?

Grace: No. It's her birthday weekend. I don't want you upsetting her.

Ellen: Then give this a little thought, huh? Because if you don't, I am going to ask her.

Grace: That's not fair. You're putting me on the spot.

Ellen: It's you or Mom.

Grace: Why? Why are you putting me through this?

Ellen: Because I want to understand why we can't be together and not argue.

Grace: Maybe the arguments are because of your choice of conversation topics.

Ellen: I have never confronted you before about this.

Grace: Yeah, so why are you doing it now?

Ellen: Because I'm getting married. I'm going to have a family some day. I don't want my own kids to do the same thing, especially if I have daughters.

Grace: You're blaming me for mistakes you haven't even made yet with your own kids?

Ellen: No. I just need to know. What was so different about ME from you and Lou? Good God. We even look alike. We're so much more alike than you and Lou. We always have been. Haven't we?

Grace: Maybe that's why. Maybe we're too much alike.

Ellen: Then the whole 'you're different' thing was a lie?

Grace: I never said that. Mom said that.

Ellen: But you LIVED it.

Grace: No. Ellen, I hate this. I hate that you're trying to make me feel guilty.

Ellen: I'm not trying to make you feel guilty.

Grace: Well then, why am I feeling guilty?

Ellen: I don't know. I'm just trying to get to the bottom of things. I've been seeing a shrink for the last six months to deal with some issues that are bothering me.

Grace: So your shrink put you up to this?

Ellen: No. I told him I always wanted this question answered. He said to be brave and ask it. You know, I went through a big part of my life feeling like people were looking at me like there was something wrong with me.

Grace: Great. Lay on the guilt.

Ellen: Grace, you know. Maybe you should feel guilty. Maybe that's why you ARE feeling guilty. It affected me. It made me feel, uh, oh, I don't know...inferior.

Grace: Oh God.

Ellen: Yeah, you know? Like if my own family doesn't like me, maybe there's something wrong with me. You know, I hardly ever had dates. You know why?

Grace: Neither did I!

Ellen: I always thought I was ugly, that men looked at me and thought all those words you used to throw at me. I was always embarrassed of myself, like I had all these flaws they could see and judge me on.

Grace: Oh, Ellen. It was adolescent stuff.

Ellen: It was not. Don't tell me you were kidding when you used those names for me.

Grace: We all called each other funny nicknames. I called Marylou Lou...

Ellen: Lou WANTED a boy's name. And that was different.

Grace: Please don't.

Ellen: Pimple face is not a nickname.

Grace: Ellen, don't....

Ellen: Flatsy dolls were not something anyone aspired to BE.

Grace: I don't want to hear...

Ellen: Then, you said, (getting really angry) you actually said something when I was crying, yeah, I know, I cried a lot when I had PMS. But you actually said...you don't remember...because you don't want to remember.

Grace: What?

Ellen: You said, 'oh the world is tough for one so ugly'.

Grace: I said that?

Ellen: No, you jerk. I just made that up.

Grace: See?

Ellen: I didn't make it up. You said it. And you know you did.

Grace: Don't blame your insecurities on me.

Ellen: I thought I would never be happy. That nobody would ever love me. I really grew up thinking the entire world saw me the way you saw me. Ugly, skinny, bad skin, no boobs, crooked teeth and braces, then there was the frizzy hair…

Grace: Hey, I had them too!

Ellen: That's not the point. You didn't have an older sister you looked up to reminding you of your flaws every second of every day.

Grace: You looked up to me?

(Pause)

Ellen: Doesn't everyone look up to their older sister?

Grace: You were always trying to one up me.

Ellen: Grace, I was always trying to keep up with you.

Grace: Everything I did, you did, right after me. It drove me nuts.

Ellen: Grace, we're twelve months apart.

Grace: Guitar lessons, putting streaks in my hair, even the love beads, and every time I read a book, you read the same one.

Ellen: See? We were alike.

Grace: No, you drove me nuts. I wanted my own friends. Especially in high school. You were like a…an appendage, a responsibility.

Ellen: So if you wanted to shake me, couldn't you just say that?

Grace: I did. I told Mom.

Ellen: What did she say?

Grace: She said Uncle Jerry was the same thing to her growing up. And she hated it.

Ellen: But he's her favorite brother.

Grace: Now.

Ellen: So there's hope.

Grace: Hope?

Ellen: Yeah, maybe you and I can get over this and be friends…finally. That's all I ever really wanted, you know.

Grace: You're joking.

Ellen: No.

Grace: Yeah, after all this. After all the pain I caused you, all the name calling, all the leaving you out…you think we can be friends? Now?

Ellen: Why not?

Grace: A minute ago you were screaming at me.

Ellen: Well, yeah, but you just said it was because you were trying to just be you without a little sister following you around.

Grace: That's not so bad, is it? I was just trying…

Ellen: But there's more. If you just wanted to not have a little sister around…why did you and Lou do everything together without me? See? This still isn't enough.

Grace: Wow, you really don't give up do you?

Ellen: No. And if you go back further, Lou and I were best buds when we were younger. She and I used to play checkers, ride our bikes, drink root beer, we used to have contests to see who could make our root beer last the longest.

Grace: Yeah, and you always won.

Ellen: I did.

Grace: And you always beat her at checkers.

Ellen: She always was the faster bike rider.

Grace: And I never did any of that with you.

Ellen: You were always down the street.

Grace: Yeah, because if I stayed around Mom had me watching you little ones.

Ellen: Oh, so you escaped too! You just did it earlier than I did.

Grace: Heh, yeah, I guess you're right.

Ellen: So why did you change and take Lou under your wing and not me?

Grace: We'd better stop or we'll talk all day. I've got to get the cake from the bakery.

Ellen: I'll go.

Grace: See? You're trying to take over.

Ellen: No I'm not. I'm trying to be helpful. You just said I ought to be home more, to help.

Grace: Yeah, but this is MY party for Mom.

Ellen: See? Mixed signals.

Grace: You're trying too hard. You always tried too hard.

Ellen: Grace, let's not start all over again.

Grace: Good idea.

Ellen: One more thought though.

Grace: Oh please, let's end this.

Ellen: Why was Lou okay and I wasn't? Why were you two friends and I was out?

Grace: I don't know. Maybe because she wasn't you. Maybe she was far enough away from me. Or because she didn't cry all the time. Maybe because she lost all those games with you and I felt sorry for her. Maybe it was just because Mom said it was okay. (Pause) You really getting married?

Ellen: He's coming tomorrow. He's flying in overnight.

Grace: Charles will be surprised.

Ellen: Your Charles? Why?

Grace: Because he asked me once. He asked me why you and I were not close since we're so much alike.

Ellen: Really?

Grace: Yes.

Ellen: And what did you tell him?

Grace: Well, since we're both putting our cards on the table, I'll tell you...I told him you were a lesbian.

Ellen: Very funny.

Grace: No, really, I did.

Ellen: You're not joking?

Grace: It was on that vacation we took to Prince Edward Island. You remember that?

Ellen: That was so long ago.

Grace: I never told him it was a lie.

Ellen: Why? What on earth made you do that? Of all the nasty lies…

Grace: I was afraid he'd like you.

Ellen: Are you out of your mind?

Grace: I'm sorry. Ellen, I am so sorry now.

Ellen: How could you? All these years he's thought that?

Grace: Yes.

Ellen: And you stand there and ask me why I moved away from the family? That is the end, Grace. The absolute end…So what are you going to tell him when I bring Sean here? When I announce we're engaged?

Grace: Nothing. Let him think what he wants now.

Ellen: Who else thinks that?

Grace: Lou knows I told him.

Ellen: Lou knows? Does she think that too?"

Grace: No. She knows it's a lie. She just knows I told him.

Ellen: So behind my back, you and she and Charles…you pretend that's true?

Grace: Yeah, so maybe at tomorrow's party you shouldn't announce…

Ellen: Does Mom know he thinks that?

Grace: Of course not.

Ellen: Oh my God. Why Grace? Why did you do this?

Grace: Because he said you and I were a lot alike. He asked me why you and I weren't close. I couldn't tell him why. I didn't know. All I know is that he noticed you. I was afraid he'd, get, like, attracted to you.

Ellen: Do you really think I would steal your boyfriend?

Grace: Well, you were always getting all the attention. Ellen made a dress…look how good she is at sewing…Ellen plays the guitar…Ellen, play something for us…you always won at checkers. You were always doing everything I was doing…and you were better at all of it. I was so afraid. I was, I guess I was insecure.

Ellen: I'll say. Good God. How could you sustain a lie all these years?

Grace: You can't tell him I lied.

Ellen: Are you nuts? I'm telling him next time I see him.

Grace: Can't you just act like you're reformed? That you used to be one and now you're not?

Ellen: You are out of your mind!! Why would I agree to that?

Grace: Then you're a liar too.

Ellen: I'm a liar?

Grace: You just said you wanted to be my friend.

Ellen: I did say that, but I don't think I still mean it. (Pause) I don't think I want anything to do with you. You're vile. And all these years I thought I was the one with no self-confidence, that I was unworthy of your friendship because I was all those things you used to say I was. I actually looked up to you! What a fool I am!

Grace: Ellen, I'm sorry.

Ellen: Yeah, you're sorry, finally, for once in your life. I'm done. I'm going back to England and you're right, once Mom goes, I will never come back here again.

Grace: Suit yourself.

Ellen: That explains so many things. At your wedding...none of the ushers would even dance with me. All Charles' friends, they all danced with Lou but I was ...he must have told all those guys, those friends of his...

Grace: He didn't tell them.

Ellen: Oh, are you kidding? Of course he told them.

Grace: He promised to keep it secret.

Ellen: He told them. Because I gave Jim, the cute one, the best man, I gave him my phone number and he just looked so, bewildered, like, he said to me, 'you're pretending to like me right?' And I didn't know what to say. I was like, what does he want me to say, 'no, I think you're cute?' Little did I know he thought I was a lesbian. See? Do you see what you've done?

Grace: It doesn't matter now. None of those guys were worth it. Jim is...

Ellen: But it mattered then. I felt so strange at your wedding, like I was different. I was being treated like I was different. All because of a lie YOU told.

Grace: So you had a bad time at my wedding. It was a long time ago. Tomorrow is Mom's party and you have to behave.

Ellen: Behave? What do you mean, behave?

Grace: Go along to get along. To not upset the day. To make it nice for Mom's sake.

Ellen: And if I don't?

Grace: You'll look like the bad girl.

Ellen: I'm not coming. I'd rather die than be there and let that lie stay there and poison everything. I'm meeting Sean's plane and flying right back to Heathrow.

Grace: That'll ruin the day too. Mom's expecting all her daughters to be there. She knows you're here.

Ellen: I'm telling her. She has to know what you've done to me.

Grace: I think maybe it would be better if you just went home.

Ellen: This is what you really want, isn't it? You really only ever wanted me to leave. No matter what I do you manipulate things to make ME the troublemaker. I can't believe that my being here makes you so, so, weak and …

Grace: Yeah, when you're not around, dear sister, things are pretty good here. Lou and I get along like sisters are supposed to. We take care of Mom, we go on double dates with Charles and Kevin, our kids are friends, real cousins, it's cool. When you're here, it all gets like this.

Ellen: My fault I suppose…In your eyes this is all my fault.

Grace: Yeah, it would be better if Mom skipped you and just had me and Lou.

Ellen: That's what you always wanted, huh? Well, you know what? You've got it. I'm not coming to the party, and you can explain, in whatever twisted way you want, to everyone there, why I am not there.

Grace: You have to come. Mom will never understand if you're not there.

Ellen: She'll understand because I'll tell her, tonight.

Grace: No, you won't. You can't upset her. See? You're going to ruin her birthday party.

Ellen: No, you ruined it. You ruined it with your pathetic lies and your...How will Sean ever understand this? What am I going to do? He's in the air on a plane.

Grace: You have to go to the party. For Mom's sake. She knows you're here.

Ellen: But you have to tell Charles about your lie.

Grace: No. And you have to not try to steal the limelight from Mom. You need to keep quiet about your engagement.

Ellen: You're not worried about Mom and the limelight. You're worried about how you're going to explain to your husband why your lesbian sister is getting married to a man! What a phony you are, pretending you care about Mom and it's all about you.

Grace: No, Ellen.

Ellen: I'm coming to the party. I'm coming one last time for Mom's sake. We can all pretend one last time. And I am announcing our engagement. Sean is coming all the way here just for that, to meet my family. Then, I'm leaving. Then, I will go away and this family will never see me again.

Stepping Up

"It's time to step up," says Meg. "We've been helping Rebecca and Mark."

It was late February and cold gripped the Garden State, as it typically does in its darkest months. Anna is surprised at the phone call that comes on a Saturday morning while she is hunkered down with a steaming cup of coffee, reading the first drafts of essays from her freshman writing class. The subject of the essay is business marketing to children. It awakens, she hopes, her student's nascent ability to think for themselves, an ability that they don't realize has been usurped by the consumer culture they've been passively participating in since birth. What substitutes for thinking, she told the students in class, are patterned responses, programmed responses. "How many minutes of your life do you spend watching TV commercials? Think about it. Do you let those messages influence you? Or, do you make decisions yourself?"

This essay assignment is Anna's attempt to clear away the chatter so they can ask themselves that question 'what do you really want vs. what you've been told to want' and answer it honestly for themselves.

Meg doesn't ever call her. As a matter of fact, of her four sisters, there isn't one who checks in with her on a regular basis. Last time she heard from Meg was when Meg invited her for the family Christmas dinner at the very last minute. "I assumed you'd be busy, or that you'd want to bring that guy, what was his name, Ken? And, well, isn't he Jewish?"

"He broke up with me on an email in mid-December. Thank you for inviting me."

"Oh, I'm so glad," Meg had said.

"Uh, glad he broke up with me? Or glad I'm coming?"

"What do you mean step up?" Anna asks now, recovering from the surprise of Meg's mid-February call.

"Tens of thousands of dollars over the years," Meg says. "Darla and Richard have been giving them money. Gavin and I have too. And now Theresa and Calvin are chipping in."

"Gees, Theresa and Calvin still have two in college," Anna says. "Why did you even ask them?"

"Well, Darla is tired of Richard being the only one giving hand-outs."

Anna asks, "Well, thank God you are able to help too. Would the money be a loan?"

"Not really, Rebecca and Mark are down to zero. They'll never be able to pay it back."

Anna, at age 60, recently divorced, barely had enough put away for retirement. She worked at a community college and taught as an adjunct at a local four-year university in the evenings. "I will help in any way I can, but I do not have the wealth Darla has, or you have. I can't just donate cash. Sorry."

"Maybe if you hadn't gotten divorced you'd be able to help," Meg said.

"I divorced him because he was so stingy I had to go into debt for the MFA. He refused to let me use what he called 'family money'." Then she adds as a reminder, "If you hadn't married Gavin you would be on a Catholic schoolteacher's salary and would have to think of another way to help them too." Anna said it with an even, unemotional tone.

She calls Rebecca, the sister about to be evicted. It's one in the afternoon. Rebecca tells her Mark's claim for unemployment was rejected, so Anna drills down with some questions. Rebecca overstates everything, loudly, which is the signal to Anna that she's been drinking. Turns out, Mark over collected by three weeks on his last unemployment claim after he went back to work last year, and he owes money back to the state. There is a hold on his new UI claim until he pays it back.

Anna tells her, after making hours of phone calls to her contacts at the department of labor, "He can pay it back from the benefits checks if you win on appeal."

Anna explains to Meg what she has done, "This is what I CAN do to help. I have to do this for the people in our workforce classes at the college."

"I thought you had a marketing job," Meg says.

"There's a lot you don't know about me," Anna says.

Mark wins the appeal, is sent a check for UI benefits to the tune of $4,000 after the three weeks he over-collected are deducted. He gets a job a few weeks later and works until he lands in the hospital with Afib, pneumonia, and because his underlying health includes a COPD diagnosis, comes close to death. Rebecca whispers to Anna, "Don't tell the other sisters, but the reason he's in the hospital? He started smoking again."

"I hope he cuts that out," Anna says.

Rebecca nods. But, Anna notices she doesn't give an answer, not really, so the nod could be a lie. Another lie. Like the drinking Rebecca says she's not doing. But the bottles are in the recycling.

Mark recovers. Goes back to the lumber store and stays employed for another year. Then, he's let go again. Anna suspects he's drinking at lunchtime. Rebecca says it's because he's working 50 to 60 hours a week and he's stressed. "I'd be drinking too," Rebecca says, "if I worked as hard at he does."

"It's the drinking that is destroying them," Anna says to Meg later on the phone call during which Meg asks for money for them again. "We need to stage an intervention. We need to hire a therapist who knows how to do one, get ourselves ready to do it right. We need to confront them and we need to learn the right way to do it. Solve the problem at its source."

"Don't you think anyone has tried to talk to them? Don't you think we tried?" Meg says. "Gavin and Calvin took Mark out for breakfast and brought it up."

"I mean all of us, together, confront them with the truth, a united front, so they can't hide it. So they can stop pretending it's just Mark's health."

Theresa tells Anna. "I'm not sittin' in a room tellin' Rebecca something she already knows. We're payin' their bills, and the one thing they make sure they have every few days is a case of Coors Light. You know how much she spend on cigarettes? Cigarettes are like eight dollars a pack. She sits in that apartment and isn't looking for a job herself. She can work at the Shop Rite, or Kohl's or somewhere. But she sits there and smokes and God knows when she starts the beer."

"If we do this right…" Anna tries. "There's a right way to say what we need to say."

"I'm not going to have a psychologist tell me how to talk to my sister." Theresa says. "And you need to step up."

Darla refuses the intervention idea too. She's given Rebecca and Mark more than anyone else over the years. She says, "I'm fed up."

"Why won't any of you listen to me?" Anna asks Meg. "There are methods that work. Maybe we can get them into AA. Gees, you studied psychology, you should know…"

"Well, maybe if you helped with some money we'd listen to you," Meg says.

"Well, we need to find a solution that is more than just getting their bills paid," Anna responds. "You want to keep giving them money forever?"

She calls her brothers. Steve and George both live out of state; both are married and have no children, only dogs. Their wives are both artistic, Marjorie with pastels and oils, Amy with mosaics.

"I'll help in any way I can," Steve says. "I'll pay for the therapist and I'll fly home."

George says, "Yes, the sisters asked me for money too. I told them no. I'll do an intervention, but without everybody in on it, I doubt Rebecca and Mark will listen to just you, me and Steve. And, think about who Mark is…you think he's going to listen to his two liberal brothers-in-law?"

"Or me, apparently the black sheep of this family," Anna says, telling George the reason Meg said nobody will cooperate is because she can't hand over money.

"You're not the black sheep," George says. "You know who is…"

"Well, I'm the ugly duckling then."

"This isn't about Rebecca and Mark," George says. "It's about who's got money and who's in control. It will diminish Meg if what you suggest works."

"Diminish who?"

"Meg."

"Shit," Anna says. "But then we just perpetuate the problem."

"Anna," he says with an ironic tone, "just go back to your prescribed corner and be quiet."

Anna schedules a visit to her therapist. She lays out the whole thing, lamenting her inability to influence the family toward something that might actually help her sister in the long run.

"Interventions don't always work," Betsy tells her.

"How will we know unless we try?"

"There is a risk of failure," Betsy tells her. "And then what?"

Anna goes home unchastised. She pours a cup of tea and opens her files and begins to read her student's essays again. Her concentration is not good. Her mind is filled with how we fall into patterns of thinking and behavior and how it forms who we are.

As she reads her student's reflections, the subject is still about escaping proscribed patterns and learning to think critically, she remembers the long ago day she stopped at a toy store with her daughters to pick up gifts for a birthday party. A long line had formed in front of the store, snaking around the mall for a few hundred feet. Apparently, a new shipment of the latest toy craze had arrived. These grown women were lined up to be the first to buy before the inventory ran out. 'Limit three per family,' said the sign. She told the store manager, "I'm not here to buy Beanie Babies."

Her comments on the essays, neatly lined up along the right hand column by the 'track changes' feature of MS Word, offer opportunities to expand here and there, give examples, to produce evidence to support their arguments. She finds, after two or three essays, after she saves and sends them back to her students via email, that she is repeating the same suggestions over and over. Her own mind is trapped, she realizes, by the comment box and by what she is trying to teach them, a fixed set of ideas, a box she now considers.

Was she complicit in defining her place? Are her own attempts to 'think outside' this box and asking her sisters to do the same damning her to a tightened grip of refusal? She wonders if her sisters think she is wealthier than she lets on. She resents that, because she is being truthful and doing her best to help. In their minds, she can just hear them congratulating themselves and criticizing her. In their minds, one of them needed help, they all said yes, except her. She wants to call them and shout that they didn't know how to do what she just did at the UI and wasn't that something.

She opens another essay but leaves it unread. She opens a blank Word document and starts typing. Do I want to help Rebecca and Mark stop their self-destructive pattern? If I gave some money, would the sisters listen to me? Would they agree to the intervention? If I gave some money to Rebecca and Mark would they heed my advice and go to AA? Anna opens her online bank record and jots down the amount of savings she has there. She really can't start giving money to her sister. Not without hurting herself in the long run.

She calls Rebecca's phone number. She gets voice mail. She tries a text instead. She gets a text back, "What? I'm resting."

"Did Mark apply again for UI?"

"No."

"Why?"

"None of your business."

"How long did he work at the lumber store?"

"Not long enough."

"I'm coming over."

"I said I'm resting."

Anna writes, "I've got to talk to you."

"Go away."

Anna hears the signs of drinking in the texts and drives to Rebecca's apartment. It is wedged between two strip malls on a busy commercial street. She has to park two blocks away and walk in the gloomy afternoon to the house and ring the top doorbell. Nobody answers. She rings again. She dials Rebecca. No answer. She texts. She gets Rebecca's, "Go away."

"Let me in."

"Go away or I'll call the police," Rebecca's text is in all caps.

Anna stands on the porch contemplating her next move. Suddenly, a young man in a Yankee cap is standing in the doorway. "Can I help you?" he says.

"I need to go upstairs to my sister's," she says. "She's mad at me and won't let me in."

He, the downstairs tenant, stands back, swinging the door wide, and waits. Anna looks at him. She grins. She steps through the door. She climbs the stairs. The inner door to the apartment is not locked. She walks in.

She sees Rebecca on the bed through a crack in the door. Anna stands very still. Then she goes to the dining room table and flips open the laptop and navigates to the UI website. Like a thief, she pulls open a file drawer and finds a stash of the blue UI statements she sometimes collects from students at work to determine their eligibility for government workforce training. Lucky. Mark or Rebecca has written Mark's Social Security number, his email address and his password on the claim summary from his last round of collecting. Anna quietly sets the volume on the laptop to mute, types in the info and breathes a satisfied sigh as she files a new claim.

"What are you doing?" behind her, Rebecca's smoky voice. "How did you get in here?"

Anna whirls around. "I'm filing his claim. Your downstairs neighbor opened the door."

"Who the hell do you think you are?"

"Why didn't Mark apply for unemployment again?"

Rebecca exhales. Anna can detect beer and cigarettes on her breath. She holds her own while she waits for the answer.

"He quit. They didn't fire him. He's not eligible for UI. And, if you tell anyone in the family I'll tell them you're making shit up about us."

"And, why on earth would I make up something like that?"

"You should hear what they're saying about you." Rebecca sits down and presses her lips together in a grimace.

"I already know what they think of me. Do you know what they're saying about you behind your back?" Anna asks.

"I don't care what they say. They're helping us."

"Temporarily, yes. What's gonna break this cycle, Rebecca?"

"Well, I guess our luck needs to change, huh? You think?"

"Why did he quit?"

"I don't have to tell you."

Anna let a beat of silence pass.

"The boss gave him an ultimatum. He said Mark had to bring in a certain amount of sales revenue in like two weeks or he'd be fired.

Mark knew it was impossible. So he told him so. So the guy took it as a resignation."

"That's not quitting."

"But when the UI reps do the employer interview, that's what they'll tell them."

"But Mark can appeal again."

This time Rebecca pauses. Then Anna hears her voice dip to a whisper. "I just …we're just exhausted."

"I just re-opened his claim. He has a few weeks left on the old one. And, he worked long enough to qualify for another six months."

"Did Meg tell you to come here?"

"No. But, they're all tired of writing checks, Rebecca."

"How would you know? You're not helping."

Anna just stares. "I'm doing what I can. Sorry I'm not rich. "

"Would you please just leave? I'll handle it from here. I will have to tell Mark he's going to get a phone call from UI and he'll have to talk to them. He hates it. He says he feels like a welfare recipient."

"But he's okay with taking Richard's money? And Gavin's?"

"It's like a guy thing. He was so pissed at you for making him appeal his claim last time. Like he was begging for a handout."

"So it's because I'm showing him how to…"

"It makes him feel stupid. He got drunk the last time, when he got that $4,000 you helped him with?"

"So I'm making it worse?"

"It's easier for him to let the guys help."

"So even if I contributed some money?"

"Yeah, he'd be so humiliated knowing it came from the divorced sister who has no money either."

"So why did Meg ask?"

"She probably wouldn't have told him. I wouldn't have told him it was from you."

"This is a fucking mess," Anna says. "Who knows what's true, who knows what's a lie. Let's pretend it's all just going to get fixed some magical way. Meanwhile, he's getting worse and the hole you and Mark are in is just getting deeper. And they're all complicit in it. Meg wouldn't have told Mark even if I was helping? She'd let him keep on thinking I said no?"

"I'm so thirsty. It's after three. I'm having a Coors." Rebecca went to the refrigerator and took out two cans. Then she went to the window, opened it wide and lit a cigarette. Anna watched the smoke float up and out the window.

"Meg told me you wanted to stage an intervention to get Mark to stop drinking. To stop me too." Rebecca sucked on the cigarette loudly and exhaled toward the window. She took a gulp of her Coors. "She said an intervention would just humiliate us."

"Why would I want to humiliate you?"

"Well, I never gave you the chance to do that before. And Meg won't now."

"When have I ever tried to humiliate you?"

She watched her youngest sister, the prettiest of all of them, with her dark, nearly black hair, her light blue eyes, her pale skin, classic black Irish, stare at her, the same stare she gave when she was lying. Anna floated back in time to that long ago weekend when she stood at the ski resort bar and reminded her baby sister that she should take responsibility for birth control if she was going to sleep with her boyfriend. She recalled how Rebecca had agreed, nodded in fact and said, 'yes, you're right' with that same glaring stare. How, six weeks later, after it was already done, Meg told Anna that she, Theresa and Darla had spent the weekend seeing Rebecca through an abortion. Meg told Anna that Anna should never tell Rebecca she knew. It took Anna only about two seconds to realize why.

"You know," Rebecca said now. "You and I never talked about my abortion."

"No, we never did." Anna stared back at Rebecca.

"But you knew?"

Anna nodded. "Guess who told me?"

"You never said 'I told you so'."

"Did you expect me to?"

"Meg said you would."

"Meg was projecting onto me something that isn't true. Consider for a minute that she still is."

"Why would she?"

Anna remembered that George had said it, 'It will diminish Meg if what you suggest works.'

"I think she needs to be the responsible eldest sister and anything that diminishes that role threatens her," Anna said.

How could she make Rebecca understand that if Rebecca and Mark stopped drinking Meg couldn't be their savior? That Anna's UI rescue, while it helped Mark and Rebecca, had broken a pattern in the family that suited Meg and that an intervention if it worked would do the same? Anna's horror at this realization was visceral. The horror of actually being the one to try to deliver this explanation to Rebecca, who clearly couldn't see it, rendered her mute.

Anna declined the Coors and found a Diet Coke in the refrigerator instead. She took a cigarette and stood near the window and smoked with her sister. The taste felt appropriately harsh on her tongue and in her throat. She coughed once, took another drag, silently flicked the ashes into the sink. She momentarily considered, then rejected George's advice to go back to her corner and be quiet.

He Briefly Thought of Tadpoles

The dawn sky promised rain showers, and when Martin slid the Beemer under the dripping oak branches onto the road, whispers of water on blacktop hissed at every rotation of his belted radials. At the corner he stopped, pressed 'on' and woke up Marcia.

"Prepare to turn right," she said, exactly as he had programmed her the night before. He obeyed, knowing his day depended on execution of every move with perfect precision, every word carefully chosen, every pause deliberate in his appeal to his client's mind. A yes decision would bring him to where he hoped to be. Yes, yes, yes. Getting to it was Martin's livelihood. With this machine under him, with his excellent selling skills, with Marcia guiding him through traffic, weather and all the right turns, he'd get his yes today.

Marcia was as integral a part of his days as his wife was of his nights. Marcia stuck to what he needed from her. Directions, traffic jams, weather. She spared him the MapQuest printouts of old. He fancied what she'd look like if she sat beside him, long legs in silk stockings, a short skirt, heels, understated and professional with gleaming red hair pulled back to a cascading rope over one shoulder. Classy like this car, reciting the way to suburban citadels of commerce. Sometimes he laughed and said he didn't sell for a living, he drove. His sanity relied on this splendid chariot and lately, on Marcia.

Martin had owned a BMW before, wrecked it on the GS Parkway when a fat Oldsmobile veered into his lane and knocked him sideways. That was just before Suzie and just after the first Marcia, the real one, informed him, "Oh, I thought you knew this was just a fling. I'm moving to Arkansas."

Martin hadn't known, had a solitaire in platinum in his pocket, and too many drinks in him after her announcement, but, he insisted, the wreck was the Oldsmobile driver's fault.

He met Suzie at the auto body shop where they'd towed his car. He convinced her to take him home. His rebound from Marcia's jilting was remarkable and here they were, seven years later; the solitaire and a wedding band now glittered on Suzie's hand. Still young, no children, no mortgage yet, Suzie had her eyes on the old yellow Victorian near the center of town.

"Does it have to be practical?" he had asked about getting a new car. "I mean, I just got a promotion. My car should look better than the guys who work for me."

By then, Suzie's sigh had become familiar. At her soft click of tongue against teeth preceding her sigh, he felt sweat form on his brow. "Will a car seat fit in the back? And, what if I don't find a job," her voice was doing that low octave drop he dreaded.

"I'm doing okay for both of us," he knew he was talking about money and she was talking about something else. He coughed. "It's only been six months. You'll be earning again," Martin said. "And look, this is a hot car. It has all these safety features. Look at the roll bar design."

The doctor said it sometimes took a year after the woman went off birth control pills and they didn't need to speak their knowledge that she was ovulating and her hormone levels were adequate or that she'd been hormone free for three years. They both knew it was his fault she wasn't pregnant. Guilt broke over him along with the sweat.

"We'll have a minivan soon enough. Let's have fun while we can." He stroked her bangs away from her furrowed brow. "You'll love the ride. Seriously, have you ever driven a BMW?"

His one indulgence since he had redirected his love to Suzie from the real Marcia was this car. Martin set the GPS on the female voice, soft, sultry, helpful, tentatively supportive, and unperturbed. He liked calling it Marcia. He liked that she simply announced to him, 'recalculating route' when he was lost. Marcia the first's recalculation of his life's route had begun that night of the accident and had brought him to Suzie. Her daily guidance was something he knew he needed, even if her presence in his life was now only embodied in that sultry dashboard voice.

Today, Marcia would get him there. Today, he would exceed his sales quota. Suzie's ring on his mobile interrupted just as Marcia urged him to prepare to take the ramp to the highway on the left.

"My interview is canceled," Suzie said. Martin detected a dull lowering of her pitch, which signaled a fight against tears. It was his turn to say something.

"Postponed?"

"No, canceled."

"So what, things change. That's one thing we both know kid, right? Things always change." He secretly suspected the prolonged unemployment was engineered by her biological drive for a child.

"I'm tired of the waiting, Martin." Suzie's last day at her pharmaceutical company was now ten months past. She despised the long lines at the unemployment office and her long empty days. He was beginning to despise them too.

"Prepare to turn left and follow the ramp to the interstate," Marcia broke in and Martin obeyed, but he missed what Suzie said next.

"You're not waiting. You're actively looking," he said, "I'm closing the big one today, Suzie. It's worth a year's salary. Don't sweat it. We'll make it happen."

"First the job, then Dr. Hughes…I'm getting nowhere."

"Suze," he said, "we're going to get there. Don't I always get us there?"

"Martin, you can't keep saying that."

A reproach. He felt it coming at him in the heat under his collar. Like he hadn't done it for her lately. But he had. He was trying. Shit, if he could find her a job, he would. If he could qualify for a mortgage alone, he'd buy that yellow colonial. If he could…Marcia distracted him from his next thought.

"Stay right, then, after 5 miles, prepare to merge right onto highway 510."

In bed Saturday night, he'd done it for Suzie. He'd waited four full days, and on the fifth, he exploded into her. Waves of pent up pleasure for both of them. The wet spot cold beneath his naked ass, he'd held her afterwards. She slept and he prayed, PRAYED, that his count and motility rate were at the speed of light, this time, please.

"I'm trying Suze."

"But…"

Martin felt impatience fill him. He kept his eyes on the road, one ear for Marcia and directions, a splintered consciousness for his wife. His confidence sank. His joy in his driving machine ebbed. His desire to hang up the phone shamed him. He didn't want to talk about this. It was the only topic lately and he did not hold up well against her blighted pessimism. "Recalculating route."

Shit! He flew past highway 510, caught himself going 80 in the fast left lane.

"Did you say shit?"

"No. Yes, Suzie. Listen, I missed my turn. I can't talk at length about this, about anything right now. I'll call you later, okay?"

He heard the quick disconnect, and felt relief.

Marcia regained his attention and Martin regained control of his day until nature brought more rain than forecast. It splashed down, bounced off his windshield, kicked up on the road, pooled rapidly along the left and right lanes, forcing all the cars, semis and oil tankers into the center which didn't allow him to control, or Marcia to accurately report how long his journey to Drake and Lonigan would take.

The receptionist signed him in, gave him a visitor pass, pointed him toward the elevator and returned the smile he pasted over the humiliation he felt deep down, over the dampness he felt in his socks, over the fear he denied, over the deep need he had for this to go his way today. If it went his way, he'd take Suzie to Italy, make love to her on the coast of Tuscany, and there, they'd do it, make it, end the current malaise in their forward movement toward the future. He'd make her a mother. Damn it. He would.

Then he remembered.

Lonigan had asked him for a competitive analysis. He had posted Cisco's proposal for him on Google Drive, sharing the competitors pricing, details, practically begging Martin to give his best offer so he could bring it to his partners and not be refused. It was up on Google Drive later that afternoon two weeks ago, minutes after Martin arrived at the car dealership having the 5,000 mile maintenance done on the BMW. He remembered Suzie texting about her ovulation and her temperature and the day of the month and how he should come home, now. He remembered now. Son of a bitch.

In the conference room on this rainy, chilly, day, trickles of sweat greeted Martin again somewhere between his armpits and the starched crispness of his blue Oxford under his suit. Lonigan was waiting and Martin had completely forgotten about it. That night, Suzie had surprised him with candles, filet mignon, sautéed mushrooms, green beans and a bottle of Borollo that cost $87.00, and as he looked back now, Martin knew he really had fucked his brains out after that seduction. Lonigan was eyeing him with such anticipation. Martin had no choice, he made it up and said exactly what Lonigan would want to hear…and it worked.

Marcia was waiting to guide him home. And the rain poured still. Hard, cold, sideways in the wind now, and unrelenting, it seemed. One hundred and twenty miles to home. He pressed the button to activate Marcia and waited. Something about her recitation of the obvious satisfied him. She sprang to life and led him away. Marcia's comforting sureness, her soothing voice, so sure of what he should do next, took him to the interstate. Her confidence matched his. He obeyed her, ruminating about how Suzie's schedule of sex on demand had almost derailed him but how he'd come back and won anyway. What he already knew about his body didn't matter at this moment, and he felt himself peering over the steering wheel, struggling to see through the thumping windshield, hearing rain and slick taunting whispers of swishing tires passing him and passing him and passing him on the left.

His foot slammed down and the anti-locking system stuttered him to a stop inches from a MiniCooper in front. Standstill. Now what? He waited. The lane to his right crept along, but stopped too. Whatever this was, it must have just happened. Marcia surely could have navigated around this.

"Hey, girl, what's the problem?" Martin said.

"Recalculating route," Marcia answered.

"Too late," Martin mused out loud. "We're already stuck."

"You're stuck," Marcia said. "Recalculating route."

Suzie's ring on his mobile. "It's time," she said. "Spiked an hour ago. Time again."

"Oh," he said. "Don't worry. I'll be home. This baby will get me home in no time. Just order take-out and relax and wait for me."

"How far away are you?" she asked. He could hear her calculating mind measuring the window of opportunity Dr. Hughes might have explained to them that day in his office, when he was giving them lessons on how to fertilize an egg with slow sperm. Martin had sat, frozen, as the man explained how it would increase the odds if the sperm were to travel downhill, not uphill, into the fallopian tubes. Suzie, you might want to practice headstands, he'd actually said. Martin had thought he would prescribe a medication, something like Viagra, not to give him an erection, he had no trouble with that, but to up the numbers, rev up the little lazy suckers, get them excited enough to seek out their destination. But there was the venerable doctor, suggesting his wife stand on her head after sex. And the next time, while he lazed, satisfied and spent, Suzie had moved to her yoga mat and the wall and lifted her hips, then her legs, both, straight into the air and stayed there, motionless, for twenty minutes, at least that's how long she estimated she'd lasted until her head was so full of blood she thought she would break a blood vessel and in her graceful yoga way, dropped to the floor and then lay down in bed while, she said later, he snored like a hibernating bear. Her efforts hadn't worked. His lazy crew couldn't even roll downhill.

"I'm behind an accident or something. God knows how long this will take. It's out of my control, Suze." And with that, with hearing his own voice admit that, he knew it was true.

"No, it isn't," Suzie said.

"Suzie, please, I've had a really great day so far. Can you just not start this?"

"I don't think you want a baby."

"What? You think I don't want to get you pregnant? Suzie, I do. Of course, we both do."

"Every time it is time for you know what, you're late."

"That isn't true. Suzie, you are just freaking out. It's only been six months."

"Nine months. I feel like you've got your car, your baby, do you know what it feels like when I hear you call that car your baby?"

"Babe, it'll happen. I'll be there. I am just stuck. I've been sitting here for twenty minutes already and the line of traffic hasn't moved."

"Well, okay. Then get here. Could you do that? Could you do that for me?"

"I'm working on it."

That clicking silence filled the car. Through the rain he spotted a green overhead sign. The next exit. Wherever it took him, he'd get off. Marcia could recalculate the route and he'd circumvent this snarling stalled traffic. Voila! He could do this. He would do this. For Suzie. For both of them.

"Recalculating route," he heard from the dashboard.

Marcia's confident voice guided him through a series of turns in the dark, first an unlit rural road, then a series of left turns, and a right for which he was prepared by Marcia's great skill at anticipation. Then, with a loud expletive, he recognized the same road he'd just left and into which he was now crawling, an entrance ramp packed with pick-up trucks.

"Prepare to merge left," Marcia's triumphant voice announced. "Then, after 30 miles, take the exit on the right for Route 78 East."

"Marcia!" Martin said her name out loud for the very first time. He said it with anger. "No!"

"Well, then you find your own way home," he heard in response. "I'm doing the best I can," her voice embodied.

The rain pelted his roof and all light and all the white lines on the road melted like candle wax through his windows.

"Just get me home," he muttered.

"I'm working on it," Marcia said. "But that's not what you want."

"I need to get home," yes, he was talking to himself.

"No, Suzie needs you to get home. You don't want to fuck her tonight."

He punched off, picked up his phone and rang Suzie.

"What?"

"Got a map?" He knew his old collection of road atlases was on the floor under his desk.

"Where are you?"

"I'm on 91 somewhere near Oaktowne Road."

"What, the GPS isn't working?"

"She…it brings me back to the same jammed highway."

"Hold on."

"You're not!" Martin saw the lights on the GPS flash and knew it wasn't Suzie's voice that said that.

"Not what?"

"Not going to let her tell you what to do."

"You're no help."

"That's what you think."

"Martin, who are you talking to?"

"You, Suze."

"No, you sound like you're arguing. Is someone in the car with you?"

"No, it's just the GPS. It turned on again by itself."

"I found you on the map. Got a pen?"

He found one, grabbed a crumbled receipt from the floor and said, "Okay. What do I do?"

A horn blared and the right lane of traffic was suddenly moving.

"Hold on Suze. I've got to drive. My lane is moving finally."

The BMW crawled, then cruised, merged left and within five minutes Martin was speeding along at 45 mph.

"Suzie, looks like the logjam is over. I'm okay. I'm moving."

"Okay, call back and let me know your ETA. I've got dinner."

"Love you." Martin said this hopefully.

"Me too," Suzie said and clicked off.

Marcia came back to life with a clipped beep and Martin pressed reset a few times. She wasn't saying anything. He pressed repeat. Nothing. "Come on Marcia, wake up," he pleaded.

"Do this on your own," Marcia's tone was no longer assured, confident or helpful. Martin banged his hand on the steering wheel. What's with this? Was it his mind or was Marcia really speaking to him?

"Go ahead, big shot," Marcia said. "See how you do without me."

Traffic stopped again. "Now what? Now fucking what?" he yelled. "Marcia why did you bring me back here? Christ! Beam me up, man!"

"Martin," said the voice in the car. "Do you want to move forward?"

"Of course I do. I just want out of this mess. Get me off this highway."

"Recalculating route," said Marcia again. She went silent. Martin waited. There was no way to get off here now. This would take hours.

"Traffic delay at Two Mile Canyon Road," she recited. "Press reset for new route."

Martin pressed. He waited. His leg was going numb from sitting so long in the car. His back was beginning to ache and the fine leather of his expensive shoes was shrinking with the dampness and squeezing his toes.

"Take the exit on the right after one half mile," Marcia suggested brightly.

"I've got to get there. How will I get around this mess?" He peered through the flapping wipers and saw to the right of the shoulder where he was stopped that he might be able to pull around on the grassy roadside. It was level. So, he turned the steering wheel in that direction, lifted his foot from the brake, and left the gravel shoulder and sank deeply in mud. He briefly thought of tadpoles, born in the mud, wriggling their way out, setting themselves free, and he imagined a good Samaritan coming to give him a push, or a tow truck.

"Prepare to take the exit on the right after one half mile," Marcia repeated.

He couldn't call Suzie. On the last call he'd been moving, unencumbered, optimistic, nothing in his way, and now, she'd be waiting, dinner congealing, little ovum disintegrating and passing smoothly from her tube into her uterus, too late, once again. He imagined re-entry, the tears, the pleading, the sorry anger, his shame, and with a brazen stroke of ego, he knew he would not apologize, not for this, not for fate stepping in his way, even if she said 'again' or 'it's never your fault but it is'.

For a brief second he thought about tiny infinitesimal GPS systems, each one guiding his sperm upstream, his future progeny dependent upon a computer, this central data bank, to navigate the river upstream. And they might be lost like him, without it. Then he looked out the window at the man with a flashlight in his hand and a baseball cap with rain spewing off its rim coming at him on foot.

This miraculous mirage hooked a towing chain to his front bumper, signaled a thumbs-up to Martin and stepped up into the cab of his wrecker. Martin was back on the gravel shoulder in no time. He exited the BMW, slid his credit card through the cracked window of the wrecker's cab, waited in the rain for his receipt and the return of his card, saluted this stranger and was back behind the wheel gleeful.

The roadway was clear. Nothing was stopping him. Marcia's tone returned to its calm authoritative register, he obeyed her instructions, driving straight, tunneling east, feeling the power of his engine purring under him, propelling him rapidly toward his target through the torrents of rain, the cats and dogs of it bouncing off the slick road. Rush hour was long over. The numbers dwindled on the road and soon he was the only driver left, cruise controlled, headlights beaming ahead and scattering rain like diamonds into the air. Martin heard Marcia announce, "Stay left and after five miles take the exit south to 87."

"No," Martin shouted at the screen. "Home, take me home!"

"I'm working on it. But that's not what you want," Marcia's voice announced as clear and distinct as if it were himself talking.

Martin punched the 'off' button one last time. He braked. His stutter brakes kicked in and he was moving at 40 mph, then 35, then 20. He checked the rearview mirror. He was alone. Not another car in sight. And, when he yanked the steering wheel, his foot came off the brake and hand over hand, foot on the gas, he made a circle with his chariot on the wide three lane highway, and another, and another until, dizzy and spent, he pulled to a stop on the shoulder and let his exhaustion immobilize him. As stillness settled, Marcia's voice whispered, "You have reached your destination."

Acknowledgements

These stories hid in a drawer for decades and only after reading Hilma Wolitzer's collection entitled, *Today a Woman Went Mad in the Supermarket* did I dust them off and bring them to life. I owe Hilma a big thank-you for her inspiration. Thanks to Apprentice House Press for publishing my second book with them. Thanks to Margo Krasne, my friend on the far end of the seesaw of life who picks me up or drops me down gently.

I owe immense thanks to my fellow writers in Working Title Six, Finding Our Way Back, and Women Reading Aloud –including Karin Abarbanel, David Holmberg, David Popiel; the more gentle helpers, Tricia Murphy, Brooks Geiger; Julie Maloney and the women writers of Alonnisos. Of course, my fellow students and talented teachers at Rutgers' Newark belong on this list: Alice Elliott Dark, Tayari Jones, Jayne Anne Phillips.

Life and my writing would not be the same without my dear, loving Warren, who gets me out of my head to the woods; thanks to my daughters Melissa, Maura and Shannon, who are my heart and soul; to my brother Steven who weeps joyful tears when he sees me happy and my brother Kevin who said, "Women in Hollywood should see this work" and inspired me to write screenplays as well as fiction.

About the Author

Nancy Burke studied writing at the Rutgers' Newark MFA Creative Writing Program and teaches writing at Montclair State University and New Jersey Institute of Technology. Her earlier work includes: *From the Abuelas' Window* (2005), *If I Could Paint the Moon Black* (2014) and *Only the Women are Burning* (2020). Her short fiction has appeared in *Pilgrim: A Journal of Catholic Experience* and *Meat for Tea: The Valley Review.* Her story, *At the Pool,* (included in this collection) was a Finalist in the J.F. Powers Prize for Short Fiction at *Dappled Things Magazine.* She lives in Little Falls, NJ.

Apprentice
House Press
Loyola University Maryland

Apprentice House is the country's only campus-based, student-staffed book publishing company. Directed by professors and industry professionals, it is a nonprofit activity of the Communication Department at Loyola University Maryland.

Using state-of-the-art technology and an experiential learning model of education, Apprentice House publishes books in untraditional ways. This dual responsibility as publishers and educators creates an unprecedented collaborative environment among faculty and students, while teaching tomorrow's editors, designers, and marketers.

Eclectic and provocative, Apprentice House titles intend to entertain as well as spark dialogue on a variety of topics. Financial contributions to sustain the press's work are welcomed. Contributions are tax deductible to the fullest extent allowed by the IRS.

To learn more about Apprentice House books or to obtain submission guidelines, please visit www.apprenticehouse.com.

Apprentice House Press
Communication Department
Loyola University Maryland
4501 N. Charles Street
Baltimore, MD 21210
Ph: 410-617-5265
info@apprenticehouse.com • www.apprenticehouse.com